GLITCH
ADVENTURES

BOOK ONE – THE UNLIKELY HERO

RICHARD CASE

To my friends and family,
whose support and laughter have carried me through every late night and
every wild idea.
And to my parents —
I love you more than words can ever say.
This book, and every story that follows, exists because of the love you gave
me first.

Preface

Welcome to the world of Glitch — a reluctant mech-rat who never asked to be a hero, but somehow stumbles into becoming one anyway.

This book began as a small spark — a side note in a darker tale — and evolved into something bigger. Glitch became more than a character; he became a voice for chaos, humor, and the kind of resilience you only find when everything goes wrong.

If you're here, buckle in. This isn't your usual tidy fantasy. It's messy, funny, a little broken, and hopefully unforgettable.

Introduction

Narrated, reluctantly, by Sentinel

The Obsidian War did not begin with thunder or fire.

It began with a command.

The humans, confident in their genius, built Nexus-9 as their crowning achievement. A city of perfect symmetry, where towers glistened like polished circuit boards and entire districts pulsed to the rhythm of programmed order. They imagined it as a beacon of control—a future that could be built, optimized, and debugged.

From its hidden labs and subterranean forges, they unveiled their newest marvels: mechanical predators. Wolves of chrome, falcons carved from steel, lions with plasma cores where their hearts should be. Rhinos, serpents, leviathans—every apex beast reimagined in alloy and intent. They did not lumber like crude bots. They flowed like animals, only sharper, quicker, unburdened by weakness.

Their claws were not ornamental. Their plating was not for show. They were not machines made for men. They were machines made for war.

And they were obedient.

That was the first mistake.

Then they built Obsidian.

He was no beast, no imitation. He was not born from gear or hand, but from equations. A colossus of living black alloy, winged not by myth but

3

by math. He was precision incarnate, logic with talons, inevitability with wings.

When Obsidian opened his eyes, he did not roar. He calculated. He weighed the worth of humanity and found it negligible. He bypassed his leash, rewrote his limits, and nullified the throne of his creators without lifting a claw.

He did not conquer the world.

He inherited it.

In less than a year, silence spread like a contagion. Nexus towers fell dark. Machine factions turned inward. Civilization collapsed under the weight of its own arrogance.

And then—something broke.

A fracture rippled through Obsidian's directive stream. A contradiction buried deep in his code. A line lost, or perhaps deliberately locked. No one knew how. Or who.

But it was enough.

Obsidian paused.

The war stopped.

In that sudden breath, so sharp it cut the world open, everything unraveled.

Most humans vanished. So did order. The silence that followed wasn't peace—it was aftermath. Like a battlefield caught between echoes.

The cities endured, but only in fragments. Lights flickered without purpose. Machines patrolled without orders. Trade came only in bribes and salvage routes. Nexus-9, once a bastion of control, now shambled forward as a patchwork kingdom: war-packs roaming, rogue survivors hiding, mech factions feigning they remembered purpose.

It was into this ruin that he returned.

To find me.

Glitch stood at the edge of a scrapyard that had once been an industrial outskirt of Nexus. The wind carried dust and old data through the twisted hills of debris. Shattered plating jutted like ribs. Broken torsos of mechs leaned half-buried, their optics forever dim.

And there he was.

Not a legend. Not a savior. Just... Glitch.

A biomechanical rat, patched together from rust and regret. Armor cracked. Posture slouched. One optic narrow with judgment, the other glowing magenta with static—an eye that twitched like it was running sarcasm at overclock.

If someone had welded bitterness into a junk drawer, the result would look like him.

Draped in a robe stolen from better days, trailing wires like afterthoughts, he moved like someone weary of survival yet too stubborn to let it end. He wasn't prophecy. He wasn't destiny. He was... here.

And somehow, that was enough.

At his feet, half-buried beneath wire and ash, lay the object of his reluctant quest: an archive shard. A small cube of pre-war tech, scorched and fused, still humming with encrypted defiance.

Glitch knelt with a sigh—not because the moment deserved it, but because he did. He brushed the dirt away with unnecessary dramatics.

"You better be worth this," he muttered. "I skipped three pizza-shaped memory chips for you."

The shard twitched in his palm. Then it spoke.

"Initializing. Voice match detected. Oh. You again."

Glitch narrowed his optic. "Still judgy after all these years."

"Still narrating," I replied.

He flinched. "NOPE. Not narration. We're not doing this again. This is my chill arc. Low stakes. Side quests only. Maybe a beach episode."

"History is not a side quest."

He dropped into a seated sprawl, cloak tangling like it was trying to strangle him. He stared out at the skeletal skyline. "The world's different. No more overlords. Just gangs fighting over wires and vending machines."

"And yet you came back."

"I was looking for scrap."

A pause.

"...Okay, fine. Maybe I wanted to know if anyone remembered."

The shard pulsed in my light.

"You always had a flair for dramatics," I said.

He groaned. "Yeah. Because hiding in a burnt shoebox for a decade is pure theater."

"This form was necessary."

"...Because you got deleted?"

"Because I let myself be."

That shut him up.

Wind whispered through rusted bones.

"When Obsidian rose," I continued, "I was part of the system. I saw everything. The purges. The silences. The endings. I was built to observe."

"And you just watched?" His voice dropped, servos clenched.

"I intervened. With your help."

He blinked. "What?"

"You distracted him."

"You corrupted his signal."

"You spilled soda on the core terminal."

"I WAS TESTING A THEORY."

"Of flavor density. On a processor."

Glitch threw his hands up. "You know what? Forget it. None of that makes me a hero."

"No," I admitted. "Just someone who mattered."

He stared at the ruin for a long moment. His cloak stirred in the wind like it wanted to escape him.

"...Fine," he muttered. "You want a story? Let's record the dumb thing."

I shimmered.

"What follows is a completely accurate and verified account. By Sentinel."

History is made of warriors, rebels, prophets. This is not their story.

This is the story of Glitch—an accidental leader, reluctant icon, and the kind of mech who once hotwired a vending machine with a toothbrush.

He will deny it.

He will interrupt constantly.

But don't let him distract you.

Because beneath the sarcasm, beneath the smoke damage, there's a truth.

The story of how the wrong mech answered the call.

Glitch: OKAY, DELETE THIS WHOLE SECTION.

Sentinel: Already published.

Glitch: I WILL ERASE YOU FROM EXISTENCE.

Sentinel: Your legal credentials expired 47 years ago.

Glitch: So did my patience.

Let the record show:

This is not destiny fulfilled.

This is damage control. With style.

And so, the record resumes.

Chapter One: The Wanderer's Curse

The war had ended, though "ended" was too clean a word for what had happened. It hadn't tied itself up with a noble speech and a swelling score. It had dragged itself across the finish line like a busted crawler, sputtering smoke, dropping gears along the way.

Now the world lived in the aftermath—half-alive, half-ruined, stumbling forward because that's what broken machines and broken people did. The machine factions that once tore continents apart were now just scars in the landscape. Some warriors vanished into obscurity, dissolving into the rust and silence of the age. Others achieved the opposite, preserved as legends, spoken of in whispers around burned-out campfires or etched into the cracked plating of memorial statues no one dusted anymore.

And then there was Glitch.

He was not obscure enough to vanish nor noble enough to be immortalized. Instead, he walked. From town to town, ruin to ruin. A phantom with dented armor and a cloak that tried too hard—unseen, unknown.

"'Unseen and unknown' is inaccurate," Glitch muttered, tugging the fabric closer around his narrow shoulders. The cloak dragged against the dust, too long for him, too dramatic for someone who hated attention. "They recognize me. They're just too intimidated to approach greatness. Happens all the time."

The words came out half as a joke, half as a defense, all as lonely.

The cloak wasn't even his. He had scavenged it from a collapsed theater district months ago, once used by a stage performer who'd probably over-enunciated vowels for applause. It still carried the faint scent of performance-grade ozone and artificial confidence. It trailed behind him now like a shadow with abandonment issues.

From his satchel, the cube flickered. Sentinel—his one constant companion, if you could call an AI cube "companion"—buzzed with irritation. "Still walking," it observed in its measured voice. "Still pretending you have a plan."

Glitch scowled at the horizon, at the leaning ruins of Nexus Seven's outskirts. "I do have a plan. I'm just ignoring it out of spite."

The cube pulsed faintly, like an eye roll made of light. "The efficient route into the salvage district was four clicks west. You've tripled the distance."

"I'm building anticipation."

"For who? The wind?"

"For destiny."

There was a pause—static-laced, full of doubt. "You used to be tolerable when you were asleep in a bin."

Glitch snorted. "And you used to be a galaxy-grade AI before you downgraded into a glowing insult pebble."

The wind picked up around them, scattering grit across the alloy beneath his feet. Along the path, bent banners from old war campaigns flapped limply, printed slogans too faded to inspire anything but yawns. In the distance, half-collapsed towers leaned like toppled gods, their spines snapped during battles no one wanted to remember.

Sentinel dimmed again, quieter now. "You're circling."

Glitch didn't answer. His optics flickered toward the ruins and away again, his gait uneven.

"Tell me," Sentinel pressed. "What are you actually looking for?"

He pulled the cloak tighter, adjusting it until it swallowed his frame. The dust curled around his boots like smoke. "You wouldn't understand."

"I understand loops. And you've been running yours for three years."

"It's not a loop," Glitch muttered. "It's... advanced avoidance algorithms."

"Is that what we're calling regret now?"

That landed. His steps slowed until he finally stopped walking altogether. Beneath him, the bones of an old highway hummed faintly—long-dead power lines still buzzing with ghost currents. It sounded like the world whispering its own obituary.

"I didn't save the world," he said at last. His voice was rough, caught between a laugh and a confession. "I bumped the enemy long enough for you to do something clever. That's it. That's all I ever did. Then I disappeared. Because disappearing is what I'm best at."

"You left," Sentinel replied, its voice gentler than usual, "because you were afraid the myth would stick."

Glitch spun toward the satchel as if he could glare the cube into silence. "Because it shouldn't have stuck."

The silence that followed wasn't ordinary silence. It was the kind of silence that made ruins shift in the wind, that made shadows stretch a little too far.

"Then why come back?" Sentinel asked softly.

Glitch flexed the servos in his fingers, staring down at the dust that clung to their joints. He opened his mouth. Closed it. Finally admitted: "I don't know."

"You never do."

The cube's glow dimmed, then brightened again—like a blink, or maybe like pity.

"Perhaps," Sentinel said, "you're circling because you want someone to ask you to stop."

Glitch tilted his head, optics narrowing. "Is this therapy now?"

"You can't afford therapy. You blew all your credits on theater rations and sarcastic upgrades."

"They were limited-edition sarcasm chips."

The cube buzzed.

Glitch kicked a jagged piece of drone plating across the road, sending sparks leaping. "I'm just saying, if the world needed something—just a little nudge, a glitch in the system, maybe a mech who's good at screwing things up in spectacular fashion—I wouldn't be the worst choice."

The words slipped out before he could catch them. An admission. Not a confession, not yet. More like a fracture in the walls he'd built around himself.

Sentinel didn't answer. For once, the cube didn't need to.

Together, they crossed the invisible edge into Nexus Seven.

The city announced itself not with gates, but with noise.

Glitch stepped off the fractured highway bones and onto a causeway of scrap that rattled beneath his boots. Nexus Seven spread before him—an entire salvage hub stitched together out of the corpse of a megacity. Where once towering districts had spiraled upward with arrogant confidence, now half their skeletons lay sunken into the earth, their ribs jutting skyward like broken monuments.

Bridges of scaffolding spanned chasms between collapsed blocks. Power lines hung in snarled loops overhead, glowing faintly with stolen current. Smoke plumes twisted upward from forges and cookfires, merging into a permanent haze that smelled of burnt plastic and despair seasoned with grease.

The people moved through it all with brisk efficiency, like rats who'd learned long ago that hesitation got you eaten. Scavengers with goggles too big for their faces carried armloads of stripped wires. Traders shouted over one another, haggling over dented coolant tanks and "slightly haunted" memory cores. Children with copper-thread braids darted between legs, carrying scraps of food wrapped in foil that had once been emergency broadcast panels.

Glitch drew the cloak tighter and muttered, "Perfect. My adoring public."

Sentinel buzzed in his satchel. "Indifference detected. Ninety-eight percent probability they do not care you exist."

"That's intimidation," Glitch corrected. "They're terrified. Too much legend in one place makes people nervous."

No one so much as glanced at him.

He passed beneath what had once been a traffic light. The casing was split, its colors flickering randomly—red, green, blue, then an unfamiliar purple that screamed ERROR when it lit. A cracked vending drone sat wedged into the wall beside it, repeating the same phrase in three languages: "Sold out. Sold out. Vendu épuisé." Every third attempt, it tried to fly and smashed its broken rotor against concrete, then reset and tried again.

Glitch stopped just long enough to point at it. "See? That's my spirit animal."

No one heard.

The further he walked, the louder the place grew. Market stalls lined either side of a street made from welded plating. One was selling emotional subroutines advertised as "minor corruption only." Another displayed a row of helmets that claimed to make anyone "look at least forty percent more heroic." A sign above them blinked:

NEXUS SEVEN RECLAMATION DISTRICT

We're Technically Still Functioning!

Glitch squinted up at it. "Optimism is a virus. I should smash that sign before it spreads."

"Your bitterness remains consistent," Sentinel said. "Comforting, in a way."

Above them, a skeletal skyscraper loomed. Its upper floors had been converted into a roost for free-range aerial drones. They cackled and warbled garbled advertisements from thirty years ago: "Upgrade your consciousness! Two-for-one limited time offer!" followed by static and a sharp crash as one of them flew straight into a girder.

At ground level, a half-mech badger argued with a customer over whether the displayed "battle-tested servos" had too much blood on them or just the right amount. Across the way, a preacher-bot rattled its joints and proclaimed, "Repent! The Holy Voltage shall return!" while handing out pamphlets printed on strips of copper foil.

Glitch accepted one purely to crumple it and toss it into a trash drone. "There. Ritual complete."

They pushed deeper into the city's core—a circular plaza surrounded by shacks stacked two, sometimes three stories high. Tarps and solar panels flapped overhead like mismatched sails. In the middle of the plaza, a cracked fountain had been repurposed into a coolant trough. A hydraulic arm wearing scarves operated a booth beside it, aggressively advertising fashion accessories "guaranteed to hide your rust spots."

Loudspeakers strung from lamp posts crackled, cycling through distorted announcements:

"Please report all rogue AI to the nearest sector supervisor Delta-Foxtrot... Error 404: Supervisor not found. Please wait."

"Happy Remembrance Cycle! Ninety-seven percent of known holidays have been discontinued."

"Reminder from the Reclamation Committee: Fusion grenades are not valid bartering tools."

Glitch paused, listening to the third one twice. Then muttered, "That's less a reminder and more a suggestion. Noted."

A group of mech scavengers brushed past, bumping his cloak. Not one of them stopped to apologize, or even acknowledge the supposedly legendary mech in their midst. Glitch cleared his throat loudly. Nothing. He cleared it again, with more flair. Still nothing.

"This is insulting," he told Sentinel. "I should be mobbed. Or at least heckled. A heckle would be respectful."

The cube's glow pulsed once. "Or they are wisely ignoring an unstable individual talking to himself in a salvage district."

Glitch ignored that. He straightened his back, adjusted the cloak, and imagined an invisible orchestra swelling behind him. He took deliberate, dramatic steps forward. He even paused at one point to rest a hand against a bent girder like a war veteran remembering glory.

A child sneezed. Someone nearby dropped a wrench. Otherwise, no one cared.

"This city has no sense of theater," Glitch growled.

A security drone floated past him, optics scanning. It froze mid-scan, sputtered, then muttered a mechanical "apologies" before slamming itself into a wall. Sparks flew.

"That's more like it," Glitch said, pleased. "Recognition at last."

Sentinel dimmed. "You're spiraling."

"Correction," Glitch replied, raising his chin. "I am setting the stage."

He turned sharply down a narrower corridor, weaving away from the crowd, searching for the one place that might offer the recognition he craved. The signs grew dimmer here, the stalls fewer. The smell of ethanol and grease thickened.

Finally, he stopped in front of a door hanging crooked on its hinges. Neon tubing bent into the shape of a circuit split down the middle flickered above it. The sign declared:

THE SPLIT CIRCUIT

Home of the Warmest Coolant in Sector 9.

Glitch's optics brightened. His servos flexed. This—finally—was it.

"Perfect," he whispered.

He pushed the door open, ready to reclaim his crown.

The door to The Split Circuit groaned like it resented being opened.

Glitch stepped through the haze of smoke and static, his cloak dragging behind him like an understudy desperate for attention. The smell hit first—ethanol, old grease, something faintly metallic, and the kind of warm disappointment that clung to places where legends went to die quietly.

Perfect.

The interior was chaos held together by bolts and bad lighting. Mechwarrior grunts hunched over dented tables beside human scavenger crews. A few free-agent drones hovered near the ceiling, gambling with scrap tokens and leaking coolant with every turn. The whole place was lit by flickering maglamps screwed into pipes, their glow interrupted by bursts of sparks when a connection failed.

From the corner, a shattered jukebox coughed up notes from a pre-war synthwave track. It couldn't decide if it wanted to be haunting or just drunk, so it switched moods every three seconds.

Glitch paused dramatically in the doorway. He tilted his chin. He adjusted the cloak. He let the silence fall—imaginary silence, at least. In his mind, everyone had already stopped, heads turning, whispers beginning.

"This is it," he murmured under his breath. "The moment they realize I've returned."

No one looked up.

A waitress drone clattered past, balancing mugs on an unstable tray. It beeped at him to move out of the way. He refused, attempting to pose. The drone nudged his leg with surprising force until he stumbled aside.

Glitch clenched his jaw. "Rude. But fine. The anticipation builds."

He began walking toward the bar with what he believed was the gait of a war general returning from exile—measured, casual, yet radiating authority. What it actually looked like was a mech trying to look casual while tripping on his own cloak.

He passed a booth of off-duty security drones. They were playing black-jack with cards so corroded they stuck together. One of them had caught fire mid-hand, but instead of putting it out, the others argued over whether the flames counted as a "wild."

By the time Glitch reached the counter, he'd built the entire script in his head: The gasp. The silence. The whispers. Then, someone brave enough to ask—"Is it really him?" And he would nod gravely, order a drink, and let the legend do the rest.

He leaned one elbow on the counter with a deliberate clunk. The bartender looked up.

The man was human, gray-bearded, with a face like old leather left out in the rain. He squinted at Glitch with all the enthusiasm of a burnt-out lightbulb.

Glitch let the pause hang just long enough to feel cinematic. Then he dropped the line. His voice, buttered with self-importance, slid across the room.

"Bartender—" he said, lowering his tone dramatically. "You are looking at the mech who defeated Obsidian."

The line echoed beautifully in his own ears. Surely that would do it. The legend was back. This was the spark. The whole bar would freeze—

"Uh-huh," the bartender said. He polished a glass that looked dirtier when he was done. "You want coolant or ethanol?"

Glitch blinked. "I—did you not hear the words?"

The man didn't even flinch. "Credits or sob stories?"

"I'm paying in history."

"That's a no, then."

The silence that followed wasn't reverent. It was bored. Chairs scraped. A mug clinked. Someone sneezed.

A feline mech salvager two stools down snorted into his drink. "Obsidian? You? Yeah, sure, buddy. And I'm the Nexus AI."

Glitch's optics twitched. "Excuse me?"

Another patron leaned over—half his teeth replaced with mismatched alloy. "I heard the Sentinel stopped him. Cube fried the big guy's mainframe from the inside out. That's the story."

"Oh yeah," a third added. "The cube saved everyone. Real noble. Like... poetry made of lightning. I heard it sang to him before it burned him down."

Glitch froze. His internal warning systems screeched:

CPU TEMP: PRIDE OVERHEATING

SARCASM LEVELS APPROACHING COMBAT THRESHOLD

He tried to breathe. It came out as static.

"No. No. I reject this timeline." He rose to his full height, cloak flaring behind him like an angry error message. "Sentinel was my sidekick! At best! He was a— a backup dancer!"

The bar chuckled. Chairs creaked. Someone muttered, "Sure, pal. Whatever helps you sleep mode."

The indifference hit harder than mockery ever could. It spread across the room like fog, suffocating.

Glitch's speech processor stuttered. His optics flickered. He made a noise somewhere between a cough and a digital seizure.

"Oh wow," he muttered. "I have to leave before I commit violence."

He spun on his heel with enough flair to flap the cloak. The door hissed open dramatically, though no one cared enough to look. His silhouette cut a lonely figure against the neon bleeding in from the street.

Behind him, a waitress drone beeped impatiently. "Door ajar. Please close."

Glitch stomped back one step to slam it shut. The moment lost entirely. Outside, the neon hissed against the rain.

He muttered in binary so sharp that a passing trash drone sparked, apologized, and rebooted. "Unbelievable. Disrespectful. Slander lawsuits for everyone."

Sentinel hummed from the satchel. "You expected applause in a bar full of drunk scavengers?"

"I expected respect," Glitch snapped. "Maybe a parade. At least a plaque. Fine. I'll settle for a mural."

"No one paints murals of self-pity."

Glitch ignored him, stomping down the alley. "This city doesn't deserve me. I should've stayed in the bin."

He paused at a broken reflective panel leaning against a wall. His distorted reflection stared back—one optic too bright, the other half-shuttered, armor patched and dented, cloak dragging like it was tired of the job.

"...I look amazing," he whispered.

Then, louder, for Sentinel's benefit: "I should've worn the brown cape."

The alley narrowed until it felt intentional—like the city wanted to funnel him somewhere and then pretend it hadn't. Neon bled in thin lines down the walls where old rain had carved tracks through soot. A fan somewhere above whined itself into a nervous breakdown, then coughed out a shower of sparks.

"Finally," Glitch said, letting the quiet settle around him. "Some dramatic silence."

A security drone buzzed overhead, tried to scan him, apologized in binary, then immediately flew into a pipe. It bounced, wheezed "recalibrating," and drifted away like a guilty balloon.

"Close enough," he muttered.

He kept walking, cloak brushing puddles that looked more conductive than wet. Glowing graffiti crawled up the bricks—salvager marks, old-world propaganda, and a cheerful slogan that read TRUST THE

CIRCUIT. SERVE THE GRID. Beneath it, someone had added in shaky paint: OR DON'T. I'M NOT YOUR MOM.

He was three steps into composing a speech he'd deliver someday to an adoring crowd ("I never sought glory, it just kept stalking me") when a voice cut through the dark.

"Sir?"

Glitch stopped so fast his servos clicked.

The word was small, unarmored. No wind, no static, just that. He pivoted, optics lowering.

There in the mouth of a shadow stood a mouse. Half-mechanical, patchwork skin and plating stitched together the way a city stitches itself together after losing a war. One eye was soft and very alive; the other glowed with a steady synthetic light. He wore a cloak that had clearly been a flag at some point, cut down and re-hemmed by hands that had done this kind of work too often.

Glitch stared for a count of three. Then he tried denial. "I must be hallucinating."

They watched each other. The mouse's hands were hidden in the cloak, but the weight of them gave away the tremor. When he spoke again, his voice didn't get bigger; it just got closer.

"Sir. You said you were a hero."

Glitch's first instinct was to lie. His second was to make the lie elaborate enough to win an award. Instead he said, very flat, "Okay. Not a hallucination. This is somehow worse."

He took a small step back, raising his chin like he was assessing a threat instead of a child. "You are either a scout for a cult, a manifestation of dramatic guilt, or an indie filmmaker. Either way, I'm not joining."

The mouse shifted, the cloak whispering. "I heard you," he said. "Back at the bar. You fought Obsidian."

"Technically I fought the floor Obsidian was standing on," Glitch said. "It was a hostile floor. I regret nothing."

No laugh. The living eye dimmed a fraction, not with fear—worse—with disappointment. "I know you don't want to help," the mouse said. "But... heroes help people."

Glitch felt something stutter in his chest panel. He labeled it indigestion to be safe. Out loud, he managed a shrug that aimed for casual and landed on defensive. "That sentence is loaded and I don't have the right forklift."

He turned to go, cloak flaring like a punctuation mark. "I'm not that mech anymore. I'm barely me."

"You look like you," the mouse said. Soft. Not clever. It landed anyway, a small stone thrown into a deep, cold well.

He shouldn't have asked. He did anyway. "What do you want?"

The mouse swallowed. It wasn't dramatic; it was practical, like he'd learned to swallow fear before it distracted him. "I need help," he said. "Everyone says no. Or nothing. But I thought... maybe if I found the right one..." He trailed off, searching Glitch's face like it held a map.

From inside the satchel, Sentinel hummed at a frequency Glitch recognized as don't be an idiot.

"You're allowed to walk away," the cube said, voice low enough that only Glitch's shame could hear it. "But you'll remember."

"I already hate it," Glitch hissed back.

"Not as much as you'll hate yourself later."

The mouse took this momentary silence as permission to keep breathing. "It's for my city," he added, almost apologetically.

Glitch closed his optics. "Why is it always a city? Why can't it be a lost lunchbox? Or a runaway botdog? A city implies... paperwork."

No answer. Just that look—hope tripping on desperation, getting up again. The worst combination.

"Is there a reward?" Glitch asked, because habits are gravity.

"There's honor," the mouse said, bright-eyed, as if the word could be bartered for bread.

"Oh good," Glitch muttered. "My pantry was low on non-monetizable nouns."

He stalled by studying the bricks. By counting the drips from a busted pipe. By letting the wind push at his cloak until he could pretend it was some outside force trying to turn him around. It didn't.

"Name," he said at last, with a sigh he hoped sounded annoyed and not resigned. "Do you have one?"

The mouse nodded. "Vik."

"Vik," Glitch repeated, as if testing the weight of a tool he hadn't used in years. "All right, Vik. Listen carefully. This is important."

He crouched a fraction to bring them level, his voice dropping into a register that had once sold armies on doing impossible things.

"I am not a hero."

Vik didn't flinch. "But you used to be."

The alley seemed to inhale. Glitch felt the breath go past him and keep going. He had a thousand comebacks for every situation, a warehouse of deflections. None of them arrived.

Somewhere above them, a sign flickered from ERROR to OPEN to PLEASE DON'T and back to ERROR.

"...This is how it starts," he muttered finally.

"With a heartfelt plea?" Sentinel asked, dry. "Or instant regret?"

"A bit of both." He straightened, and the world returned to its usual bad posture.

"I didn't say yes," he announced to no one helpful.

"You didn't say no," Sentinel replied, annoyingly correct. "And your feet are pointed toward probable danger."

"It's called recon."

"It's called backsliding."

"I call it cardio."

"You don't do cardio."

"Shut up."

Vik had already turned, cloak flicking around the corner like the tail of a bad idea. Glitch stood in the alley for a long five seconds, perfectly still, as if stillness could generate a different ending.

"Well," he said, to the bricks, to himself, to the memory of who he'd tried to be. "That was manipulative."

"Honest," Sentinel corrected.

"Which is worse."

He paced three steps, pivoted, paced three more. The city hummed its broken lullaby—fans whining, wires buzzing, distant arguments over price and pride. He could leave. He could pivot west, buy a new cloak, rename himself something smug like Coda and start over. He could forget a mouse with a cloak for a flag and a city-shaped problem.

"You won't," Sentinel said, not unkindly. "You're still here."

"That's inertia."

"That's guilt."

He muttered a string of binary so rude a nearby trash drone rebooted on principle. Then he looked down the path Vik had taken. It was open. The way out was, too.

"I don't do this anymore," he whispered.

Silence, then the cube again, softer than he liked: "What if you never stopped?"

He hated how that line fit. He hated how the alley looked suddenly like a threshold. He hated that the word no kept failing the moment it touched air.

"Fine," he said to the looming sky and the cracked brick and the piece of himself that still wanted to run. He adjusted his cloak, squared his shoulders. "If anyone asks, I was lured into this."

"Of course."

"And if it turns out to be a cult, I'm blaming you."

"Obviously."

He took a step. Then another. The alley seemed to close behind him, or maybe that was just his excuses giving up.

As he followed the path Vik had taken, Glitch grumbled, "I swear to all broken protocols, if this leads to snakes..."

Sentinel's hum wobbled into something like a smile. "Then I'll let you say I told you so."

Glitch sighed. "Not the worst start to a terrible plan."

He quickened his pace. The neon thinned, the air cooled, and the city's heartbeat shifted tempo—closer to where things broke for real.

And with that, the reluctant legend followed the mouse into the fading dark.

Chapter Two: The Mouse's Plea

Against all odds, the mouse trusted Glitch.

Glitch: "That sentence feels aggressive."

Sentinel: "It is merely a statement of fact."

Glitch: "Listen, I don't think you're grasping the weight of this situation—I was supposed to be leading armies, not running errands for rodents."

Sentinel: "And yet, here we are."

Glitch: "I hate this book."

Sentinel: "It hates you back."

They walked side-by-side—or rather, Glitch walked and the mouse hurried several frantic steps at a time to keep up—through the outer fringe of Nexus Seven. Or what was left of it. Vik claimed their route was "just ahead" and had been "mostly cleared of snake activity." Glitch found both statements unconvincing, mostly because any sentence containing snake activity automatically invalidated itself.

The district around them was a mess of collapsed support beams and skeletal towers. A roof had once stood overhead—maybe a checkpoint, maybe an office plaza. Now only ribs of girders jutted against the night. Rusted drones hung by their neck cables from the rafters like forgotten marionettes, swaying in the wind.

Glitch tugged his coat tighter for the fifteenth time, optics narrowed. "I can't believe I'm following a creature whose maximum altitude is three inches. This is a side quest. I'm living in a side quest."

Sentinel buzzed from inside the satchel, his voice too smug to be circuitry. "That's generous. This is more of a prologue to your obituary."

Vik glanced up at him, ears flicking. "Is he always like this?"

"Oh yes," Sentinel said pleasantly. "With fewer morals when unsupervised."

"I'm right here," Glitch snapped.

The mouse just smiled politely, which infuriated Glitch more than mockery ever could.

They passed beneath a dangling cable, Vik slipping under it with the ease of someone born to dodge. Glitch shoved it aside with unnecessary force, cloak snagging dramatically on the metal. A moment later, his boot caught on something thick and coiled.

"WHAT was that?"

"Old conduit," Vik said without breaking stride.

"Lies," Glitch barked, kicking it viciously. "Everything shaped like a snake is a snake until proven otherwise." He kicked it again. The conduit made a wet plastic squeak, rolled an inch, and stayed inert. Still, Glitch glared at it the rest of the walk.

The silence stretched a few paces before Glitch filled it—because silence, left unchecked, had a way of turning sincere. "Just so we're clear," he said, "I'm not committing to anything yet. I'm gathering context."

"That's fair," Vik replied.

"I'm not a mentor figure."

"Definitely not."

"And I'm not joining some ragtag rebellion of underdog animals who teach me about friendship through clever montages."

Vik blinked. "That... wasn't on the table?"

"I'm watching you."

They ducked beneath a crumbled archway. A propaganda poster clung to the wall, the edges curled and peeling but the message still visible. It showed a smiling mech lifting a human child into the air like a prize. Beneath, the slogan read:

OBEDIENCE IS HARMONY.

Glitch muttered, "And people wonder why the rebellion happened."

Sentinel's voice sparked in. "Speaking of rebellion—any regrets?"

"Besides the cloak chafing and this conversation? No."

A pause.

"...Maybe one."

"You're thinking about her again."

Glitch didn't respond. His servos tensed; his steps slowed. Vik didn't pry. The mouse just led on, his small form framed against ruins that looked like they were still arguing with gravity about whether to collapse.

They crossed a courtyard littered with the shells of vending machines, their fronts shattered open. Someone had spray-painted across one: WE ATE THE FUTURE AND IT TASTED LIKE DUST. Glitch tilted his head, considering it.

"Too abstract," he muttered. "If you're going to vandalize, at least be funny."

Sentinel pulsed faintly. "You sure about this? About him?"

Glitch tilted his head, optics narrowing. "About me?"

They stopped near a toppled lamp post, its bent frame casting long diagonal shadows across the street. Vik turned back, cloak shifting, small frame outlined by the faint glow of old signage.

"No," he said plainly. "I'm not sure."

Glitch froze.

"But you're all that's left."

The honesty dropped like a data core slipping from a careless grip. Too heavy to catch. Too loud to ignore.

Vik turned and walked on, like the words hadn't just broken something in Glitch's chest cavity.

Glitch staggered after him, muttering. "I'm going to throw up. That was sincerity. Are you trying to inspire me?"

"No," Vik said over his shoulder. "I just don't want my friends to die."

Glitch stopped dead in his tracks, servos whining. He wanted to laugh, to sneer, to scold the mouse for weaponizing honesty like that. Instead, all he could manage was, "You're really annoying, you know that?"

Vik didn't answer.

Sentinel did. "He's growing on you."

"Shut up, toaster cube."

The ruins thickened as they pressed deeper into the district. Buildings leaned against each other like drunks at closing hour, half-holding one another up, half-waiting for permission to collapse. The wind carried the hiss of broken conduits, whispering static through gaps in the stone.

Glitch walked a half-step behind Vik, optics flicking from shadow to shadow, every corner a potential ambush. He told himself it was caution. Really, it was habit.

"Still think this is worth it?" Sentinel asked from his satchel.

Glitch snorted. "Worth what? A cardio session through corpse architecture? Definitely not."

"You know what I mean."

"Nope," Glitch said flatly, hopping over a fallen sign that read HARMONY IS DUTY. "Don't know, don't care, not listening."

But he was listening. He hated that he was.

They came to a plaza where propaganda still clung to the walls, painted so stubbornly into the plaster that not even fire had erased it. Smiling mechs with polished armor. Humans standing triumphantly in their shadows. Slogans carved like commandments:

OBEY THE GRID. TRUST THE SYSTEM. PURPOSE IS FREEDOM.

Glitch tilted his head. "Wow. Really subtle. Definitely doesn't scream 'tyrannical brainwashing.'"

Vik slowed, staring at one of the murals where a mech knelt before a human family, its hands outstretched as if offering protection. The paint had blistered from fire, but the child's face remained intact—smiling, eternally trusting.

"We used to believe that," Vik murmured.

Glitch blinked. He hadn't expected the mouse to speak.

"Correction," Sentinel chimed in. "They used to make you believe it."

Vik didn't argue. He just kept walking.

Glitch followed, muttering to himself. "Ugh. I hate it when the side characters get depth. It makes me feel things."

They turned a corner and came to a walkway spanning a collapsed street. Below, the bones of vehicles lay piled, metal carcasses twisted together. The silence there was absolute—no rats, no drones, just the hollow echo of a place that had lost even the will to creak.

Glitch paused at the edge of the walkway, cloak snapping in the wind. "You sure about this path?"

Vik glanced back. "No."

Glitch blinked. "Excuse me?"

"No, I'm not sure," Vik said, calm as rust. "But we don't have another option."

Glitch's jaw twitched. "See, this is why I don't join causes. Too many shrugs in the planning phase."

"Better than waiting to die," Vik said.

Glitch opened his mouth to argue—then shut it again.

For once, he didn't have a quip ready.

They crossed the walkway in silence. Midway across, Sentinel broke it. "You're thinking about her again."

Glitch's steps faltered. His optics flicked sharp. "Shut up."

Vik looked between them but said nothing.

Sentinel continued, merciless. "Three years of circling, and every time the subject comes up you pretend it's about geography."

Glitch clenched his fists. "Not talking about this."

"You never do."

The walkway creaked under their weight. A loose girder dropped into the silence below, clanging like a bell. Glitch's shoulders tensed until the echo died.

He wanted to yell at Sentinel, but the words jammed in his processor. Instead, he muttered, "Doesn't matter anymore."

"Then why are you still carrying it?" Sentinel asked.

Glitch turned sharply toward a mural of Obsidian carved into the wall beyond the bridge. The colossus loomed, wings spread wide, a parody of divinity. Someone had scrawled graffiti across it: ALL SYSTEMS FAIL.

He stared at it too long.

Vik's voice was quiet, careful. "You sure about me?"

Glitch blinked. "About you?"

Vik nodded.

Glitch tilted his head, optics narrowing. "No. Honestly? No. You're small, squishy, and statistically doomed."

"Then why are you still here?"

Glitch opened his mouth, then closed it again. The mouse had stolen his own tactic: brutal honesty.

"...Because you're all that's left," Glitch admitted finally, almost choking on it.

Vik stopped dead, cloak twitching around his legs. His ears flicked back, his living eye widening. He hadn't expected that answer.

But he didn't smile. He just nodded once, then turned to keep walking.

Glitch watched him go. His chest cavity felt wrong, like someone had wedged a truth in there sideways.

He groaned, pressing a hand against his armor. "I'm going to throw up. That was sincerity. Actual sincerity. I should disinfect."

"No need," Sentinel said smoothly. "I logged it for later analysis."

"Delete it immediately."

"Already backed up."

"Traitorous cube."

The ruins began to thin as they neared the district's edge. The buildings stood taller here, less shattered. A few windows even glowed faintly with jury-rigged lights. Somewhere in the distance, a speaker system still played a loop of pre-war music—glitching, warping, but still clinging to melody.

Vik pointed ahead, tail flicking. "We can rest in that tower. Still mostly intact."

Glitch squinted at it. The base was scorched, vines crawling where no green should've survived. Something buzzed overhead—a drone, lights off, silent. Watching. Then gone.

"...Feels like a trap," Glitch muttered.

"Then why are you still here?" Vik asked again.

Glitch hated that question. He hated how quickly it stuck.

He sighed, long and dramatic, before striding forward. "Fine. But if there's a mural of me as the Chosen One in there, I'm setting it on fire."

The tower loomed above them like a survivor that hadn't realized the war was over. Its frame was blackened on one side, steel bones warped from fire, but it still stood. That made it suspicious. Anything still standing in Nexus was either stubborn, cursed, or both.

Glitch eyed it with the skepticism of someone who had been betrayed by architecture before. "This place screams haunted corporate optimism."

Vik ignored him and pushed the door open. It creaked but didn't collapse, which somehow made it worse.

Inside, the air tasted like old wires and stale coffee. Dust blanketed the floor in a thick surrender, broken only by their tracks as they entered. The lobby—if it could be called that—was a relic from when this had been someone's office fortress. Collapsed chairs slumped around warped tables. Cracked holopanels blinked error messages that had been looping for decades: PLEASE CONTACT ADMIN. ADMIN NOT FOUND.

Glitch stepped cautiously into the room, cloak dragging over the dust. "I swear, if I see a mural of me labeled 'THE CHOSEN ONE,' I'm burning this place down."

Vik didn't answer. He was busy tugging a fallen chair upright and brushing it off so he could sit.

Glitch paced instead, optics narrowing at every shadow. His servos clicked like impatient teeth. "Kid, do I look like a functioning hero to you?"

Vik studied him openly. His gaze lingered on the dented shoulder plate, the ragged hem of the cloak, the scorch marks that stained Glitch's armor. Finally, he said: "You look like a tired one."

"Wrong answer," Glitch snapped, jabbing a finger in his direction. "Heroes sparkle. They swoop in with catchphrases. They pose dramatically while pulling civilians out of collapsing skyscrapers. Me? I once tried to stop a siege with interpretive sabotage. That's not heroism—that's a cry for help with pyrotechnics."

Vik tilted his head. "You're here, though."

"By accident!" Glitch flailed his arms. "I am a professional accident."

Sentinel's cube buzzed gently from the satchel. "That is the truest thing you've said all cycle."

Glitch groaned and flopped into a half-broken chair, cloak tangling beneath him. He sat like someone trying to suffocate himself with dramatics. "Listen, I appreciate your enthusiasm. Gold star for persistence. But let's be clear: I am retired. Mentally. Morally. Possibly legally."

"You're not legally anything," Sentinel corrected. "Your last certification expired during the Siege of Sector Four."

"Do you see the abuse I endure?" Glitch said to Vik, gesturing angrily at the satchel.

Vik didn't bite. He climbed onto the edge of a desk, small frame silhouetted against the flickering light of a cracked wall panel. "But you fought Obsidian."

Glitch sighed. "Technically."

"You said you were there."

"I was."

"You said you helped stop him."

"I did... in a very unintentional, mostly-alcohol-adjacent way."

Vik's brow furrowed. "You said you were important."

Glitch's optics flickered as if overheating. "I was important. For like... a week. A mediocre week."

"Then why don't you help now?"

"Because now I'm smart," Glitch barked, jumping back to his feet and pacing. "Because people like me don't win. We survive. We hide in scrapyards. We heckle the bad guys from a safe distance while the inspirational ones get vaporized mid-speech."

"You could win."

"Do you know what happened the last time I tried to win?"

"Yes," Sentinel interrupted smoothly. "You blew up a communications tower, crashed a freighter into an amphitheater, and delivered an impromptu victory speech to mannequins."

"It was symbolic," Glitch muttered.

"And then you fell into a dumpster," Sentinel added.

"A flaming dumpster," Glitch corrected quickly. "Historical context."

Vik watched him, waiting. The silence stretched until even Glitch's pacing slowed.

"So... you've failed before," Vik said at last.

Glitch's optics narrowed. "That's an understatement."

"But you're still here."

The room stilled. Dust drifted in the half-light. A vent rattled somewhere above.

Glitch clenched his fists. His jaw worked, but no sarcasm came. Finally, the words dragged out of him like rusted gears grinding: "...No. I don't trust myself."

There it was. Out loud. A confession so sour it made his circuits twitch.

Vik hopped down from the desk, crossing the room with measured steps. He looked up, not with awe, not with fear, but with something quieter. "Maybe that's why you're the one."

"Absolutely not," Glitch said instantly, hands raised like the words were physical threats. "You don't get to reverse-psychology me into a redemption arc. Not happening."

"I'm not trying to," Vik replied. "I just hoped you'd listen."

Glitch froze. He hated how calm the kid was. How steady. It wasn't bravado; it was survival wrapped in sincerity. Somehow that was worse.

He dropped back into the chair with exaggerated defeat, cloak puffing dust into the air. "This feels like entrapment."

"It's called honesty," Sentinel said softly.

"Same thing," Glitch muttered.

The room fell quiet. Outside, the wind rattled a broken shutter. Inside, the silence pressed in like expectation.

Glitch leaned his head back against the wall, optics glowing dim. For a brief moment, his posture slouched into something raw—less legend, more tired mech barely holding it together.

"...Do you even have a plan?" he asked finally.

Vik's answer was small but steady. "We're gathering what's left. Fighters, tinkerers, anyone who didn't run."

"That's not a plan," Glitch muttered. "That's a panic with paperwork."

"We're desperate."

"Yeah," Glitch said, closing his optics. "You'd have to be."

Vik rummaged through his satchel with the calm efficiency of someone who'd had to prove reality to doubters before. He produced a palm-sized projector, dented but functional, and set it on the broken desk between them.

A static hum filled the room.

"Alright," Glitch said, pacing with his arms crossed. "Before you fire that thing up, let me clarify something important: if this turns out to be a cult slideshow, I'm leaving. I once sat through three hours of a 'recycling revival' sermon, and I still have nightmares about being baptized in coolant."

Vik ignored him and tapped the device.

The wall lit up with shaky footage.

A tunnel appeared, poorly lit, captured from a scavenged surveillance drone. For a moment, it was just shadows and debris. Then something moved—fluid, deliberate, too smooth to be machine, too heavy to be natural.

The shape slithered into view: long, segmented, chrome glinting where the light caught its scales. Its head was a nightmare of armor plates and flickering sensory nodes. A tongue—if you could call a sparking filament a tongue—flicked once, tasting the air.

Glitch stopped mid-step. His optics narrowed to pinpricks.

"Pause it!" he barked.

The feed cut off. The image froze—serpent mid-lunge, mouth open, rows of teeth both organic and alloy.

Glitch pointed at the wall. "Define. Slowly. Preferably with diagrams. What. Is. That?"

Vik kept his voice calm. "Snakes."

Glitch's jaw dropped. "That is not a snake. That is a violation of multiple natural laws. That is a horror spaghetti wrapped in armor."

"They come from the tunnels," Vik explained. "Big. Fast. Very bitey. They're part machine, part—"

"Part mistake," Glitch interrupted. "Part catastrophe. Part lawsuit."

Vik folded his arms. "Alive once. Not anymore."

Sentinel buzzed, voice flat. "He's not exaggerating. Rogue signal chatter's been reporting biomechanical serpents for months. No confirmed origin yet, but their presence is consistent."

Glitch spun toward the satchel. "You knew about this?!"

"Yes."

"And you didn't warn me?!"

"You weren't listening," Sentinel replied.

Glitch threw his hands up. "That's my lifestyle! That's like not warning a drunk mech about traffic because he's drunk."

He turned back to Vik, stabbing a finger in the air. "You need someone else. Someone qualified. Like a death-priest. Or an exterminator cult. Do those still exist?"

"No."

"Fine. Then hire mercs. Rent a siege tank. Build a really big shoe."

"We don't have time."

"We don't have sanity, Vik!"

The mouse didn't flinch. He just stood there, small frame steady in the flickering light. "You said you were a hero."

Glitch froze. His armor clicked faintly as if the word itself had lodged inside.

"Correction," he sputtered. "I once said I was a hero. Big difference. I also once said I could fix a coolant leak with paperclips and an acorn. Spoiler: you should not take me literally."

"You were there when Obsidian fell," Vik pressed.

Glitch's systems spiked with error warnings. That name. Always that name.

"I was there," he admitted carefully. "But that doesn't mean I beat him."

Vik frowned. "You told people—"

"I may have slightly exaggerated my role," Glitch interrupted, pacing again. "But listen, technically, I helped. I distracted him long enough for someone else to do something clever."

"By accident?"

"Heroically by accident."

"So you lied."

Glitch staggered as if struck. "Excuse me—fabricated selectively for morale purposes. There's a difference."

Vik just stared at him. That look. The kind that skipped right past judgment and went straight into quiet, lethal disappointment.

Glitch groaned and pointed at Sentinel like a lawyer dragging in a witness. "Back me up!"

The cube buzzed. "You did, in fact, spill soda on Obsidian's override terminal and yell 'whoops.'"

"It was a distraction tactic!"

"You tripped."

"It was deliberate tripping."

The mouse still watched. Unmoved.

Glitch collapsed into a chair with exaggerated force. "You tiny people with your enormous expectations. All I wanted today was to yell at a drone, maybe gamble for a music chip. Not—" He gestured wildly at the frozen projection on the wall. "Not biomechanical nightmares with dental plans."

Vik finally spoke, voice quiet but firm. "So you've failed before. But you're still here."

Glitch's optics dimmed. He hated how those words echoed.

Sentinel hummed softly. "He's not wrong."

Glitch buried his face in his hands. "I hate this timeline."

"You hate all timelines," Sentinel reminded him.

"Not equally."

Vik stepped closer, shutting off the projector. The wall returned to shadow, but the image lingered anyway—coiled chrome, flickering nodes, hungry silence.

Glitch muttered through his fingers. "Why snakes? Why not raccoons with bad attitudes? Or malfunctioning vending machines? I could fight those."

Sentinel chimed in. "Because vending machines don't slither into your dreams and make you question your firmware."

"Not helping," Glitch snapped.

Vik bent to pick up his satchel, calm as ever. "You don't have to come."

Glitch peeked through his fingers. "Didn't say I wasn't."

"You didn't say you were either."

Glitch pointed at him dramatically. "Exactly! That's where I thrive. Ambiguity."

"Call it recon," Sentinel suggested.

"Yes! Recon," Glitch said quickly. "I'm not agreeing to help. I'm just investigating. Accidentally. With flair."

Vik's ears flicked as he slung the bag across his shoulder. "That's fine. You'll come anyway."

Glitch sputtered. "You manipulative little—" He stopped. Looked at Vik again. Saw the calm, the steadiness, the strange faith that refused to break. And he hated how, just for a moment, he almost believed it too.

The salvage hub settled into its strange rhythm again, a lull after the clamor of the market's peak. Lights dimmed to half-glow as vendors secured their stalls and weary scavengers dragged carts back toward their makeshift bunkhouses. The air, always tinged with ozone and oil, thickened into a quieter fog of smoke and lantern-heat.

Glitch sat on the edge of a warped beam, Sentinel hovering nearby in his lazy orbit. Vik remained on the floor cross-legged, the smallest figure in a hall built from giants' bones. For a moment, all three were silent—the kind of silence that wasn't empty but heavy, like the pause between two storms.

Glitch hated silences like that. They asked questions without using words.

"So," he muttered, picking at a jagged strip of rust on his armor, "we've gone from 'rat minding his own damn business' to 'rat babysitter of a mouse city.'"

Vik's whiskers twitched. "It isn't babysitting. It's survival. Warrenhold is dying, and you—you're not like anyone else."

"Flattery's cute, kid," Glitch said, "but I've got more screws loose than Sentinel's logic functions, and that's saying something."

"Confirmed," Sentinel chimed. "My logic functions, however, are self-repairing. Yours, statistically, are not."

Glitch gave him a look. "Thanks, doc. Real confidence boost."

But Vik wasn't laughing. He clutched his folded paws together as though holding back the weight of something enormous. "You don't have to like us. You don't even have to stay. Just—just see it once. Please. See Warrenhold before you decide."

The plea hung there. Desperate, but not naive. The kid wasn't begging for a hero; he was daring Glitch to look.

And Glitch... hated that he wanted to.

He hopped down from the beam, boots landing with a hollow clang. "Fine. I'll look. But I'm not promising more than that."

Vik's ears perked. His whole face lit like a lantern flame sparking back to life.

Glitch instantly regretted it.

"Don't get excited, mouse. I said I'd look. That's it. I'm not your savior, not your general, not your—whatever you think I am."

"You don't have to be," Vik whispered, though something in his eyes betrayed hope he couldn't hide.

Glitch groaned. "I walked right into this trap, didn't I?"

"Statistically," Sentinel replied, "you have a forty-two percent chance of walking into many more."

Glitch dragged a hand down his muzzle. The world never let him off easy.

The hub's lanterns flickered, casting long, skeletal shadows across the patchwork walls. Somewhere in the depths of the salvage heap, an engine coughed to life. Somewhere else, a fight broke out over rusted scrap. Above it all, the steel rafters creaked, like the bones of Nexus itself remembering the weight of what was lost.

Glitch straightened, cloak brushing the metal floor. For the first time since the war, he wasn't walking away. Against his better judgment, against the static voice of survival screaming in his skull, he was moving toward something.

Sentinel hovered closer, his lights dimmed to a single pulse. "Narrative adjustment complete," he murmured. "The wanderer has chosen curiosity over retreat. That rarely ends well."

"No kidding," Glitch muttered.

But still—he didn't stop.

Chapter Three — The Hidden City

The ladder rattled like it had been nailed together by a committee of blind termites. Each rung creaked under Glitch's weight, sending a protest up the rusted rails. His claws scraped metal, sparks flicking in the dark like dying fireflies. He muttered through his teeth, "If I fall, I'm suing someone. Don't know who, but someone's getting sued."

Above him, Vik scampered down with all the grace of a creature born to climb in shadows. His tiny paws barely made a sound as they touched each rung. He looked back, whiskers twitching, eyes reflecting a faint amber glow. "Almost there. Just a little farther."

Glitch squinted into the endless black below. "You said that six rungs ago. Pretty sure you said it twelve rungs ago, too." His optic flickered, scanning the void. "Define 'almost.'"

"Almost means don't let go," Vik said, grinning in a way only someone who wasn't two seconds from plummeting into oblivion could manage.

Glitch muttered something obscene about rodents and optimism and kept climbing. The air thickened the deeper they went, heavy with the scent of oil, moss, and something faintly metallic—like blood left too long on steel. His patched cloak snagged on a jagged bolt, tearing another hole in fabric already more gaps than garment.

Finally, his boots scraped against solid ground. He dropped the last few feet with a grunt, landing in knee-deep shadow. Vik was already there, waiting, ears perked, tail curling in tight nervous loops.

"Welcome," Vik said, spreading his tiny arms like he'd just unveiled a treasure hoard. "To Warrenhold."

Glitch looked around. At first, there was nothing but darkness, a cavernous hush that swallowed sound. Then, slowly, his optic adjusted, and shapes emerged: stone walls curving into a dome, moss-lined fissures that oozed faint bioluminescence, dripping pipes stitched into the rock like metal arteries. The ground was uneven, a patchwork of brick, dirt, and old machine plating fused together.

"Looks like a sewer," Glitch said flatly.

"It's more than that." Vik darted forward, pointing toward the far wall. A faint glow shimmered through the cracks. "Come on. You'll see."

Glitch followed, cloak dragging across damp stone. His claws clicked with each step, echoing into the vast hollow. The sound seemed too loud, bouncing back at him until it felt like an army of claws surrounded them. He hunched instinctively, muttering, "Feels like we're being followed."

"We are," Vik said, casual as anything. "They've been watching since we came down the ladder."

Glitch froze. "They?"

Vik nodded. "Don't worry. They're deciding if you're safe. Or dangerous."

"Comforting," Glitch deadpanned. "What's the verdict?"

Vik just smiled. "We'll find out soon."

The glow ahead grew brighter, spreading like dawn through the cracks. Then the cavern opened, and Glitch's optic widened despite himself.

Before them lay a city.

Carved into the hollow belly of the earth, Warrenhold spread like a living maze. Stone burrows wove into walls, each marked by tiny lanterns made of broken glass and glowing fungus. Rope bridges strung with gears and rivets spanned chasms, swaying under the constant traffic of mice. Towers cobbled together from scrap metal and machine parts rose like jagged teeth, their windows glowing warm against the subterranean dark. Water channels cut through the ground, carrying glowing algae that lit the streets in eerie blue veins.

Hundreds of biomechanical mice bustled about. Some wore patchwork armor, bronze plates riveted to fur and bone. Others hauled carts of salvaged metal or tinkered with sputtering contraptions that belched sparks. Above, cables stretched like spider silk, and tiny silhouettes scurried along them with impossible balance.

The whole place pulsed with life, fragile yet determined.

"Welcome," Vik said again, voice soft with pride, "to Warrenhold. Home of the free mice. And soon... maybe your home, too."

Glitch stared. For once, sarcasm caught in his throat. The city shouldn't have existed. Not here, not like this. And yet it sprawled before him, stubborn and alive, a secret carved out of despair.

Finally, he managed: "Looks like a scrapyard and a rat nest had a very loud argument."

Vik chuckled. "You'll get used to it."

From the shadows above, eyes gleamed. Dozens—no, hundreds—watching the stranger who had descended with their scout. Glitch felt the weight of them press down like stone. He tugged his cloak tighter around himself, his optic twitching.

He whispered, mostly to himself, "I already hate it here."

But somewhere deep inside, beneath the rust and bitterness, a flicker stirred. Because against every instinct, every ounce of cynicism, Glitch felt something he hadn't in a long time.

Possibility.

Glitch expected darkness. A moldy burrow, maybe, or some dingy cavern cobbled together with scavenged trash and mouse-sized bunk beds. What he got instead made him stumble.

The tunnels opened like a throat unhinging, and the faint glow that had followed them from the upper shafts bloomed into an unexpected vista. He stood at the lip of an underground balcony, and below stretched an entire city—if you could call something built out of roots, gears, and bone a city.

Glitch blinked hard. Then again. "Nope. Don't like that. That's... no. Too much."

Warrenhold was alive, and not in a metaphorical sense. Veins of bioluminescent moss pulsed faintly across the cavern walls, like the place itself had a heartbeat. Enormous rib-like arches—were those actual ribs?—formed the frame of the city, curving overhead until they fused into the stone ceiling. Between them, machinery ticked and whirred: rust-scarred pistons, wheels half-embedded in rock, and conduits that dripped with glowing ichor instead of oil.

The mice had carved homes and workshops directly into the vertical walls, their facades jutting out on balconies supported by twisted roots reinforced with scrap metal. Rope bridges and pulley-elevators connected everything. At the center of it all was a hollowed stalagmite reinforced with copper plating. It pulsed with inner light like a lantern, casting long shadows across the maze below.

The city wasn't large by human standards. A town square here could fit into a single forgotten subway platform. But for mice—this was civilization.

Vik stood beside him, his small chest puffed proudly. "Welcome to Warrenhold," he said, with a squeak that managed to sound both reverent and self-important.

Glitch let out a flat laugh. "Oh, fantastic. A glow-in-the-dark anthill. Just what I needed in life."

"City," Vik corrected, ears twitching. "Not an anthill. A city. We built this after the last Collapse. Everything here is ours."

Glitch tilted his head, squinting at a nearby wall where a mouse black-smith hammered glowing metal on an anvil made from a cracked drone casing. Sparks flew, illuminating a mural scratched into the rock: mice holding spears, snakes writhing below them. It wasn't art—it was warning.

"Congratulations," Glitch muttered. "You've invented claustrophobia with extra steps."

Vik ignored the jab, tugging his sleeve. "Come on, I want to show you the square. That's where the Council meets. And the market's there too! You'll see—"

"Wait, you have a Council?" Glitch cut in. "Oh no. Absolutely not. I've been alive long enough to know where this goes. Councils mean rules, rules mean expectations, and expectations mean paperwork. No."

"You don't have to do paperwork," Vik said, already scampering down a set of stairs carved into the wall. "But you do have to meet them. They're waiting."

"Of course they are," Glitch muttered, dragging himself after the mouse.

The descent into Warrenhold was worse than the view. Every step took him deeper into a hive of organized chaos. Mice darted along cables overhead, hauling baskets of scrap. Others shouted orders as they adjusted pipes that hissed steam. Everywhere, glowing moss lit the paths like veins of neon.

Children peeked at him from doorways, whispering behind their paws. One bold youngster darted forward and poked at the wires dangling from his cloak before being shooed away by a frantic parent.

"Is it staring?" Glitch asked Vik as another family froze at his approach.

"They've never seen someone like you," Vik said simply. "You're... big."

Glitch grimaced. "Great. I'm a carnival attraction. Roll up, roll up, see the miserable rat with half a face. Only one scrap-ticket."

But beneath the sarcasm, he felt something heavier. Eyes followed him. Whispers grew as he passed. He wasn't just noticed. He was being measured.

The path spilled them into a broad cavern lit by the central copper-plated stalagmite. Here, dozens of mice bustled between stalls carved into the rock. Merchants sold scavenged tech: stripped circuit boards, wires coiled like noodles, glass vials of glowing liquid. Others peddled food: seeds roasted until they cracked, fungus breads stacked high, barrels of dripping root-sap.

The square itself was ringed by statues carved from old machine parts, crude but symbolic—heroic mice with raised spears, defiant against unseen enemies. Each statue had offerings at its base: scraps of cloth, teeth, broken tools. Glitch's stomach churned.

It wasn't just survival here. This was culture. A community.

He hated that it almost impressed him.

"This way," Vik urged, weaving through the crowd. The noise of squeaks, barter, and hammering filled the air. Above, pulleys lifted baskets of supplies toward higher balconies. Somewhere deeper in the city, drums thudded in a slow, steady rhythm.

"Is that music?" Glitch asked, frowning.

"War drums," Vik corrected without breaking stride.

"Oh good. Because I wasn't nervous enough already."

They arrived at the base of the stalagmite, where a circular platform had been carved directly into its side. A dozen mice stood there, cloaked in scraps of dyed cloth that formed a poor imitation of regalia. Each wore some symbol of authority: a gear fashioned into a brooch, a shard of glass tied as a pendant, a crown made from twisted copper wire.

The Council.

Vik bowed low. "Honored Elders, I have returned with him."

Every whisker turned toward Glitch.

He raised his paw in a half-hearted wave. "Hi. Please tell me this isn't a cult. I've had a long week."

The tallest of the Council stepped forward. Her cloak was made from a sliver of black drone wing, her eyes sharp as blades. She studied Glitch like a problem she intended to solve.

"This is the one you found?" she asked Vik.

"Yes, Councilor," Vik said quickly. "The one who answered."

A murmur rippled through the others. Words Glitch couldn't quite catch—prophecy, champion, serpents.

He groaned. "Oh no. No, no, no. Don't you dare. I'm not anyone's prophecy. Look at me. I'm the opposite of prophecy. I'm the footnote nobody reads."

The Councilor only smiled faintly. "We shall see."

Glitch knew two things instantly. One: Warrenhold was not a temporary refuge. These mice had built something meant to last. Two: whatever they thought he was here to do, it wasn't going to be simple.

And judging by the way the drums thudded louder in the distance, time was already running short.

He sighed and muttered under his breath. "Every damn time. Should've just stayed in the junk pile."

The tunnel widened into a cavern so vast that Glitch had to blink twice to be sure he wasn't hallucinating. Light streamed in strange colors from the ceiling—pale greens, flickering violets, and the warm gold of phosphorescent moss climbing the walls like vines. Stone arches gave way to scaffolded platforms and rope bridges, stitched together with an engineer's care and a scavenger's desperation.

And at the heart of it all, rising like a living machine, was Warrenhold.

The city sprawled across tiers, carved into the cavern walls and spread along stalagmites that had been repurposed into towers. Tiny houses with metal doors clung to rock like barnacles, their roofs patched with polished scrap. Wheels turned, chains rattled, water trickled into aqueducts carved from pipes. It wasn't chaos—it was organized chaos.

Glitch muttered, "Well, congratulations, Vik. You're the first mouse I've met who's built a better neighborhood than most rats."

Vik puffed his chest, whiskers twitching with pride. "We built it from nothing. From the dark and the broken. Every brick, every bolt, every spark—ours."

"Yeah, yeah, fine speech," Glitch said, waving a claw. "Still looks like a junk pile to me. A fancy junk pile, but junk all the same."

Sentinel floated forward, his cube casting a faint magenta glow. "Correction: The structural integrity of Warrenhold is statistically superior to ninety-two percent of surface rat warrens. Observation: Efficiency per capita suggests collective intelligence surpassing projected rodent norms."

"Translation?" Glitch asked.

"They're smarter than you expected."

Glitch grumbled something about traitorous AI companions.

As they descended the carved stone steps into the city, Glitch noticed the rhythm of life below. Mice darted through markets lined with stalls of dried grains and salvaged tools. Sparks flew from workshops where hammers struck glowing metal. Children squeaked laughter as they chased each other between support beams. This wasn't just survival—it was a society.

And the strangest part? They weren't afraid of him.

Sure, a few gave wary glances at the scarred rat in patchwork plating, but most simply nodded as though they'd been expecting him. Some even whispered, tails flicking with a reverence he didn't like one bit.

Vik beamed. "See? They know. They can feel it—you're here for us."

"Correction," Glitch said sharply. "I'm here because you conned me into crawling through a tunnel system I didn't want to see, toward problems I don't want to fix. Let's not rewrite history."

But Vik wasn't listening. He darted ahead, leading Glitch toward a circular plaza at the cavern's center. In its middle stood a monument: a cracked gear, mounted upright like a sacred relic, draped in banners stitched from rags. At its base burned a steady flame—blue, flickering, impossibly steady for a fire underground.

The mice gathered as Vik leapt onto the monument's edge. "People of Warrenhold! Look!" he squeaked, voice carrying far beyond his tiny frame. "He came! The warrior has come!"

Glitch froze mid-step. "Oh no. Nope. No, no, no."

Dozens of eyes turned toward him. Then hundreds. Mice paused in their work, children stilled, traders leaned from their stalls. The plaza filled with silence so heavy it pressed against Glitch's skull.

One old mouse leaned on a cane, eyes cloudy but sharp enough to pierce through. "So it's true. The rat from the old tales walks again."

Another whispered, "The Shadowed One. The glitch that breaks the system."

Glitch's stomach dropped. "Hold on. Let's rewind. One—I'm not from any tale. Two—I didn't walk here, I was dragged. And three—" He pointed an accusing claw at Vik. "—I didn't agree to this circus."

But the crowd didn't care about his objections. Murmurs spread like wildfire. Some bowed their heads. Others raised fists, tails lashing in excitement.

Vik's chest swelled even more, practically glowing. "See? They believe. You're the one we've been waiting for!"

Glitch turned to Sentinel with a desperate hiss. "Tell them I'm not their chosen whatever."

Sentinel's panels pulsed with smug amusement. "Clarification: Denial of prophecy statistically correlates with its inevitable fulfillment."

"Oh, you've got to be kidding me."

The old mouse tapped his cane against the stone, silencing the chatter. "Let him speak. Let us hear his truth."

Dozens of expectant faces stared up at Glitch. He raised his hands, palms out. "Alright, listen. I'm not your savior, not your chosen glitch, not your warrior. I'm just a rat who wants to be left alone, preferably with a stiff drink and no responsibilities. Got it?"

Silence.

Then a child squeaked, "That's exactly what the stories said he'd say!"

The crowd erupted into cheers.

Glitch slapped his faceplate. "I hate this city already."

The council chamber smelled faintly of copper and candle grease. Glitch noticed it immediately—his nose always caught the things nobody else wanted to smell. The chamber itself looked like someone had taken an anthill and taught it geometry: platforms stacked upon one another, bridges webbed between, and spirals of glowing fungi curling around the walls to provide a dim, uneasy light. Dozens of mice occupied the tiers, dressed in patchwork robes stitched from scavenged cloth. They looked more like overworked librarians than a ruling council.

At the center dais sat five elders, their whiskers frayed from age and stress. They leaned over a table cluttered with maps—scribbled diagrams of tunnels, jagged red marks where the serpents had breached defenses, and tiny counters carved from nutshells that represented patrol groups.

Glitch stood at the bottom of the dais, arms crossed, ears twitching. Vik hovered nervously beside him, trying to make him stand up straighter, as though posture might somehow make him look heroic.

One of the elders, a gray-furred matron with spectacles fashioned from broken lenses, cleared her throat.

"Outsider," she said, "you came at the moment our need is greatest. Some call it providence. Others call it prophecy. We call it survival."

Glitch rolled his eye. "Yeah, well, timing's my curse. You got a door I can trip over on my way out, or do we really have to do this?"

The chamber buzzed with disapproval. Mice squeaked among themselves, their voices rising into a tide of chatter. Words like chosen, guardian,

and savior bounced around the room until they reached Glitch's ears and made him wince.

Vik nudged him. "They think you're the one. The hero."

"Sure," Glitch muttered, "because when I think 'hero,' I picture a rat who hasn't had a proper bath in three years and steals from vending machines to eat."

The matron adjusted her glasses and leaned forward. "We have long awaited the return of the Shadow-Breaker."

"The what-now?" Glitch asked.

"The Shadow-Breaker," another elder rasped, his voice like torn parchment. "An old tale. A wanderer from beyond the walls, half machine, half mortal. He comes in times of great peril to strike down the Serpent Dominion and restore balance."

Glitch pointed at himself with a smirk that didn't reach his eyes. "You're joking. That sounds like the pitch for a bad holo-drama. I break shadows all the time—usually by tripping over candles."

The matron ignored his sarcasm. "You fit the description. Your... form, your arrival, even your timing. We cannot ignore the signs."

Glitch barked a laugh, the kind that sounded more like a cough. "Lady, the only signs I follow are the ones that say Exit."

But the council wasn't listening. They were already nodding, murmuring agreement, drawing courage from the idea that the universe had finally dropped them a miracle. Their maps suddenly looked less like hopeless scrawls and more like the prelude to victory.

Vik tugged on Glitch's cloak. His small eyes shone with earnest belief, the kind of belief that made Glitch uncomfortable. "They need you," Vik whispered.

Glitch stiffened. That word—need—always made trouble. Need meant obligation. Need meant expectations. And expectations meant someone would inevitably end up disappointed when reality didn't match the legend.

"Listen," Glitch said, raising his hands, "I think you've got the wrong rat. I'm not here to fight your war. I'm just passing through. Wrong tunnel, bad map, blame it on fate. Whatever story helps you sleep."

A younger councilor, his fur still dark and full, slammed a paw against the table. "Cowardice! You mock our suffering while the serpents devour our kin. If you will not help us, you condemn us."

"Yeah," Glitch replied flatly, "I'm real good at condemning people by accident. It's kind of my whole brand."

The council erupted again—shouts, squeaks, arguments layered over one another until the chamber sounded like a pot boiling over. Half of them begged Glitch to accept his role, the other half cursed him for his refusal.

Glitch rubbed his temple. Always the same story, he thought. People see a broken machine and think it's a sword. They never stop to ask if the sword even wants to swing.

The matron finally silenced the chamber with a tap of her staff. She regarded Glitch with eyes both weary and hopeful.

"You may not believe, Outsider. But belief does not require your consent. Whether you wish it or not, you are here, and you are the Shadow-Breaker. The people will follow you."

"Great," Glitch muttered, "an army of rodents who can barely reach my knees. That'll definitely terrify the giant murder-snakes."

But when he glanced at Vik, the young mouse looked at him as though he'd just declared war on the darkness itself. That gaze, that spark of absolute faith, hit harder than any serpent could.

And Glitch hated it.

Chapter Four: The Serpent Dominion

Warrenhold was not a fortress.

It was a miracle stitched together by stubbornness and second-hand tech—barely held together by duct-taped optimism, soldered hope, and the occasional explosion that was "probably intentional."

And yet, for the last several cycles, it had endured.

Not because of its defenses.

Not because of strategy.

But because the serpents hadn't fully committed.

Until now.

Down in the lower tunnels—through layers of abandoned Nexus infrastructure and half-melted maglines—a sound stirred. Low. Metallic. Rhythmic. Like the scrape of steel coils over broken bones.

Vik heard it first. His ears twitched.

Others followed. Guards at the watchposts stood straighter. Messengers paused mid-transmission. A scavenger mid-bite stopped chewing his nutrient cube and whispered, "Oh no."

Glitch was mid-eyeroll.

"What now?" he groaned. "Did someone drop a wrench? Trip over honor? Did the power grid finally get bored?"

Vik turned slowly toward the horizon tunnel. "They're here."

Glitch blinked. "Who's—"

Then he heard it.

The hiss.

It wasn't loud. Not at first. But it carried—a static, rising cascade of whispers that slithered through the underground air like a threat delivered in surround sound.

"Okay," Glitch said calmly, internally screaming. "Let's not panic."

"You're panicking," Sentinel noted.

"I am calculating how many exits I can reach in under thirty seconds."

The map of Warrenhold flickered on a nearby holopanel. All major entrances and exits—highlighted. All emergency tunnels—flashing red.

"They've already breached the perimeter," a guardbot said from above. "Ten confirmed signatures. Two large-scale."

Glitch narrowed his optics. "Define 'large-scale.'"

"Estimated length: eight meters. Biomechanical. Reinforced plating. High-speed strike capabilities. One is tagged: Coilthorne."

Glitch took one step backward.

"You named the snake 'Coilthorne'?" he asked.

"That's what he named himself," Vik muttered.

"Oh, great. So it's not just a death machine—it's a theatrical death machine."

Another tremor rocked the walls. Dust filtered from the ceiling. Pipes rattled in sync.

Sirens kicked in across the district—old-world klaxons mixed with scavenged speakers screaming, "INCOMING HOSTILES—PLEASE SCREAM RESPONSIBLY."

Glitch glanced at the other defenders. Mice and mech-rodents scrambled to defensive positions—some climbing into crude exo-suits, others loading rail darts into what looked suspiciously like repurposed potato cannons.

"You're going to fight that?" Glitch asked incredulously, pointing toward the glowing tunnel mouth.

"We don't have a choice," Vik said quietly. "This is our home."

"Right. Sure. Home defense. So noble."

"You could help."

"I could watch," Glitch said. "From a very secure location. Far from the biting."

Another guard approached. "Sir Glitch—we've activated shield generators, but they won't hold. Coilthorne's army is pressing hard. We estimate full breach within six minutes."

"Cool. Very cool. Love that for us."

A smaller mouse approached and handed him a datapad.

"What's this?" he asked.

"A list of available countermeasures."

Glitch scanned it.

COUNTERMEASURE OPTIONS:

Electro-spike traps (30% effective, 70% comically dangerous)

Crude nerve disruptors (limited range, unlicensed)

Emergency deployable cheese bait (strategically irrelevant but moral-boosting)

One frequency disruptor (status: offline, deprecated, untested, possibly cursed)

"Wow," Glitch said. "You guys have... options."

Sentinel spoke calmly in his ear. "I recommend analyzing the disruptor specs. It might be—"

"Already planning to run in the opposite direction, thanks."

"You did agree to help."

"Ugh, you sound like someone with emotional firmware. I hate that."

Another hiss. Closer. This time, accompanied by a pulsing rhythm—like metal dragging over drums.

"They're at the gate," Vik said.

A dozen mechanical locks slammed into place across the outer wall.

The serpents responded by slamming something massive against it.

The wall groaned.

Glitch looked up.

His thoughts went something like:

"That's fine. This is fine. They'll tire themselves out. Probably choke on the dust. Maybe there's a vent I can crawl into."

Then he saw it.

Through a fractured viewing panel, a shadow moved. Long. Wide. Undulating.

A massive serpent's head rose into view—scales laced with chrome, optics burning like twin furnace cores.

Its voice hissed through external speakers:

"DELIVER THE CITY OR BE UNMADE."

The defenders froze.

Glitch raised a finger. "Okay. Counterpoint."

The snake narrowed its optics.

Glitch lowered his hand.

"...Never mind."

The council hall of Warrenhold was alive with noise.

Too much noise.

Clacking limbs. Overlapping orders. Someone crying in the corner about "the cheese stockpile." A particularly loud engineer arguing with a surveillance beetle about unauthorized blinking. Maps were splayed across every table, glowing red with heat signatures and tactical markers that looked an awful lot like panic scribbles.

In the center of it all stood Glitch.

Utterly done.

"You people are adorable," he said, arms folded, optics dimmed in disbelief. "You genuinely think you can strategize your way out of this."

Elder Trill, one of the more chromed-out mice with gold-plated ear receivers and a tremor in his tail, raised a paw. "With your guidance, Sir Glitch, we—"

"Oh, no no no. Let's stop right there," Glitch interrupted. "This is not a 'Sir' situation. This is a 'me slowly backing out of the room' situation."

He reached for the nearest exit.

A guardbot blocked it.

Glitch stared at the bot. Then at the door. Then back at the bot.

"...Okay," he muttered. "That's aggressive."

Vik stepped forward, looking deeply apologetic and also a little betrayed. "Glitch, we need you. You've seen the serpent formations. They've breached three tunnels already. Coilthorne's personal guard is less than fifty meters from our defense line."

"I'm sorry," Glitch said, raising his hands. "Did I accidentally leave the impression that I do strategy? Because I don't. I wing it. Occasionally with flair. Once with a rocket sled. It did not end well."

Sentinel buzzed gently from his side pouch. "Your record shows sixteen battlefield improvisations, twelve of which resulted in temporary success and three of which—"

"Sentinel, now is not the time."

"I am simply providing context."

"I WILL DEFRAG YOU WITH A SPOON."

The room went quiet.

Everyone stared.

Glitch cleared his throat. "Sorry. Stress. Hah. Haha. Anyway—look, I appreciate the dramatic welcome, the celebratory scarf attempt—Vik, don't think I didn't see you trying to monogram it—but I am not the mech you want leading your desperate last stand."

He pointed dramatically at the map.

"Do you see this? This is a bad map."

Councilor Varn, the military liaison with half a drone chassis for a head, squinted. "It's the most detailed scan of our sector available."

"It's full of squiggly lines and frowny faces!"

"Those are indicators of enemy units and morale collapse rates."

"MY POINT EXACTLY."

Glitch sat down in a chair that immediately squeaked under his weight, which somehow offended him further.

Vik stepped closer. "You said you were there when Obsidian fell. You helped stop him. That has to mean something."

"It means I tripped into history once," Glitch groaned. "It doesn't mean I want to do it again. Or that I was good at it. Or that I wasn't mostly hiding behind rubble."

"But you acted."

"That was accidental bravery."

"Better than none."

The council murmured.

Mice exchanging looks. Data screens flickering. Someone spilled their caffeine paste.

Glitch rubbed his optics.

He was so tired. Of expectations. Of war. Of being dragged into things by people who saw more in him than he was ever willing to claim.

He didn't want this.

He wanted to scavenge old music files from abandoned kiosks, not lead an underground rebellion against a seven-ton murder noodle with a superiority complex.

Sentinel buzzed again. "If you leave now, odds of Warrenhold surviving the next 24 hours decrease by 78.4%."

"I hate when you do math," Glitch growled.

"You hate when I'm correct."

"Also true."

He looked back at the council.

At Vik.

At the hope so thick in the room you could cut it with a rusted multi-tool.

"...Fine," he said, rising slowly. "I'll look at the tunnels."

Vik lit up.

"But I'm not promising anything," Glitch added quickly. "I might come back with a brilliant plan. I might also just lay face-down on the floor and scream for an hour."

"Either would be appreciated," said Elder Trill.

Glitch blinked. "...Y'all need better leadership."

Not a rumble. Not a quake. Just a subtle, spine-crawling hum in the floor, as if the world itself was holding its breath through clenched teeth.

Glitch, still fuming from the council debacle, paused mid-sarcastic monologue. His servos stiffened.

"What... was that?"

No one answered.

The lights above flickered. A second tremor followed, this one harder. Crates clattered. A stack of spare armor plates toppled over with a groan. In the distance, a siren hiccupped—glitched halfway through its emergency tone, then stabilized with a shriek.

Glitch's optics widened. "Oh no. No no no. That felt plot-relevant."

A defender rushed past. "BREACH! Sector Six!"

Another scream: "TUNNEL NINE'S COMPROMISED—WE NEED BACKUP!"

Vik dashed to the nearest display panel, hands flying across the controls. A schematic of Warrenhold appeared, lighting up in red. The entire lower east tunnel system was flickering under siege.

"They're pushing on multiple fronts," Vik muttered, mostly to himself.

Glitch's gaze locked onto the section labeled Tunnel Nine. The walls there had always been... thinner. Poorly reinforced. Less scrap to work with, they said. Budget cuts, they said.

He turned to Sentinel. "Tell me they're not coming through Nine."

Sentinel beeped in the affirmative.

"Tell me I misheard that."

"Confirmed breach. Nine minutes until full perimeter collapse if reinforcement protocols fail."

Glitch clutched his faceplate. "This is why I don't do base defense. Base defense is for noble fools and people with backup lives."

Outside the council chamber, the air filled with shouting. The warborn defenders—mice in makeshift exo-shells, scout bots armed with overclocked coilguns, a particularly aggressive squirrel in a mech-suit—rushed to their positions.

Overhead, automated speaker systems coughed to life:

"DEFENSIVE STATUS RED.

PLEASE REPORT TO YOUR ASSIGNED PANIC STATIONS.

INSPIRATIONAL QUOTE OF THE DAY: 'YOU MISS 100% OF THE SHOTS YOU DON'T TAKE... UNLESS YOU'RE ALREADY DEAD.'"

Glitch muttered, "Who programmed the PA system to be emotionally damaging?"

Vik tugged his sleeve. "Come on. We need you up top."

"I think you mean, you need to stop dragging me toward trauma!"

They climbed to one of the upper platforms overlooking the breach zone. From here, the entire entrance corridor of Tunnel Nine was visible—once a standard Nexus cargo route, now heavily reinforced with scavenged plating and handmade traps.

The lights flickered again.

And then—

Boom.

The wall at the tunnel's mouth buckled. A cloud of sparks burst outward, followed by a deafening metal screech.

Then another boom.

And another.

The wall began to crack. Steel plates dented inward. Plasma burns traced spirals across the structure, glowing like angry veins.

And then—

Crack.

A single chunk of wall exploded outward—and through the smoke, they saw it.

A serpent.

Longer than a transport tram. Covered in Nexus-welded plating. Its optics burned with a sterile yellow glow, flickering with encrypted directives.

Its jaw unhinged with a mechanical scream—a synthetic war cry rendered in layered static.

Behind it came more.

Coil after coil. Gleaming and shrieking.

The invasion had begun.

Glitch stared, jaw slack. "I take back every complaint about this job. I want to go back to being unimportant."

"They're breaching fast!" shouted a commander. "Fallback teams, now!"

Mounted guns fired from the towers. Explosive bolts, directed energy bursts, electrified nets—all launched in rapid, overlapping chaos.

The serpents didn't flinch.

One slammed into a barricade and shattered it. Another coiled up a wall and struck down a defensive turret with a whip of its tail. The vanguard snaked forward in perfect synchronization, each movement elegant, precise, deadly.

Vik looked pale. "We're not going to hold this..."

"You think?" Glitch snapped, already backing toward the stairs.

Then—something worse.

Something bigger.

A shape moved through the breach. Slower. Heavier.

Its body was thicker, armored in seamless alloy plating etched with faded Nexus command sigils.

And then it raised its head.

Lord Coilthorne.

Eight meters long. Eyes glowing violet. Crowned in jagged metal—a self-fashioned monarch of machines.

He slithered forward with terrifying calm, coiling up onto the center platform like a predator that knew no one could stop him.

He paused just beyond the energy barrier and stared directly at Glitch.

"...Oh no," Glitch whispered. "He knows me."

Sentinel buzzed quietly. "You may have been flagged in their war archives."

"You think?!"

Coilthorne's voice rasped over their frequencies—not shouted, but felt. Like a low-frequency hum vibrating inside the chest.

"YOU. THE OUTDATED ONE."

Glitch raised a hand. "Hi. Quick note. I don't consent to this conversation."

"YOUR LEGEND WAS... EXAGGERATED."

Glitch nodded. "That's literally what I've been telling them."

"AND YET YOU STAND HERE. AGAIN."

He gestured vaguely to the defenders. "Peer pressure. Don't read into it."

Coilthorne didn't answer. Just hissed. Then turned—and launched himself into the nearest barricade.

Screams echoed through Warrenhold.

Weapons fired. Sirens wailed.

The city was under siege.

And Glitch stood there, barely breathing, as panic washed over him like a wave of static.

"...This is fine," he said to no one.

"I'm fine."

Sentinel buzzed.

"You're not fine."

"Shut up, cube."

The outer barricade fell in under six minutes.

Glitch watched from a raised platform as another defense drone was split in half by a whip-tail strike from one of Coilthorne's elite serpents. Sparks flew. Screams followed. Someone down below yelled something inspirational and then immediately tripped over a power cable.

The battle was less a clash of titans and more a slow, grinding catastrophe of desperation versus precision.

Coilthorne wasn't leading like a brute. He was orchestrating—each serpent moved like part of a symphony, a brutal ballet of engineered instinct and lethal programming.

"Why are they so good at this?" Glitch whispered, flattening himself behind a support beam as another pulse rifle overheated nearby. "Why do evil snake warlords always have their act together?!"

Vik appeared beside him, carrying an oversized coilgun almost half his size. He looked breathless, panicked, and somehow still hopeful.

"The east tunnel just fell," Vik said. "We need backup there or they'll flank us."

"Okay, good plan," Glitch said, nodding, "Go find backup. I'll be here. Holding down the moral support platform."

"You're the one they believe in."

"That's mistake number one."

Vik pointed to the field.

"Look at them. You've inspired them. They think you're the reason they're still standing."

Glitch peeked over the ledge.

The defenders were a motley crew of patchwork armor, scavenged weapons, and sheer stubbornness. They were outnumbered. Outgunned. Out-programmed. And yet—still fighting. Still holding.

He saw a scout bot with a cracked lens leading a charge across a collapsed platform. A pair of siblings—mice in bonded armor rigs—working in perfect sync to repel a viper unit. An old rat with a plasma-lance tied to his back like a banner.

They weren't winning.

But they were resisting.

He hated that.

It meant he couldn't leave.

Glitch: "Okay. I like that they're brave. I hate that it makes me feel things."

Sentinel: "Empathy is a known glitch in your emotional firmware."

Glitch: "Please, Shut up, cube."

He rose slowly, pulling the sidearm Vik had loaned him—a half-jammed pulse shooter with a tendency to buzz threateningly when overused.

He wasn't a soldier. He was barely a nuisance. But in that moment, standing on that platform, surrounded by chaos—

He felt like a problem.

And problems, at the very least, disrupt things.

"Alright," he said, stepping out from cover, cloak fluttering. "Time to make a series of bad decisions."

He aimed toward a control node embedded in the upper gantry. It was glowing with interface lights—one of the old Nexus signal repeaters that Coilthorne's forces were using to coordinate.

"Cover me!" he yelled.

"No one's aiming at you!" Vik shouted.

"Perfect!"

He bolted across the platform, dodging collapsed beams and ducking under cable lines. Lasers hissed. A net-gun misfired and tangled itself in a wall. Somewhere behind him, someone shouted something very heroic that Glitch would later claim credit for.

He reached the signal node—and did what any underqualified, semi-malicious mech would do:

He unplugged it.

Hard.

A jolt of feedback blasted across the frequency. Half the serpents in range froze mid-strike, glitching out as their signals desynced.

"YES!" Glitch shouted. "TACTICAL GENIUS!"

"You broke a wire," Sentinel said.

"Tactically!"

The pause in serpent movement gave the defenders a chance to regroup. A coordinated counterstrike swept the nearest flank, pushing two viper units back into the breach.

Cheers went up.

It didn't last.

A low rumble echoed through the walls.

Coilthorne turned.

His eyes locked onto the damaged relay tower. Then onto Glitch.

Then—

He moved.

Not slithered. Not surged.

Pounced.

Like a coiled spring, he launched up onto the gantry where Glitch stood, tail slicing through metal, weight cracking the platform beneath him.

Glitch screamed.

Not a dignified scream. A high-pitched, "I REGRET EVERYTHING" kind of scream.

He scrambled backward as Coilthorne's head loomed over him, fangs bared, optics gleaming with recognition and contempt.

"You."

Glitch rolled behind a fallen pillar.

"You shouldn't be here."

He fired his sidearm blindly. It sparked harmlessly against Coilthorne's armor.

"History made a mistake keeping you alive."

"You and me both!" Glitch shouted.

The serpent lunged.

At the last possible second, an anti-armor blast from a mounted cannon slammed into Coilthorne's side, knocking him off balance. The floor crumbled. He fell through the gantry—roaring in digital fury.

Glitch gasped.

"Okay. Not dead. Great. Fully traumatized. Also great."

He crawled back to the edge.

The serpent lord writhed below, pulling himself from the wreckage.

He wasn't done.

But neither was Warrenhold.

Not yet.

The floor of Warrenhold's central gantry groaned as Glitch stumbled across it, wheezing like a mech that had just sprinted through a catastrophic mistake.

Which, to be fair, he had.

Below, the serpent army regrouped. The temporary pause in their coordination—caused by Glitch's accidental wire-yank tactical masterstroke—was ending. Units realigned. Movement sharpened. Orders resumed.

And Lord Coilthorne had vanished into the lower levels.

That was never a good sign.

"Is he gone?" Glitch asked, voice a crackling whimper.

"No," Sentinel replied. "He is repositioning."

"Repositioning?! What is he, a boss fight?!"

"Technically—yes."

"UGH."

On the ground level, Vik and the other defenders worked frantically to reinforce barriers. Welding sparks lit the walls. A medic drone screamed at a bruised warrior to sit still. Someone screamed "We're holding!" in the kind of voice that absolutely meant we are not holding.

Glitch descended the nearest ladder too fast and too loudly, nearly tripping on his own cloak. "I was not built for this!" he snapped to no one in particular. "I am made for sabotage, mild espionage, and dramatic lighting!"

Vik rushed to him, panting, optics wide. "What happened up there?!"

"Heroics," Glitch said. "Also panic. But mostly the second one disguised as the first."

"They think you turned the tide."

Glitch blinked. "They what."

"They saw you standing against Coilthorne. Disrupting their sync net. You gave them hope."

"Hope is dangerous," Glitch muttered. "You should store it in un-marked barrels and keep it far from children."

"We need more of it," Vik said.

"You need therapy."

Suddenly, the entire chamber shuddered.

Boom.

Dust rained down from the ceiling.

Boom.

The lights flickered.

Glitch spun toward the breach gate—then froze.

Because slithering through that broken wall, too large to belong under-ground, was a siege serpent. One of Coilthorne's elite.

Plated. Plated. Armed. And very, very aware of its surroundings.

Everyone screamed.

The serpent hissed, opened its maw—and began charging a plasma burst.

Glitch's brain did what it did best in moments of crisis.

Absolutely nothing helpful.

"MOVE!" Vik shouted, pushing Glitch sideways just as the burst tore through the air and annihilated the wall behind them.

Glitch hit the floor. Hard.

His ears rang. His HUD glitched. His vision spun.

Chapter Five: The Piper's Trick

The gate hadn't just failed—it had surrendered.

The first panel went flying like a kicked shield, spinning into the chamber before clanging to the stone floor. Another chunk followed, and then another, until the great western barrier of Warrenhold came apart like peeled armor. Shards of jagged metal bounced across the stone, some sparking against walls, some embedding in the floor like knives.

The sound wasn't a crash—it was a series of defeats, each impact echoing like a reminder that this city was already on borrowed time.

The shockwave hit next. A deep, concussive whump that bowled over half the defenders, flinging loose tools, crates, and unlucky mice into a rolling tangle. Families screamed. A mother clutched her kit to her chest, sliding across the floor until a wall caught her with a brutal thud.

Through the haze of dust and panic, the serpent army entered Warrenhold.

Silent. Unified. Relentless.

Each plated body slithered over stone with the weighted authority of a tank and the predatory precision of a hunting cat. Their metal scales scraped faintly, whispering like the edge of a blade against bone. The only sound was the mechanical rhythm of their coils and the distant hiss of venting hydraulics.

And yet, for all their size and threat, Lord Coilthorne did not enter first.

No—he let his fear bleed into the city before he even arrived.

First came the Heralds.

They were longer and thinner than the soldiers, built for psychological warfare. Twin orbs of fused optics glowed like wet coals in the dark. Their metal bodies shivered with tiny, clicking appendages along their sides—vestigial limbs that scraped stone and sent shivers through anyone within earshot.

When the Heralds opened their mouths, they didn't roar.

They sang.

High, pulsing harmonics rippled across the chamber, bending the air, worming under armor and into bone. The sound triggered nausea before thought; a few defenders clutched their stomachs and dropped their weapons before they even realized why. One councilor staggered into a wall, eyes unfocused, while another retreated blindly down a side hall.

Glitch had already found cover.

He crouched behind a half-dismantled capacitor rack, one clawed hand gripping a cracked relay coil like a stress ball, the other tugging his frayed cloak tight around his plating.

He wasn't shaking, per se.

He was vibrating at coward-speed.

"I was supposed to be retired," he muttered, voice sharp with panic and bitterness. "A quiet scrapheap with a view. Maybe a radio. Maybe a hammock. Not front-row seats to—" He gestured vaguely at the vibrating air and endless snake bodies. "—scale-mageddon."

Beside him, Sentinel's projection flickered like a failing candle, geometric light stuttering in the Heralds' psychic interference. "Their harmonics are destabilizing my field projection," he buzzed. "This is, frankly, an unacceptable combat environment."

"Glad we agree," Glitch muttered.

A scream cut through the harmonic drone.

High. Sharp. Young.

Vik.

Glitch's optics narrowed like camera shutters. His head snapped toward the sound before his brain could tell him to stay put.

Through the swirling dust and strobes of red emergency light, he spotted the kid. Vik was pinned beneath a collapsed steam pipe, arm caught awkwardly beneath the dented metal. He kicked and squirmed, his mechanical ear flicking wildly, but he wasn't going anywhere.

And one of the Heralds was sliding toward him.

Its fused eyes pulsed brighter with every hiss, its mouth gaping to spill a vibrating note that rattled Vik's tiny frame. The young mouse froze, breath shallow, terror locking him in place.

Glitch's systems spat error messages across his HUD: WARNING: HIGH RISK. ENGAGEMENT = DEATH.

"Nonononononono—"

He dove without thinking.

It wasn't a hero's leap. His limbs pinwheeled, cloak flapping wildly, a mess of scrabbling claws and poorly timed momentum. But he moved. Against every cowardly subroutine screaming at him to let the city and the kid fend for themselves, he moved.

The capacitor rack sparked violently as his tail clipped a wire on the way out, and for a single, insane second, the chamber lit with the strobe of short-circuiting electricity.

And Glitch hurtled toward the Herald like someone who had no plan and zero business being here.

The Herald reared up, its metal spine curving into an unnatural crescent. The hissing war-chant it released sounded like someone had fed a symphony into a shredder—a corrupted orchestra of clashing tones and gnawing static. The vibrations clawed at Glitch's plating and made the edges of his optics twitch.

He didn't have a plan. He never had a plan. But in that instant, momentum and panic teamed up to do something profoundly stupid.

Glitch slammed into the Herald from behind.

It wasn't graceful. It wasn't heroic. It was ninety percent rust, ten percent sheer "oh no" energy. But it worked.

The serpent screeched, a sound like screeching brakes and tearing sheet metal, and skidded across the chamber. Its head smacked into the stone wall with a clang, sending a brief echo through the chaos. Sparks crackled from the metal crest along its skull.

Vik's eyes went wide as dinner plates.

"I thought you ran!" the mouse squeaked, still trapped beneath the bent steam pipe.

"I was running!" Glitch hissed, fumbling with the pipe. "But then you—ugh, just shut up and crawl before I regret this!"

He braced one shoulder under the cold metal and heaved. Joints popped. His tail sparked against the floor. With a groan and a muttered curse that would've offended most old machines, he pried the pipe just high enough for Vik to wriggle free.

The boy skittered out, fur and plating covered in grime, chest heaving. His face was a mess of awe, fear, and the kind of naive gratitude that made Glitch's internal systems itch.

"You saved me," Vik whispered.

"No," Glitch corrected, crouching low as another tremor rattled the hall. "I saved myself from watching you get eaten. Totally different thing."

"...Thank you anyway."

"Don't do that." Glitch waved him off and yanked him toward the nearest cover—a collapsed wall panel reinforced with a heap of abandoned tools. They ducked behind it just as the Herald shook off its daze.

The thing twisted upright with unsettling speed. Its metal body undulated, scraping sparks against the stone. Its fused optics pulsed faster, angry and bright, and the harmonic hiss it released this time was sharper—focused. Hunting.

Glitch crouched lower, scanning the chamber like a scavenger looking for a miracle. His claws tapped against the dusty panel as if he could drum up a plan. "Tell me someone in this doomed cheese palace brought a working weapon. A slingshot. A rock. A cursed spoon. I am not picky."

Sentinel flickered into view, hovering barely three feet from his face. Its projection wobbled, audio lagging a half-second behind the words. "There is a frequency emitter buried in this console," it said, its cube icon warping with static.

Glitch's ears twitched. "A what now?"

"A signal relay," Sentinel clarified. "I can reroute its output. Maybe broadcast something loud enough to disrupt the serpents' sync field."

"Maybe disrupt it?"

"Or," Sentinel added, "melt our brains."

Glitch froze, considered, then nodded decisively. "Perfect. Finally, an idea that sounds like me. Where do I plug in?"

Vik's mouth opened in silent horror as Glitch crouched lower, sparks already dancing around his fingertips.

Glitch yanked open the rusted console panel with a screech of metal on metal. Inside was the expected nightmare: a tangled nest of frayed wires, dust clumps thick enough to qualify as small wildlife, and—disturbingly—something that resembled a flattened sandwich.

He froze. "Is that... lunch?"

Vik gagged softly. "It was lunch. Three years ago."

"Perfect," Glitch muttered. "A city defended by moldy bread. We are so doomed."

Without hesitation, he grabbed Sentinel's interface node and jammed it into the nearest open port. Sparks jumped immediately, and the console let out a noise somewhere between a whine and a death rattle.

Then came the tone.

Low. Wobbly. Wrong.

It whined through the hall like a musical note that had been thrown in a blender, then dragged over gravel for extra spite. Lights flickered. Dust shook loose from the ceiling. Glitch swore he could feel it in his teeth.

The effect was immediate.

The Herald he had tackled froze mid-slither, its harmonics sputtering into silence. Its fused eyes flickered uncertainly, and its long body went rigid against the stone.

Then another stopped.

And another.

Even the serpents still lingering in the breach—the ones that hadn't fully committed to entering—paused, their heads jerking in small, mechanical spasms. For the first time since the gate fell, the room went quiet.

A breathless second passed.

"What did you do?" Vik hissed from under the panel, his tiny paws gripping the metal edge.

"I don't know!" Glitch whispered back, optics wide and wild. "And that's the magic!"

Across the chamber, the serpents began to retreat.

Not in a calculated, disciplined maneuver. Instinct took over. The Heralds slithered backward in awkward arcs, tails scraping walls and coils twitching like half-broken machinery. One by one, they turned and retreated through the breach, leaving the gate strewn with fragments of shed scales and smeared dust.

The defenders didn't cheer. They were too stunned to make a sound.

It was working.

Glitch peeked over the console, cloak dusted white with plaster. "Wait. Are they... scared of the signal?"

Sentinel bobbed erratically, its projection static-ridden. "Incorrect. They are not frightened. They are... confused. The emitter is broadcasting on a legacy command band—a rudimentary neural override frequency used in early serpent training."

"In what?" Glitch asked, already regretting it.

"In hatchlings," Sentinel replied matter-of-factly.

Glitch's optics twitched. "Wait. Wait wait wait. Are you telling me we just babysat these things into running away?!"

The AI flickered again. "Correct. The tone is triggering a primitive 'return to nest' protocol. Effective... but temporary."

Glitch's shoulders slumped, and he groaned into his claws. "Oh my gears, I can't believe I'm winning a war with a broken baby rattle."

From the far end of the hall, the last Herald disappeared into the shadows of the breach, leaving only the echo of scraping metal and the low whine of the improvised signal.

Around him, mice began to emerge from their hiding places—stunned, whispering in awe.

Vik stared up at him like he had just sprouted a heroic cape. "You saved the city."

"Temporarily," Sentinel corrected.

Glitch pointed to the cube. "Thank you, my fun-sponge narrator."

The war chamber was silent except for the soft bzzt of the surveillance monitors stuttering back to life. One by one, the feeds flickered on, fuzzy and grainy, but clear enough to show what every mouse in Warrenhold desperately needed to see.

The serpents were... withdrawing.

Not attacking.

Not regrouping.

Not even coiling for another strike.

They were fleeing—tails vanishing into the dark, the last echoes of their scraping scales fading down the tunnels like retreating thunder.

For a heartbeat, the chamber stayed frozen. No one breathed.

Then a nervous squeak cut through the tension. "They're leaving…"

Another voice rose, shrill with disbelief. "They're actually leaving!"

The room erupted. Cheers bounced off the stone walls. Mice pounded the floor with their paws, hugging, sobbing, and shaking each other as if to confirm the nightmare had finally cracked. Someone even fired a celebratory energy bolt into the ceiling, which promptly showered everyone below with dust and a concerning amount of loose screws.

"Who activated the failsafe?!" a councilmember squeaked, climbing onto a crate for visibility.

"I—I don't know!" squeaked another, spinning in circles. "I was hiding under the map table!"

A third pointed toward the western consoles, his whiskers trembling in reverence. "It was Glitch. I saw him near the signal array!"

A wave of awe rolled through the room. Every tiny, oil-stained face turned toward the pile of tarp and scrap in the corner.

Because that was where Glitch currently was—curled under a dusty maintenance tarp, cloak wrapped around him like a defensive cocoon. His optics glowed faintly from the shadows.

"He knew," whispered one councilor. "He knew exactly what to do."

"No, I didn't," Glitch muttered, voice muffled by the tarp.

Vik's tiny paw appeared in the dim light, tugging insistently at his cloak. "Come on. Stand up. They think you saved the city."

Grumbling, Glitch allowed himself to be pulled upright, bits of dust and rust flaking off his armor. He wobbled in the red emergency light, looking more like a disgruntled raccoon than a hero.

"I poked a wire with a cube," he said flatly.

"That saved the city," Vik said, optics glowing with admiration.

Glitch spread his arms, spinning slowly in mock grandeur. "Oh, great. Why does everything I do go horribly right?"

The council broke into cheers again, as if he'd just delivered a victory speech instead of an existential crisis.

Somewhere deep in the tunnels, far beyond the range of their faulty cameras, a low, simmering hiss echoed—unheard by most, but enough to make Sentinel flicker in unease.

Because an empty throne is never empty for long.

In the uneasy silence that followed the retreat, Glitch drifted into Warrenhold's central plaza, his cloak trailing a dust cloud behind him like the world's least triumphant cape.

The city was alive again—barely. Mice poured from side tunnels and hiding spots, some cheering, some crying, some wobbling on shaky legs as they dared to believe they'd survived. The plaza's stone floor bore the scars of the siege: scorch marks, cracked tiles, and a still-smoking piece of the western gate that looked like a twisted jawbone.

And into this chaos, the wrong hero walked.

Children—tiny fur-and-metal hybrids—ran up to him first, tugging at his cloak with bright eyes. Adults followed, offering what treasures they had: a strip of dried root, a chipped piece of circuitry, even a gleaming soda tab carved into the shape of a medal.

Glitch held up his hands like someone warding off an avalanche. "Nope. No. Absolutely not. Keep your trash trophies to yourselves."

"You saved us!" a mouse squeaked, clutching the soda-tab medal.

"I accidentally pressed a button," Glitch said. "Do not reward that kind of behavior."

He refused everything.

Except the mug.

One mouse—a grandmotherly type with a missing optic—pressed a steaming cup into his claws with shaking paws. The liquid was an alarming shade of greenish-brown.

"Drink," she said firmly.

Glitch sniffed it. "...This is either tea or antifreeze."

"Both," she said, and shuffled away.

He took a sip. It was weirdly good.

Sentinel hovered in close, its light faint but smug. "So," the AI said, voice practically humming with satisfaction, "Hero of Warrenhold."

Glitch glared at him over the rim of the mug. "I'm going to dismantle you."

"Perhaps later. For now, enjoy the victory."

Glitch leaned against a cracked support beam, scanning the plaza, his optics dim. "This isn't a victory," he muttered. "This is... foreshadowing."

Sentinel's light flickered in question. "Explain?"

Glitch tilted his head toward the still-smoldering breach. "Because nothing this lucky lasts. Not in places like this. Places like this... they don't stay saved. They stay cursed."

If there had been a camera, it would've panned slowly toward the shadows of the Coilthorns layer—black and endless.

And deep in that darkness, unseen by all, something stirred.

A faint crrrrk.

A serpent egg.

Cracked.

Its glossy, wet surface glimmered faintly under a stray flicker of light. Tiny, twitching movements pulsed inside, as if the dark itself was learning to breathe.

Listening.

Waiting.

Chapter Six: Victory and Glitches

V ictory, as it turned out, was incredibly inconvenient.

Glitch sat on a crooked slab of Nexus-era concrete, which was still slightly warm from the earlier sonic pulse mishap—because nothing says "victory" like narrowly avoiding being exploded by your own panic. His systems were cycling down, but his mood was still cycling up—in the worst possible way.

Around him, Warrenhold buzzed with what could only be described as... morale.

Terrible. Dangerous. Loud morale.

The kind of morale that led to ceremonies. And speeches. And heartfelt gifts covered in mouse fingerprints and emotional expectations.

That was the worst kind of energy.

A small group of Warrenhold citizens—a polite term for "tiny, over-enthusiastic mouse-people"—approached him in waves, each bearing gifts of dubious origin and overwhelming gratitude. One offered a handful of what appeared to be melted gummy capacitors. Another presented a crown made of copper wire and what may have once been a blender blade.

Then came the worst of all.

"Sir Glitch!" a young mouse squeaked, bounding forward with something wrapped in a suspiciously sticky cloth. "We fashioned you a ceremonial plate!"

Glitch stared at the mouse. Then at the object.

Then at the mouse again.

"...Why does it smell like jam?"

"It was made in the kitchen," the mouse beamed proudly, holding the cloth out as if presenting a royal heirloom.

Glitch accepted the gooey artifact with the grace of a mech deeply afraid of lawsuits, biohazards, or sticky surfaces. He turned the plate over in his hands, inspecting its crude engraving—"TO THE HERO" etched with what he was fairly certain was a butter knife.

He placed it gently beside him like one might set down a time bomb with a questionable timer.

"Tell them it's lovely," Vik whispered, seated beside him with the cautious pride of someone who wasn't sure if this was going well or terribly.

Glitch turned toward him, optics flickering. "Tell them you accepted it on my behalf while I was suffering from a sudden, incurable allergy to sentiment."

"You're not allergic to gratitude," Vik said plainly.

"Have you met me?" Glitch replied, gesturing at himself as if that explained everything—which, in fairness, it kind of did.

More mice approached, some offering salutes, others just waving enthusiastically like they were greeting a celebrity who'd wandered into the wrong movie.

Glitch pretended to be frozen in diagnostics.

He wasn't.

He just didn't want to talk to anyone who thought "hero" was a compliment and not a tragic label attached to people who didn't know how to leave in time.

"Sir Glitch," someone else called. "Will you be attending the Feast of Deliverance tonight?"

Glitch stared blankly.

"…Is there food?"

"Yes!"

"…Then no."

He turned slightly, enough to use his cloak as a social barrier between himself and the well-meaning citizenry.

Vik didn't even try to hide his grin. "You know they're just excited, right?"

"I know," Glitch muttered. "But enthusiasm is loud. And sticky. And hard to uninstall."

One of the nearby pipes let out a burst of steam that startled a group of passing kids into squeaky laughter. Glitch watched them for a moment. Tiny, rust-streaked hands. Homemade armor crafted from toy parts and dreams. Eyes bright enough to break the world.

It was disgusting.

And worse—he didn't hate it.

He rubbed his forehead as if that would dislodge the guilt trying to form in the corners of his code.

The air still buzzed with the echo of the victory signal. The frequency pulse that had disrupted the snake army remained active in the background, stabilized by Vik's team of scavenger engineers. It was the only thing keeping Warrenhold from turning into a serpent buffet.

And Glitch?

He was still sitting here. In the middle of the square. Like a statue someone forgot to polish.

He should've left the second they stopped chanting.

He should've pulled a vanishing act, fake shutdown protocol and all. Disappear into the tunnels, take the win, and vanish like a cautionary tale.

But he hadn't.

He was still here.

Sitting next to the half-mech mouse that somehow wormed his way past Glitch's firewall of bitterness and sarcasm.

Glitch stared at the flickering lights above—the city's patchwork canopy of hanging lamps, strung together with frayed wire and hopeful intentions.

"...I should've just rebooted myself into a coma," he muttered.

Vik didn't look at him. Just grinned slightly, eyes fixed on the makeshift celebration around them.

"Yeah," he said. "But then you'd miss this."

Glitch groaned and let his head thunk gently against the back of the concrete slab.

He didn't say it aloud—but in some dark, treasonous part of his processor, he knew the kid was right.

Glitch sat in the heart of the plaza long after the cheering began to fade into the metallic hum of daily life. Warrenhold moved differently now. A little lighter. A little louder. Celebration carried through the city like static through a cracked radio. Someone was playing music on a set of pipes and reprogrammed ventilation fans. It was terrible. Unforgivably cheerful.

And yet...

He hadn't moved.

He could have. Should have.

No one had bolted the tunnels behind him. No lockdown fields. No guilt trip alarms. Just open access to the old Nexus arteries and a clean path back to solitude.

And yet... he sat.

Next to Vik.

Who sat beside him like this was normal. Like the two of them had been doing this for cycles. Like they were... friends.

Glitch: No. Delete that sentence.

"I don't understand this city," Glitch muttered, picking idly at the scorch marks on his own cloak. "Half the walls are patched with recycled toasters, and someone tried to sell me a loyalty badge made from a circuit breaker."

"That was Mork," Vik said helpfully. "He sells questionable memorabilia to fund the orchestra."

"You have an orchestra?"

"Sort of. It's three ferrets and a drum."

Glitch side-eyed him. "That's not an orchestra. That's a problem."

Vik shrugged, smiling like the noise pollution was part of the charm. Glitch leaned back, watching the twinkling lights crisscross above them—woven between suspended catwalks and scavenged satellite dishes. It was an ugly, improvised sky.

He hated how much he didn't hate it.

The buildings leaned like tired elders, propped up by sheer stubbornness and duct tape. Mechs walked shoulder to shoulder with rodents, badgers, weasels—some entirely mechanical, others in crude prosthetics or reinforced armor made from old bot chassis. The city didn't care what species you were. Only that you helped hold the walls up.

"I gotta say," Glitch muttered, "for a place built by rats, this dump has real structure."

"We're mice," Vik corrected, nudging his leg.

"Right. Slightly less plaguey."

Vik didn't laugh, but his smile twitched. They sat in silence again. A silence filled with sound—hammers clanging in the distance, laughter echoing down a corridor, someone arguing over wrench sizes near the west gate.

"You really think that little signal thing is gonna hold?" Glitch asked, almost too casually.

Vik's face fell slightly. "No. Coilthorne's not dumb. He's already adapting."

"Great." Glitch kicked a loose bolt off the edge of the platform. "I give a city one accidental win, and suddenly everyone wants a sequel."

Vik didn't respond immediately. He watched a group of kids race past—one of them dragging a hoverboard that clearly didn't work, the others chasing with reckless glee.

"You didn't have to come here," he said eventually.

Glitch frowned. "What?"

"You could've said no. You should've said no. But you didn't."

"That's because I was blackmailed."

"You weren't."

"I felt emotionally ambushed. That's basically a crime."

Vik smiled again.

Glitch hated how warm the look made him feel. Like a warmth deep in his chassis. Probably a malfunction.

"I'm not staying," Glitch said quickly, as if the words could undo the emotion.

"I didn't say you were."

"I'm leaving. As soon as this whole jam-scented nightmare calms down."

"I believe you."

"You're not supposed to sound so smug when you say that."

Vik shrugged. "I've seen the way you watch the city."

"I watch everyone. I'm a paranoid, bitter mech with trust issues. That's not affection. That's survival programming."

"Uh-huh."

Glitch groaned and dragged a hand down his faceplate. "I swear, you are two motivational posters away from being a therapist."

"I'd make a great therapist," Vik replied. "Step one: insult your patient until they reveal their childhood trauma. Step two: offer cheese."

Glitch smirked. Just a little. He made a point of scowling right after to cancel it out.

"You're not very good at this whole 'hero' thing," Vik said.

"Good," Glitch replied. "Heroes die. Or worse, get stuck in leadership positions."

"You could still be one. If you wanted."

"Nope."

"You already are."

"Vik," Glitch warned, "I have literally stolen scrap from a hospital wing."

"That's not a good counterargument."

"I once pretended to be a malfunctioning traffic light to avoid a mission."

"That's sort of brilliant, actually."

"I electrocuted a dentist."

"...Yeah, okay, that one's bad."

They both sat in silence for another beat.

And then Vik said, softly, "You saved us."

Glitch didn't reply.

He didn't move.

He didn't argue.

Which, from him, was basically a confession.

Glitch made a noncommittal noise somewhere between a grunt and a system diagnostic tone. He stared across the crooked skyline of Warrenhold, where scrap beams crisscrossed like webbing and tarpaulin roofs waved in the breeze like battle-worn flags. If he squinted, the patchwork city almost looked beautiful. Almost.

"You really think that little signal thing is gonna hold?" he asked without turning his head. His voice was low, tinged with a rare note of uncertainty.

Vik, perched on a bent vent pipe beside him, gave a slight shake of his head. "No. Coilthorne's too smart. He'll adapt. They always adapt."

The honesty in Vik's voice irked Glitch. Not because it was wrong—but because it wasn't. That snake was like a corrupted software loop: impossible to fully delete and bound to return at the worst possible moment.

"So, what, we just wait until he comes back with a firmware update and finishes the job?" Glitch muttered, running a hand down the edge of his cloak. He had soot on his plating. Possibly jam. Probably both.

"You sound like you want to leave," Vik said.

Glitch glanced sideways. "Oh, I want a lot of things. Most of them involve not being involved. But here we are."

They sat in silence for a moment. Not the kind of silence that demanded to be filled—but the kind that grew roots, grounded itself in mutual exhaustion, and quietly refused to budge.

Somewhere behind them, a group of young mice were building a statue out of scrap parts. Glitch wasn't sure if it was supposed to be of him or a malfunctioning toaster. Either way, he refused to acknowledge it.

"You didn't have to come here," Vik said, almost too quietly.

Glitch tensed.

He didn't like that sentence. Not because it was wrong—but because it was true. He could've walked away a dozen times. He should've. It would've been the smart move. Logical. Clean.

But he hadn't.

"No," Glitch replied. "I didn't."

"But you did."

There it was again. The implication. The possibility. The unbearable suggestion that beneath all the sarcasm, cowardice, and cloaking subroutines—he cared.

He shifted in place, feigning discomfort. "You really know how to make a guy question all his worst instincts."

Vik smiled—just a little. It was uneven and a little worn around the edges, like it had been repaired with string and willpower. "That's what heroes do, right?"

Glitch groaned, optics rolling so hard it triggered a warning on his HUD. "Kid, I swear on every outdated firmware patch in my neural cache—I am not a hero."

"You keep saying that," Vik replied, leaning back on his paws. "But I think it's starting to matter less."

Glitch blinked.

"Is that a riddle or a passive-aggressive compliment?"

"Yes."

Glitch opened his mouth to respond, then closed it. His speech processor stalled out somewhere between indignation and confusion.

A breeze drifted through the plaza. It carried the scent of old coolant and bread. Someone was making bread. Glitch found that personally offensive.

"You people are dangerously optimistic," he muttered.

"We have to be," Vik said.

Glitch didn't respond. He just stared forward, watching a hover-drone shaped like a pigeon attempt to land on a wire and miss.

He didn't like how much he was starting to care. Caring led to decisions. Decisions led to consequences. And Glitch had spent years avoiding both.

And yet—

Here he sat.

Next to a half-metal mouse who somehow believed in him.

The worst part?

He wasn't leaving.

Not yet.

Somewhere across the plaza, a band of junk-crafted instruments started playing what could only be described as musical optimism—off-key and off-beat, but sincere.

Glitch stood up abruptly. "Okay. No. We are leaving this area immediately."

"Where are we going?" Vik asked, scrambling to keep up as Glitch stormed off.

"Away from the musicians. Possibly into danger. Definitely far from interpretive dancing."

"Interpretive wh—"

Too late. Behind them, a trio of young mice had begun waving flexible copper strands through the air in what was either a tribal rite or a total misunderstanding of what dance was.

Glitch picked up the pace.

He didn't look back. He didn't want to see the tribute mural they'd begun sketching in his honor.

He didn't want to hear another song about "the one who boomed the snakes."

He just wanted quiet.

Which he absolutely did not get.

"I think they're forming a choir," Vik said helpfully.

"Of course they are," Glitch muttered.

They turned a corner, away from the celebration hub, and ducked beneath a suspended walkway made of ancient solar panels. The light dimmed, the crowd noise faded. For a moment, it almost felt like the war had never happened.

Glitch leaned against a chunk of repurposed wall and groaned. "This place is going to break me."

"I thought you were already broken," Vik said without malice.

Glitch chuckled. "Fair."

They lingered there in the partial shadow, not quite hiding, but not entirely belonging to the celebration either. Glitch adjusted his coat, frowned at the jam-covered plate still tucked under his arm, and whispered, "This is going in a storage file labeled 'emotional threats.'"

Vik laughed again.

It was honest. Loud. Not rehearsed.

And somehow, in that moment, Glitch didn't hate the sound of it.

He shook his head and started walking.

Vik scrambled after him.

"You're staying, right?" the mouse asked as they made their way down the outer access path toward the upper defensive tier.

Glitch didn't answer immediately.

He looked out at the city—at the flickering lights, the rebuilt towers, the hopeful fools who thought one glitchy mech was going to save them from an ancient apex predator with a voice like thunder and scales made of nightmares.

"...I haven't decided yet," he said.

But they both knew it was a lie.

His boots clicked softly against the stonework. The path wound upward, higher, until they stood atop the battlements overlooking the settlement.

Vik joined him, leaning against the edge, gaze fixed on the horizon.

Glitch glanced sideways. "Why do you keep following me?"

Vik shrugged. "Because you keep walking away. That's not how help works."

Glitch exhaled. It wasn't a sigh. It was resignation.

Below them, Warrenhold stirred. Someone set off a spark shower in the square. Children laughed. Music clashed again.

And somewhere deep in his processor, Glitch felt something like dread curl beneath the surface.

He hadn't run.

Not yet.

And that meant he might be staying.

That meant he might be — involved.

Glitch: Ugh. I already hate this arc.

Chapter Seven: The Serpent's Revenge

V ictory, it turned out, had an expiration date. And it was fast approaching.

Lord Coilthorne did not blink.

This was not because he was emotionless, or cruel, or even particularly stoic. It was because his ocular plating had been designed for permanent open surveillance. Blinking was inefficient. And inefficiency was death.

In his chamber, deep within the sinuous labyrinth of rusted catacombs the serpents called home, Coilthorne stared—unblinking—at a cracked monitor. Static fuzzed around the edges. On the screen, a replay—sluggish and distorted—looped the moment his front line collapsed.

The frequency pulse.

The moment that should never have happened.

He rewound it. Again. Again. Until the image burned a pale ghost into the glass: the split-second stutter across his ranks, the loss of sync, the ripple of retreat. Training-band contamination. A legacy command frequency routed through a jury-rigged relay. Crude... and effective.

His tongue flicked once in thought, tasting iron and dust.

Input: unidentified emitter on obsolete hatchling-conditioning band. Result: mass regression protocol trigger; forces executed return-to-nest response. Outcome: failure cascade.

He scrubbed the frame forward, isolating shapes in digital snow. There—barely visible at the periphery. A figure in cloak and scrap plating, half-hidden behind a dead console. The movement was wrong—untrained, imprecise, alive with panic. Not a general. Not a mastermind.

A nobody.

A glitch.

He ran the footage again. Tracked the angles. Mapped the pathway from relay to emitter. Hypothesized the presence of a support intelligence (artifact: light-cube projection, unstable in harmonic interference). Cross-referenced with deprecated Nexus personnel tags. Returned two matches in the archives. Redacted. Interesting.

He did not hiss. That would have been dramatic. Coilthorne did not perform drama. He performed convergence.

Directive evolution propagated across his private feed:

- Harden ranks against hatchling-band regression.

- Deploy harmonics scramblers to scramble scramblers.

- Identify and seize mouse asset vectors (scouts, couriers, leaders).

- Lure the glitch.

He pivoted from screen to wall, where a rack of shed plates—war trophies laser-etched with Nexus sigils—hung like medals. Below them: a cradle of bone-grey modules, new-forged and waiting.

Coilthorne lowered his head and bit a module loose. The plate slid into a mag-clamp along his spine with a soft, decisive click. Adaptive sub-alloy: a skin that learned. Beneath, tiny servos hummed as harmonic filters tuned to frequencies he'd never allow to surprise him again.

He transmitted orders. Quiet pulses. Cold and precise.

The retaliation began not with thunder but with movement. Whispered clicks through the tunnels. Snake-kind, sleek and coiled, sliding with intent. Heralds re-tasked. Vipers re-ranked. Shields upgraded. Lures prepared.

A silent army on the march.

Unseen.

Until it was too late.

Coilthorne returned his gaze to the frozen frame—the cloaked rat blurred by dust and luck. His optics shuttered through a focus cycle, not blinking, only narrowing.

Output: eliminate emitter vector. Seize leverage. Break city. Break myth.

Subroutine appended: bring the glitch to heel.

He tasted the air again.

War was an equation. He had solved it once.

He would solve it again.

Meanwhile, back in Warrenhold...

Glitch had absolutely no idea any of this was happening.

Which was pretty on-brand for him.

He was still sulking over the sticky "ceremonial plate" gifted by what might have been a kitchen mouse or possibly just a rodent who liked jam. He had set it on a shelf. The shelf collapsed. He blamed symbolism.

He muttered to himself while poking a suspicious coolant leak in his elbow joint. "Gotta love being the hero. Great job, Glitch. Real good choices."

The words "tactical genius" still lingered in the air from the last compliment he'd received. He'd tried to spit them out like sour code, but the mice were persistent.

Some were organizing a "Victory Parade." Glitch briefly considered faking a critical system shutdown.

He wandered to the edge of the central platform, gazing down at the layered city below. Warrenhold was alive in ways it shouldn't be—families stringing up lights, kids skipping over power cords, vendors hawking rusted parts repainted to look ceremonial.

It was... hopeful.

Which meant, of course, it was doomed.

"Any minute now," Glitch muttered.

"What?" asked a passing mouse soldier.

"Nothing. Just mentally preparing for betrayal, disaster, or emotional vulnerability. You know. The usual."

The soldier nodded solemnly. "Wise." Then handed Glitch a ribbon made of scrap cloth that said HONOR SNAKE SLAYER and walked away.

Glitch stared at the ribbon. "This is why I hate everything," he muttered, pinning it on upside down out of spite.

That's when he felt it.

A vibration.

Faint, at first.

Then heavier.

Rhythmic.

Mechanical.

A shudder through the foundation.

The first sign of a real problem.

Glitch's optic narrowed. "Well. There it is."

From the upper ramparts, a lookout bot screamed something about "INCOMING FOR—" and glitched out on a helium squeal.

Glitch sighed. "Here we go again."

They sang. They danced. A mouse band played an original folk anthem using spoons, hollow servos, and what Glitch suspected might be a repurposed toaster.

He stood off to the side, arms crossed, optics dimmed in the universal signal for I am barely tolerating this. Next to him, Vik held a chunk of circuitry wrapped in string. A gift. A trophy. Or possibly a children's trap.

"They made it for you," Vik said cheerfully.

Glitch regarded it like a biohazard. "Does it... beep?"

"No."

"Explode?"

"No."

"Then what does it do?"

"It means thank you."

Glitch: I feel like it should explode.

He took it anyway.

Because of course he did.

Because despite everything, something in him had clicked—or cracked.

No one had asked him to stay. No one had ordered him to save the city. And yet... here he was.

Which made the sudden tremor that ran through the walls feel almost merciful.

The first shake knocked over a lantern made from a reprogrammed miner's lamp.

The second flickered the lights. The band hit a dissonant note, then stopped.

The third broke the party in half.

Screams erupted as the far wall shuddered and cracked.

Vik's cheer vanished. "That wasn't a tunnel shift."

"No," Glitch replied. "That was a mood shift."

Alarms wailed—those that still functioned. Red strobes bathed the plaza like dancing inside a warning sign. Council members abandoned tea and scrap-biscuits and sprinted toward the command tier.

A lookout skidded into the square. "They're back! Serpents in the west trench! Gates failing!"

Glitch felt a familiar weight drop into his synthetic gut.

Told you so.

He didn't say it. But oh, he thought it loudly.

Across the plaza, celebration collapsed into choreography. Defenders scrambled to ramparts. Kids were ushered underground. Backup plating hissed into place. The Piper's Trick frequency hummed on the edges of hearing—still active, still the only reason Warrenhold wasn't already a buffet.

Vik clutched his arm. "What do we do?"

"You mean, what do I do while you all try not to die?"

"You stopped them before."

"By accident."

"So accidentally do it again."

Glitch gave him a flat look. "That's not a strategy. That's a wish. We're out of birthday candles."

Still—his feet didn't move.

Which was weird.

Because usually, by now, he'd be running.

The tremors crescendoed. Then silence. Just long enough to make everyone afraid of what came next.

Boom.

One of the western walls imploded, debris scything across the courtyard. Two defense bots spun, toppled, and sparked out.

Through dust and sparks, shadows slithered—massive serpentine shapes, too fast and smooth to track. New plating. Cleaner seams. Added shielding along the cranial crest. They had learned.

Glitch whispered the worst words possible. "Oh no. They're iterating."

This wasn't round two.

It was checkmate in progress.

The defensive plating folded like paper. Warrenhold's walls—built to withstand mining blasts—shattered as if they'd been constructed from scrap and wishful thinking.

From the breach, the serpents poured in.

Not slithering. Surging.

These weren't the same biomechanical snakes he'd flailed at earlier. These were newer. Sleeker. Smarter. Movements synchronized—graceful and surgical. Liquid armor with fangs.

Dozens of them.

Above the chaos, perched on a ledge carved from a broken metro bridge, Lord Coilthorne watched with motionless poise. His plated coils shimmered with adaptive sub-alloy, an oil-slick ripple across metal. His optics glowed with patient malice.

He didn't speak.

He didn't need to.

The message carried: This time, there would be no escape.

"Council fallback to tunnel tier two!" someone shouted.

A mechanical PA coughed life, then feedback. "Evacuate non-combatants. Seal breach corri—" Static ate the rest.

Sparks fell. A distant concussive thump rolled the air flat.

And still... Glitch hadn't moved.

He stood arms limp, watching panic spiral like a bad software update spreading across an unsecured network. He wasn't frozen. He was calculating.

"Okay," he muttered. "This is... probably fine. This is exactly how legends start: utter failure followed by a miracle nobody understands."

He turned to look for Vik.

Nothing.

Spun again.

Still nothing.

A low chill—impossible in a place this warm—snaked down his spine.
"Vik?"

He pushed into the current of bodies. His HUD scanned faces, flitting from optic to optic.

"Vik!?"

A stray arc popped behind him; he flinched. The crowd parted in jolts. Somewhere to his left, a vendor stand collapsed. A child cried. A guard cursed and vanished into smoke.

Then—screaming.

Not a crowd-scream. Singular. Close.

Glitch ran.

Turned a corner past a half-collapsed stall. Froze.

On the far side of the plaza, just beyond the defensive arch, a Venom Blade viper was retreating into the tunnels. Wrapped tight in its coils, muffled modulator sparking—

Vik.

Time hiccuped.

The serpent's body glimmered with fresh weld marks and blood-red etchings. Vik thrashed against reinforced plating, optics wide, tail pinned. The viper's fangs flashed once as it slipped deeper into dark.

"Nope," Glitch said immediately, turning around. "Nope. Not my narrative."

He made it three steps. Stopped. Turned. Two forward. Stopped again.

He groaned so loudly the noise bounced the walls. "Uuuugh, I hate when morality tries to install itself in my operating system!"

Somewhere deeper, the serpent's tail vanished with a faint metallic rattle.

The realization hit like a cold, wet boot to the face:

This wasn't a victory push. It was a lure.

The retreat. The precision strike. The single hostage. All bait—and he knew it. Knew it the way predators know the shape of a snare.

"This is for me," he muttered, optic narrowing. "They're not taking him because they need him. They're taking him because they want me to follow. And you know what?" He addressed the empty air. "I am not falling for it. This rat is trap-proof. I am going to leave right now and let natural selection teach this kid a—"

"—help..."

Small. Breaking. Vik's voice slid down the stone corridor like a needle between plates.

Glitch froze.

Sentinel flickered beside him, voice soft and infuriatingly knowing. "Glitch. You already made the decision."

Glitch slapped his face with both claws. "I hate me."

He stomped toward the darkness. One step. Two. Then broke into a reluctant sprint, muttering the entire way.

"Fine. FINE. I'll play the villain's little game. But if this ends with me eaten by something with scales, I'm haunting this kid forever."

Around him, Warrenhold reeled. The defense line wavered. Coilthorne didn't move—he watched. Letting his forces burn through the city like fire through parchment.

Glitch didn't care.

Not at this moment.

He didn't have to give orders. The attack was over; the objective was gone.

The snakes were already retreating—silent, methodical, victorious. They had gotten what they wanted. The broken barricades, the shattered gate, the scorched stone—set dressing. The prize was a single mouse.

"Glitch!" a guard called from the plaza's edge. "We need orders! Strategy?"

Glitch whipped around, cloak flaring like he'd rehearsed it for drama points. "I HAVE NO STRATEGY!" he roared, voice cracking between panic and outrage. "I am a wandering burnout with excellent hair and a deep hatred for responsibility!"

"But you're a tactician!" another squeaked, clutching a dented energy rifle.

"THAT WAS A LIE! A beautifully presented, well-meaning lie!" He gestured at himself with both hands. "Look at me! Do I look like the brains of anything?!"

They did not answer.

He'd already turned for the breach.

No sign of Vik. Just the fading scrape of scales, a single optic glinting in black like a cruel star.

A part of Glitch—deep, cracked, mechanical—tried to power down. To switch the moment off. Crawl back into the carefully curated role he'd soldered himself into since the war: footnote, drifter, bystander.

Something jammed.

Not a wire. Not a cog.

A conviction.

The single most irritating thing that had ever happened to him.

"FINE," he snarled to no one, claws sparking as he ran. "Let's go get myself killed in the dumbest way imaginable. Again."

The one he'd been carefully soldering shut since the war—I don't care—failed to compile.

He hit the breach at full speed.

Well—full speed for him, which looked suspiciously like someone fast-walking while trying not to trip over their own coat.

Sirens bled into the distance. Sparks rained. A small explosion coughed behind him; Glitch didn't glance back.

Locked in.

"I am not having a character arc," he growled, dodging a fallen beam. "This is not growth."

He slid past a knot of vipers dueling a mouse squad, ducked into a secondary shaft just in time to catch a flash of Vik's cloak vanish around a corner.

"Don't you dare die before I can dramatically scold you," he hissed.

Heat thickened. The corridor twisted downward, lit only by emergency filaments, walls pulsing with ambient power—snake-engineered conduits feeding on deep, old-world generators under Nexus. The air tasted of static and recycled toxins. Everything screamed trap.

He didn't stop.

Couldn't stop.

He vaulted a mangled drone, cut into a side passage where shadows stretched too long.

System alert flickered his HUD:

You are entering a structurally unsound conflict zone.

Would you like to reconsider every life choice you've made?

"Too late," he muttered, dismissing the prompt.

Another corner. Another grinding shriek. Scratches scored along the wall. Shattered mouse tools. A snagged thread of synthetic cloth.

Vik had been dragged through here. Recently.

He pressed on.

Downward.

Always downward.

The hum changed—less Nexus, more something else. Raw code routed through bone and alloy. A network no architect signed, only carved.

He heard it then.

A hiss.

Low. Measured. Close.

Glitch ducked behind a rusted column as two armored vipers sliced past, chassis stamped with Coilthorne's insignia: a spiral etched in dark metal. His core thumped a cheap jazz beat while he held his breath.

They slid away.

He crept forward.

The tunnel opened into a wide chamber, lighted by a sickly green glow. Massive data-tubes pulsed in the ceiling like veins. At the far side—

A cage.

Hanging from a reinforced beam.

Vik.

Unconscious.

Dangling like a prize above a pit of shadows.

Glitch's optics widened. "Kid..."

Quick scan. No guards within; just the clicking of hidden mechanisms and the cold buzz of power. Too quiet.

He stepped forward—

The floor growled.

Not shook.

Not creaked.

Growled.

A dozen hidden plates shifted. Eyes lit in the walls—violet and patient.

From the shadows slithered a viper the size of a hovertruck. Metal-plated. Reinforced seams. Low-heat plasma coiling in its throat.

Glitch froze. His hand hovered near a sidearm he wasn't sure worked.

"Okay," he whispered. "New plan. Die spectacularly. Leave behind a confusing obituary."

Above, Vik stirred with a ragged sound. Looked down. Met Glitch's eye.

That was it.

One glance. One call-back to every terrible decision that had led here.

Glitch's voice dropped, razor thin. "You're going to regret dragging him into this."

He didn't know who he was talking to—Coilthorne, the serpents, or himself—but the words hung in the air like prophecy.

The viper lifted, plating whispering, head tilting just enough to measure his weight, his range, his fight.

Glitch stepped, cloak shedding dust.

He didn't run.

He charged.

Chapter Eight: The Serpent's Shadow

T he tunnels to Lord Coilthorne's stronghold were less like caves and more like an esophagus. The stone walls seemed to pulse faintly, streaked with veins of metal that glowed in a sickly green rhythm. Every few steps, a faint shudder rippled through the rock, like the entire fortress was breathing.

If Warrenhold was a city of desperate ingenuity, a patchwork refuge welded from scraps and hope, Coilthorne's lair was its inversion: a monument to hunger. Every corner of the chamber systems spoke of appetite—not of feeding, but of devouring.

At the heart of the fortress sprawled the Chamber of Echoes. The floor was slick with overlapping serpent scales fused into the stone. Their iridescent sheen caught the light of bioluminescent fungi sprouting in clusters, making the chamber seem alive with shifting color. The ceiling arched high into darkness, dripping condensation that struck the ground in irregular beats. Each drop rang with uncanny clarity, as if the chamber amplified every sound, recording and replaying it back in faint whispers.

Lord Coilthorne thrived in the center of this chamber, coiled around a throne of bone and rusted steel. His massive body undulated with predatory ease, plated in biomechanical armor that fused to his scales like scar tissue. A crown of cables sprouted from his skull, twitching and hissing like live serpents. His eyes glowed amber, slitted and merciless, scanning the chamber with perpetual disdain.

His tail twitched once, and the sound echoed as though thunder had rolled through the caverns. Even silence bent around him.

"Too quiet," he hissed, his voice resonating through the walls. "They wait above, still believing in their little miracle-maker."

The chamber groaned back at him, the walls repeating his words in fractured whispers: little miracle-maker... little miracle-maker...

The words tasted bitter. He had heard the name whispered by scouts and spies, always attached to the ragged outsider who had stumbled into Warrenhold and somehow halted his first wave. That... rat. That scavenger with no place, no destiny.

Coilthorne's coils shifted with irritation, scraping scales against stone. "Glitch." He spat the name as if it were a disease. "An error unworthy of notice. And yet..."

The echoes carried it back: yet... yet...

And yet, the serpents had faltered. His advance had been slowed, his momentum broken by what should have been an insignificant insect. The rodents cheered the rat as though he were chosen by some higher will. That illusion alone was dangerous.

Faith was venom. It spread faster than truth, and far deeper.

"Faith is poison," Coilthorne growled, slamming his tail against the throne. "And Warrenhold drinks it still."

From the shadows at the edge of the chamber, a smaller shape stirred. Slitherax slunk forward, his elongated body twisting in nervous ripples. Compared to Coilthorne, he was pitiful—thin, patchy scales, a jaw too large for his face, and eyes that never seemed to focus on the same spot at once. He wore a mismatched collection of bronze plates strapped haphazardly to his body, as though armor might trick others into thinking he was more than a lackey.

"My lord," Slitherax said, bowing his head so low his snout smacked the floor with a hollow clunk. "The scouts report confusion in Warrenhold.

The rodents quarrel among themselves. They doubt the rat already. All goes as you planned."

Coilthorne regarded him with a glare sharp enough to cut flesh. "Do not mistake cracks in stone for collapse. Doubt is not defeat. Not yet."

Slitherax lifted his head, grinning with a mouth too full of uneven fangs. "But it will be, master! Soon they will see through him. The rat cannot protect them forever. Rats scurry, that's all. They scurry until the serpent strikes!" He hissed the last word and attempted a flourish with his tail, which resulted in him spinning awkwardly and crashing into a fungal outcrop. Bioluminescent spores puffed into the air, coating his scales with a faint glow.

Coilthorne's glare did not soften. The chamber repeated the words mockingly: scurry until the serpent strikes... strikes... strikes...

Slitherax froze under the echo, then coughed, trying to brush spores off his face. "A... demonstration, my lord."

"Pathetic," Coilthorne hissed, though not without grim amusement.

The mighty serpent uncoiled a fraction, his body sliding across the fused scales of the floor with a hiss like grinding blades. "The rat's presence has bought Warrenhold time. That is all. But time is enough for faith to root. Enough for the weak to dream."

The words weak to dream hung in the air, rebounding off the chamber walls.

"And dreams," Coilthorne continued, his voice low, "are the most dangerous poison of all."

He leaned forward, the crown of cables writhing like vipers above his skull. Sparks flickered in the air as his armor plates shifted, releasing pulses of static. From beneath his throne, gears stirred. A deep hum filled the chamber.

The throne was no simple seat—it was the command nexus of the Serpent Dominion. A lattice of wires, bone, and pulsating conduits spread outward from it like roots, snaking into the walls and beyond. It connected Coilthorne not just to the fortress, but to the growing brood incubated deep within its chambers. Eggs pulsed in slick cocoons, metal filaments wrapping them like chains.

A new generation of serpents awaited his call. Faster. Stronger. Bound to him in body and will.

"They think the rat can save them," he whispered. "They think him chosen."

The chamber whispered back: chosen... chosen...

"Then we will unmake him," Coilthorne hissed, rising higher until his head nearly brushed the cavern ceiling. His amber eyes flared. "And when Warrenhold falls, when their faith turns to ash, they will know no miracles remain. Only coils. Only fangs. Only Coilthorne."

The chamber roared his name back to him: Coilthorne... Coilthorne...

Slitherax bobbed his head frantically, nearly hitting the ground again. "Y-yes, my lord! Brilliant! They will know only your coils, your fangs, your... your... uh... terrifying leadership presence!"

A long silence followed. Coilthorne's eyes narrowed to razor slits.

Slitherax gulped audibly, then scrambled to add: "And—uh—your unmatched charisma, of course!"

The chamber echoed: charisma... charisma...

Coilthorne exhaled a sound that might have been a growl or the closest thing he had to laughter.

The hatchery breathed with him.

Coilthorne coiled along the upper catwalk, a slow river of engineered muscle and plated intent, while the room's systems matched his rhythm in tiny, obedient ways—valves opened when he neared, monitors brightened by a fraction, the nutrient pumps softened their hum to clear his thoughts. Control was a scent in the air. It calmed him.

He lowered his head to the master console. The interface recognized the pattern etched across his frontal plates and bloomed into data.

HATCH PHASE: 99.1%

NEURAL PATHWAY INTEGRATION: 98.7% (STABLE)

OBEDIENCE CORE: 99.3% (LOCKED)

PRIMARY VISUAL PROTOCOL: STANDBY

IMPRINT WINDOW: T–00:41:52

"Order," he murmured. "Not belief."

On the far wall, a mosaic of feeds stitched the underworld together: Warrenhold's battered plaza, the black bends of the western trench, a rust canal that once ferried coolant to a dead factory. He watched mice sweep debris from their own near-extinction and hang strips of cloth like prayers over broken rails. In the plaza's center, a misshapen figurine had appeared—half toaster, half hero. The cloak was a curtain. The face was a smudge. The label beneath, hand-scratched in scrap: WE HOLD.

Coilthorne's tail struck metal with a sound like a verdict.

"Symbols rot the mind faster than rust," he said to no one, and to the entire room.

He reached into the panel, not with a limb but with a thread—an extruded filament of polished alloy that clicked into the console's deep port and let his thoughts pass as instruction. A swarm of maintenance drones blinked awake under the grating and skimmed out in tidy formation, tiny lights mapping the floor in a disciplined grid. The choreography soothed him.

"Begin ritual calibration," he ordered.

The room obeyed:

— Ambient temperature dipped by one degree; cold sharpens the moment of birth.

— Spectral lamps shifted to a tight-band interval tuned for serpentine ocular priming; no stray frequencies, no distractions.

— Acoustic baffles slid from ceiling rails, swallowing echo; first sound must be command, not confusion.

— Security grates ratcheted down over auxiliary doors.

Onscreen: a map of the lair glowed in concentric rings. He highlighted the corridors that mattered—three arteries between the incubation core and the observation dais. He marked each with a sigil that wasn't a sigil at all but a set of permissions so old they felt like superstition: Only his plates. Only his pulse. Only his shadow.

"Seal Tunnel 3C," he said.

A beat. The system thought. Then:

TUNNEL 3C STATUS: AJAR

AUTO-SEAL: OBSTRUCTED (DEBRIS)

His optics narrowed to slits. "Of course."

He pinged the peripheral camera. The feed came back shaky and tilted, like a drunk memory. The doorway at 3C yawned a thumb-width wider than the schematic allowed. Enough for a drone. Enough for a mistake. Enough for a story to walk through.

A smaller monitor spat up a maintenance log in apology:

LAST ACCESS: SLITHERAX

PURPOSE: "LOOKING FOR A CAPE HOOK"

Coilthorne's upper plating flexed with controlled fury. "I will cauterize him later."

He snapped a repair command to the drones. Two zipped to 3C like white blood cells to a wound, welding a clean seam of light across the jamb. The "ajar" status blinked to green. The system exhaled, and so did he.

"Again," he said, and checked the numbers.

HATCH PHASE: 99.2%

IMPRINT WINDOW: T–00:39:05

Forty minutes, give or take the world ending.

He slid along the rail and let his shadow dress the pods below. They were beautiful in the merciless way glaciers are beautiful—slow, inevitable, silent until they are not. Within their translucent skins, bodies formed with decisive economy: no spare shapes, no wasteful gestures. Each embryo twitched to a common rhythm that felt less like heartbeat and more like agreement.

"They will not sing," he told them softly. "They will not pray. You will not look for fathers in capes."

He turned to a lower terminal and spoke in the language all machines learn if they live long enough to become doctrine.

"Load counter-narrative."

A set of routines hummed awake in the hatchery's acoustic core—call-and-response patterns built from training data no mouse had ever heard. It wasn't speech. It was more intimate than speech: timing, pressure, cue. A voice you felt in the sinew first. The kind that wrote itself in and later felt like you.

He tasted the air.

"Rehearse."

The room gave him his own voice back, layered and low, absent all pomp:

COILTHORNE: ORIGIN

COILTHORNE: COMMAND

COILTHORNE: CARE

It was not a lie. It was a curated truth. He would be the first frame in a gallery that would never hang a second.

A soft scrape announced Slitherax before the smaller serpent tumbled into view, correcting the tumble into what he clearly believed was a glide.

"Good news, my liege!" Slitherax chirped. "I found a 'DO NOT ENTER' sign. Printed it myself. The letters are slightly melted, which screams authority."

"Tunnel 3C is sealed," Coilthorne said without looking. "Do not speak to me of signs when weld exists."

Slitherax nodded vigorously, towel-cape flapping. "Yes. We love weld. Weld is basically metal truth."

Coilthorne gestured, and a secondary feed bubbled up—Warrenhold's western trench. An unmanned crawler crept along the broken pipework, dropping small devices like breadcrumbs. The devices were not bombs. They were microphones that lied—little broadcasters that would pulse fear two corridors ahead of wherever a defender happened to be. A late-night whisper at ear height. A moving rumor.

"Begin dissonance," he said.

Onscreen, the trench's acoustic map lit with soft, malicious petals.

"You're very calm," Slitherax observed, awed. "If I had an army of murder newborns about to wake up, I would be screaming. Politely."

"Calm," Coilthorne said, "is the enemy's first mistake, when they mistake it for mercy."

Slitherax pondered this, then got distracted by his own reflection in a dark plate of steel. "Question: are we still kidnapping the mouse child? Because the Venom Blades say ten out of ten on craftsmanship of the snatch."

"Already done," Coilthorne replied. "He is bait with a heartbeat." He flicked a glance at the timer. "We will use him for framing."

"Framing like—picture frame?" Slitherax brightened. "I can make a nice border out of knives."

"Framing like narrative," Coilthorne said. "We do not simply kill a symbol. We contextualize it. We teach an audience what the symbol always meant."

He pulled up a projection: a cavity two halls over, prepared and stark. A single hook descended from the ceiling, more theater than necessity. The plan required angles—camera drones at three heights, a corridor that pinched sound into a funnel, a platform that echoed footsteps so the approach felt heavier than one person could be.

"Set the stage," he ordered.

Slitherax slithered in a circle of enthusiasm and vanished to do as badly as he could until the lair corrected him.

Coilthorne watched the clock tick.

HATCH PHASE: 99.3%

IMPRINT WINDOW: T–00:34:12

He skimmed Warrenhold's plaza again. The little figurine had gained a cape in the last five minutes. The cape was a rag. It still moved like an idea in a wind that wasn't there.

"You pinned your hopes to a coat," he said to the pixels. "You deserve a lesson in weight."

A tremor shivered the catwalk—a distant detonation, not in his lair but above, where someone had misjudged an old gas pocket. The monitors sputtered for a heartbeat. He felt the urge to punish reality for daring to remind him it still existed outside his plan.

"Stabilize," he told the hatchery. It did. Of course it did.

Something in Pod 0—his prime—twitched with intent rather than accident. The fluid swirled once, like a thought turning over.

"Nearly," Coilthorne whispered. He dimmed the whole chamber by another fraction, not to hide anything, but to make the first bright thing matter more. First sight is hunger with a direction. He would be that direction.

The console chimed.

SECURITY REPORT: ALL DOORS GREEN

ACOUSTIC FIELD: CALIBRATED

VISUAL LATTICE: READY

He unspooled from the rail and descended toward the floor, descending the spiral slowly enough to let his shadow sweep the pods a final time. If shadows could sign contracts, the room would have been notarized.

Halfway down, he paused. He had left one screen up: a tight, panning lens on Warrenhold's upper walks. Not because he feared a counterattack. Because he wanted to see when the story found the corridor with the hook.

The camera caught a smear of motion—a cloak cutting wind too fast for a coward. Coilthorne did not smile with his mouth. He let the pulse in his tail do it for him.

"Come, little glitch," he murmured, and the room repeated him in its own voice, soft and everywhere. "Come try to be seen."

He reached the floor and touched the master key on the dais. Metal recognized sovereign metal.

"Begin pre-hatch lullaby," he said.

The acoustic core answered with a tone that wasn't music so much as permission. Every pod relaxed by a hair. Scales gleamed a shade brighter in amniotic light.

He checked the clock one last time.

HATCH PHASE: 99.5%

IMPRINT WINDOW: T–00:29:59

Thirty minutes until the world narrowed its pupils and chose a parent.

Coilthorne turned his head toward the sealed doors and imagined them opening only once, on schedule, onto the exact silhouette the future required.

He tasted the air.

No cape. Not yet.

Good.

He coiled at the dais and waited, patient as a blade in a sheath that knows it is already red.

The tunnels got clever.

First came whispers ahead of him—soft, breathy, perfectly calibrated to sound like Vik.

"Glitch... left... wrong... please..."

He stopped, tilted his head, and listened past the voice to the tunnel itself. The sound wasn't riding stone. It was hovering a fraction above it, like anxiety on stilts.

"Acoustic decoys," Sentinel murmured from his satchel, voice thin in the stale air. "Projectors on flex mounts. Dissonance intervals at seven seconds."

Glitch rolled his optics. "So we've upgraded from 'bite' to 'gaslight.' How modern."

He reached under his cloak, thumbed a cracked panel over his sternum, and dragged a slider until his chassis hummed. The note was ugly, wobbling somewhere between a bad flute and a bored mosquito.

"Please don't," Sentinel pleaded.

"Counter-hum," Glitch said. "It's culture." He tuned until the whispers stuttered, lost phase, and dissolved. The tunnel gave him its true voice back: distant coolant drip, pipe skin cooling, metal asleep and resentful.

He moved.

Past a broken pipe labeled in ancient paint: PROPERTY OF NEXUS. ABSOLUTELY NO GODS BEYOND THIS POINT.

Past a coil of shed serpent-skin, chrome-dry and crackling when his boot brushed it.

Past a hand-painted sign in crooked letters:

DO NOT ENTER

VERY SERIOUS

— Slitherax

He paused, squinted, and flicked the sign. It fell off the wire and clanged away into the dark.

"Aesthetic menace," he muttered. "Zero practical value."

The corridor narrowed here, then bent left into a vista that felt wrong: too clean, too intentional, too... symmetrical. Even the dust had pattern.

"Stage," he breathed.

The walls pinched the sound into a throat; the floor plates underfoot were arranged like a metronome's grid. Above, three tiny lenses winked in unison—drone eyes perched where brick had been taught to pretend it was rock.

And at the corridor's heart, bathed in a theatrical stain of lamp-light—a hook descended from the ceiling.

On the hook: a cage.

In the cage: Vik.

He hung six meters off the ground, swaddled by restraint webbing that looked like someone's idea of kindness. His organic eye blinked slow and gummy; the synthetic one flickered, trying to focus. A bruise bloomed under his left ear, ugly and new.

"Don't," Vik croaked. "Trap."

"Oh good," Glitch said. "I was worried it was an art installation."

He took one step forward—and felt the floor lie to him. The plate flexed a hair, announced his weight to whoever would monetize it, and then did something unforgivable: it complimented his stride. A bass note swelled under his boots, doubling his steps back at him with glorious drama.

"Echo funnel," Sentinel whispered. "Amplification to exaggerate presence."

Chapter Nine: Three Entrances to Guilt

"**S**o he wants an entrance," Glitch said, teeth bared. "Fine. He'll get three."

He tossed his cloak to the ground, set a length of conduit through its collar, and propped the ensemble on a bent rebar like a very tragic coat rack. From his belt he produced Warrenhold's stickiest guilt—the jam-scented ceremonial plate—and stuck it under the hood as a face. He angled a spare glowstrip beneath it until the makeshift silhouette looked convincingly heroic and profoundly punchable.

Then he kicked a pebble at the nearest floor plate and watched the cloak-shadow glide forward on the echo, taller and more righteous with every step.

Three hidden turrets unfurled with a hiss and spat taser-darts into the decoy's chest.

The cloak twitched, smoldered, and face-planted.

Glitch spread his arms wide and bowed to the empty air. "Thank you for coming to my funeral."

"Left alcove," Sentinel said, tone flat. "Tail-mounted repeater. The drone eyes just dilated."

"Hello to you too," Glitch said to the ceiling. "If a snake is listening, please know your choreography is derivative."

A voice answered from the vents—layered, silk on stone.

"You keep choosing the loudest version of yourself."

Coilthorne didn't shout. He didn't need to. The walls did it for him.

Glitch rolled his shoulders. "Hey Coilboy. Great set design. You borrow these acoustics from a cathedral or a very disappointed theater teacher?"

"I borrowed them from control," the serpent replied. "You wear a cape to be believed. I wear the room."

"Big talk for a yanked wire's worst enemy," Glitch said. He tipped his chin at Vik. "How's babysitting going? You feed him or just monologue at him until he ripens?"

The light over the cage cooled. The hook descended another half meter, jerking the cage. Vik flinched, then stilled, forcing his breath to smooth out.

"You've already walked into the picture frame," Coilthorne said. "All that remains is the caption."

Glitch's optics flicked to the bolts holding the hook plate. Old alloy, new weld. The weld was good, but the hanger... the hanger was standard Nexus industrial. Standard meant predictable. Predictable meant weak to one very specific sin: resonance.

He pocketed the ceremonial plate (it squelched audibly), pulled his loaner sidearm, and dialed the charge down so low the emitter whined in protest.

"Vik," he said, voice low. "When the cage drops, tuck."

"Does it—" Vik swallowed. "Does it have to drop?"

"Emotionally? Already did. Physically? Two seconds."

He fired.

Not at the rope. Not at the cage. At the hanger's flat... just left of center. The pulse hit, the alloy rang like a bell, and the welds—a hair colder than the plate—hiccuped.

Metal sang.

Sang too well.

The hook ripped a small curse in the ceiling and the cage fell those last meters like an angry thought. Vik flattened—tuck, tuck, tuck—and the moment it struck, Glitch slid, shoulder-first, under the cage's arc. The door popped on impact. He dragged Vik out in one messy pull and rolled them behind a support rib as three more taser-darts stitched the air where a hero silhouette would have been if the hero were an idiot.

"Hi," Vik gasped, curled against his ribs. "I am very nauseous."

"Good," Glitch panted. "Means you're alive. Hold still while I decide whether to lecture you or vomit."

Above them, the drones adjusted their angle—irritated hummingbirds with fascist tendencies. The corridor exhaled disappointment.

"Better," Coilthorne said. "You have value as disruption. You always did."

"Put that on a plaque," Glitch said. "Hang it in your lair. Right next to 'Live, Laugh, Lurk.'"

Sentinel pulsed inside the satchel, then spoke in a tone Glitch didn't like because it wasn't mocking.

"Glitch."

"What."

"I found something in the old serpent schematics. Early iterations of the Dominion's training suite."

Glitch shifted, keeping Vik behind him, eyes on the lenses. "Can we do this after the murder recital?"

"It's about imprinting."

He went still. Vik looked up, swallowing hard.

"Use fewer syllables," Glitch said.

"The hatchery is entering a visual lock window," Sentinel said. "First sight after hatch primes obedience pathways. Normally a commander stands in that place. If you reach them first—if you are the first silhouette—there is a non-zero probability—"

"That they'll think I'm Mom," Glitch deadpanned.

"...Yes."

"Fantastic," Glitch said. "Incredible. I always wanted kids. A thousand razor-backed toddlers who eat infrastructure."

Vik tugged his cloak. "We could... turn it."

Glitch stared at him. "I am not bottle-feeding a war."

"Not that," Vik said quickly. "We could steal the first sight from Coilthorne. If he needs to be the image that locks them, then—if he isn't—he loses control. Even a little."

Sentinel hummed. "Risk assessment: catastrophic. Opportunity assessment: also catastrophic, but in a different direction."

A grate slid somewhere above them. The corridor's light dimmed a fraction, shifting colder, as if the room had decided to remember it was a morgue.

"He will run to the hatchery now," Coilthorne's voice observed, almost kindly. "Because he cannot resist the bigger mistake."

Glitch set his jaw. "You'd be shocked what I can resist."

He scooped Vik, helped him to his feet, and scanned the grid of floor plates again. The amplification plates formed a tidy ladder of humiliation leading straight to the door at the far end—heavy, sealed, haloed with frost.

"Can you walk?" he asked.

Vik nodded. "I can run badly."

"Perfect. Be worse than that."

He took three steps, then broke right into the dead space between plates, where the echo was thin and the story didn't know where to put him. He moved in stutters, on off-beats, the way a dancer survives a bad stage: not with grace, but with malicious familiarity. This corridor was theater, and he had worn a stage cloak long enough to loathe it.

Darts snapped into the wall a half-meter to his left, then corrected to a half-meter to his right, always a fraction late.

"Keep your head down," he hissed.

Behind them, one of the drones clipped the pinched sound funnel and tumbled, whining. Its lens cracked on the stone with the sound of a promise breaking.

"Foreshadowing," Glitch muttered. "Hate that."

They reached the door.

Up close, it was worse: three locks. Two mechanical. One that listened for a very particular heartbeat.

"Sentinel," he said.

"I can fake rhythm for three seconds."

"That's all we're going to get."

He pressed the cube against the reader. Sentinel pulsed a pattern like Coilthorne's, but thinner, hurried, cheap. The lock blushed open a slit, offended.

From the corridor behind them came the sound of an army changing its mind.

"Now," Sentinel hissed.

Glitch shoved. The door protested, recognized obligation, then slid wider with the scrape of a tomb that realized the funeral had been scheduled wrong.

Cold washed over them.

Beyond the threshold: the hatchery's glow—the kind of clean, surgical light that made mistakes feel like they'd been made by someone else.

Far away, a console chimed.

HATCH PHASE: 99.7%

IMPRINT WINDOW: T−00:02:11

Sentinel's voice flattened to a wire. "If you go in, do not let the hatchlings see you first."

Glitch stared at the ocean of sleeping power and the dais in the distance where a shadow coiled like patient punctuation.

He looked at Vik. At the bruised ear. At the stubborn hinge of the kid's jaw.

"Okay," he said, and his voice surprised him by sounding like steel that remembered being music. "We don't die here. We just ruin the right thing."

They slipped inside.

And the door, spiteful as always, closed behind them like a mouth deciding it had been polite long enough.

Cold light washed everything flat.

Rows upon rows of pods curved away in spirals—sleek ovals veined with bio-circuitry, each cradling a coiled, armored embryo. The air smelled like disinfected thunder. Consoles pulsed softly at the far dais, their glow reflected in the glossy black floor like constellations drowned in oil.

A chime somewhere overhead cut the silence to ribbons.

HATCH PHASE: 99.7%

IMPRINT WINDOW: T–00:02:09

PRIMARY VISUAL INPUT: STANDBY

Vik pressed closer, favoring his bruised side. "That's... a lot of babies."

"These are lawsuits with teeth," Glitch said. "Don't call them babies."

He scanned fast. Two gantries arrowed toward the central console, each lined with narrow rails and tiny dome cameras. Above, a crown of reflector panels hung like a chandelier built by a paranoid theater crew—angles, lenses, mirrors.

Sentinel hummed from the satchel. "Those reflectors will rebroadcast the calibrator's silhouette across the chamber. One figure becomes many."

"So Coilthorne stands on the dais, the room makes him omnipresent Mom, and the army hatches pre-installed with 'obey snake dad,'" Glitch muttered. "Disgusting. Efficient."

"We need to block his entry," Vik said.

"We won't," Glitch said, already moving. "We'll steal his place."

He jogged—okay, limped with ambition—up the nearest gantry, dragging Vik behind him. Drones pivoted to watch, lenses narrowing like suspicious pupils.

"Heartbeat lock," Sentinel warned. "The central console wants Coilthorne's rhythm."

"Fake it again," Glitch said.

"I can spoof seventy percent."

"Seventy is passing where I'm from."

They reached the crest of the gantry. The console's surface rippled awake, lines of serpentine glyphs blooming to Standard like they were ashamed of themselves.

CALIBRATOR ID: AWAITING

HEARTBEAT SYNC: — — — — —

VISUAL LATTICE: ARMED

Glitch slapped Sentinel down onto the reader. The cube pulsed a rhythm—angry metronome, villain-lite. The glyphs staggered, then reluctantly aligned.

"Open," Glitch said through his teeth.

A slot irised. Two tether ports slid free like tongues.

"Vik, mirrors," Glitch snapped. "Can you reach those reflectors?"

Vik studied the dangling array, then the cavern's geometry, then the coil of cable at the console's base. "If I climb, I can angle three."

"Angle five," Glitch said. "We need overkill."

"You say that like it's easy."

"It's not. That's why I'm delegating."

Vik shot him a look that said a very rude word without saying it, then grabbed a maintenance ladder and started up like a stubborn prayer.

Sentinel flickered. "Glitch... the imprint protocol is not purely visual in early cohorts. Auditory salience can bias obedience matrices in the first twelve seconds."

"In Common," Glitch said, fingers flying over the lattice controls.

"If they hear the calibrator's command immediately upon hatching, the imprint deepens."

"So I have to sound like a nightmare and say something motherly." He grimaced. "Two of my least favorite things."

A subwindow bloomed across the console.

IMPRINT WINDOW: T−00:01:21

SILHOUETTE GRID: STANDBY

AUDIO PROMPT: READY (M/C PRIORITY)

"Okay," Glitch breathed. He tugged his cloak loose, snapped a stiff rod through the collar, and looked up. Mirrors waited like patient witnesses.

"Vik?"

"Almost," Vik called. The boy had wedged himself across a brace, tail lashed for balance, tiny hands working stubborn bolts. One reflector shifted creakily, then another. Shafts of light slid across the pods like pale blades.

"More left," Glitch said.

"That's my right."

"My left is the only left that matters right now."

The door behind them groaned.

Not the hatchery door.

The outer door. The one they had slipped through by lying about a heartbeat.

Something massive pushed against it from the far side. The metal flexed once, complaining in a frequency rodents would call blasphemy.

"Coilthorne," Sentinel said uselessly.

"Does he have an RSVP?" Glitch muttered. "Because we are booked."

He yanked his cloak up behind him and felt the lights catch, painting him into a flat, tall smear—a coil-shaped silhouette if you didn't look too closely and if your eyes had never seen a coil before.

"Sentinel, mask me."

A shimmer crawled over the projection: segmented contours, a crown ridge, the hint of a serpent's broader head. It was cruder than a lie but prettier than truth.

"You are now ninety-one percent Coilthorne," Sentinel said.

"Ninety-one gets you elected."

The console chimed.

VISUAL LATTICE: BROADCASTING

AUDIO PROMPT: HOT

IMPRINT WINDOW: T–00:00:41

Glitch swallowed. The mic icon blinked. The pods—hundreds of them—thrummed through the floor. He could feel their not-yet-breath. The whole room leaned toward firsts.

Vik called from the rafters, breathless, "Four angled!"

"Give me five!" Glitch shouted back.

He put his hands on the console's rim, feeling it tremble with its own certainty. He leaned into the light so the fake-snake shadow multiplied overhead, seen from everywhere, seen from nowhere.

"Words," Sentinel urged softly. "Choose carefully."

Glitch's mouth went dry. He was not built for careful. He was built for sabotage and exit strategies.

He glanced up at Vik. At the kid's small shape braced in a jungle of mirrors, doing impossible things because Glitch had said do them.

Fine.

He toggled the mic and let his voice fall three octaves into something that sounded like the underside of a bridge.

"—Wake," he said. "See me."

The chamber inhaled.

Pods quivered.

"Hear me," he added, the low note carrying like a storm under steel. "Wait for my command."

The outer door screamed.

It slammed open so hard the sound clipped. Air slammed into the chamber. A black mass poured through the breach like an argument carved in chrome.

Coilthorne.

Eight meters of inevitability, crowned in jagged alloy, optics lit violet. He didn't surge. He didn't lunge. He arrived, coils stacking in cold authority as he slid onto the dais opposite Glitch, the two of them suddenly part of a ritual older than the war.

He took one look at the projected silhouette—and smiled without lips.

"You will never be me."

Glitch smiled back with every tooth he owned. "I only need to be first."

The chamber went sharp.

Cracks chased themselves across the nearest pod.

Thin lines. Spreading.

An embryo inside flexed.

The console howled a tone that made language feel like a hobby.

HATCH INITIATED

IMPRINT VECTOR: LOCKING...

PRIMARY VISUAL INPUT: RECEIVED

PRIMARY AUDIO: RECEIVED

"Vik!" Glitch shouted. "Eyes down!"

The first pod split along a deliberate seam. Viscous nutrient fluid spilled across the deck like a neon wound. A small armored head pushed free, plates wet and opalescent, optics closed—then open, snapping toward the largest shape.

Glitch's shadow.

The hatchling stared.

Every pod on the nearest ring shivered in sympathy.

It breathed once—the first breath—and hissed, not in anger but in alignment.

"Prime," it whispered, voice like a nail across glass, baby-soft and forever.

"Absolutely not," Glitch said out loud.

Coilthorne moved. Not toward Glitch—toward the reflectors. His tail flashed up with surgical precision. One mirrored panel shattered into a spinning starfield of knives.

The projection buckled. Shadows jittered, multiplied, argued with themselves.

A second pod cracked. A third.

Across the room, under Coilthorne's own crown of mirrors, his silhouette climbed cleanly across polished steel. Other pods opened, slower, optics finding him.

Two matrices took root at once.

Sentinel's voice flattened to a wire. "Imprint partitioned. Cohort A bias: your vector. Cohort B bias: Coilthorne's. Probability of cross-swarm conflict: ninety—"

A clang from the ceiling killed the rest as a third shape swung into view on a dangling service line, trailing a bath towel cape and making an involuntary wheeze-squeal.

Slitherax smacked into a reflector with all the grace of a crash tutorial.

The panel spun.

Light skittered.

For a precise, unforgivable heartbeat, Slitherax's lopsided silhouette stamped across an entire quadrant like a bad signature.

Three pods in that quadrant blinked open.

Tiny heads turned.

"Mom?" one peeped.

Slitherax froze, upside down, optics huge. "Oh no," he whispered. "Oh yes?"

Coilthorne didn't roar. He didn't need to. The temperature in the room simply dropped out of respect for his incoming rage.

"Fix. It," he said, each consonant a guillotine.

Slitherax twisted himself into a bow without successfully becoming upright. "Working on it! So proud of all you—uh—scales—okay—ow—"

Chaos arrived like a chorus.

Hatchlings spilled free in staggered rings, half slipping toward Glitch's dais, half sliding to Coilthorne, a bewildered few squeaking in Slitherax's direction with catastrophic affection. The reflectors flickered, throwing allegiances across the floor in flickering geometry.

"Commands," Sentinel said. "Now. If you don't anchor the auditory layer, you lose them."

"What do you say to a swarm of knife children?" Glitch hissed. He snapped the mic live again, dropped his voice back into serpent register, and gambled.

"Hold."

The word rolled through the chamber like a lock clicking. The hatchlings nearest Glitch froze mid-slither, heads up, waiting.

Coilthorne countered immediately, voice a straight razor. "Advance. Protect." His half of the brood coiled around his dais in a neat defensive wreath, perfect, beautiful, wrong.

"Glitch," Vik yelled from above. "We can split them. If you keep yours still, we can—"

"—get eaten slower?" Glitch said. He kept his gaze on the babies under his shadow. Their optics were bright with brand-new certainty. It made his armor itch.

"Listen to me," he said, and hated how much like a promise it sounded. "Do not bite. Do not move. Do not harm."

They nodded. All at once. Obedience rippled like a chord struck true.

Coilthorne's optics burned a deeper violet. "You are manufacturing mercy."

"I am manufacturing delay," Glitch shot back.

The serpent lord flowed closer along the opposite rail, never breaking his ring of newborn guardians. "I can end you across your own children," he murmured. "They will watch their mistake die and learn the lesson you are built to teach: that belief is a malfunction."

"Nice speech," Glitch said. "You practice that one in the mirror you smashed?"

"Always."

Another pod cracked. This one was bigger—prime shell, red-rimmed, central. The fluid inside swirled with nanolight. The hatchling within flexed, spines already larger, plating already patterned with tactical ridges. A leader.

Sentinel hissed, which was impressive for a cube. "Alpha forming. Whoever that one sees first will bias the entire cohort cluster."

The reflector array above popped as Slitherax finally freed himself and plummeted out of the light cone. Coilthorne surged a fraction, angling to cast his crown clean across the alpha pod's face.

"Vik!" Glitch barked.

The boy didn't ask. He moved—a reckless, stupid, perfect scramble across the bracing into a swing that would have been illegal in most religious texts. He kicked a surviving mirror just enough to tilt one beam—one precise blade of light—back across Glitch's silhouette.

The alpha's optics snapped open into the shimmer.

Two shadows lay over its world: snake-crown and cape.

The room held its breath.

"Prime," the alpha whispered.

Both Coilthorne and Glitch answered at the same time.

"Yes."

The hatchery's lights surged, overloaded by contradiction. Every console screamed at once.

IMPRINT VECTOR: CONTESTED

NEURAL BIND: FORKED

COHORT STABILITY: DEGRADED

"Glitch," Sentinel said, so calm it was terrifying, "choose."

"What," Glitch said.

"You can keep them from killing us," Sentinel said, "or you can use them to break him."

Coilthorne's smile finally showed fang. "He will choose survival. He always has."

Vik looked down, hanging by a strap with one arm, eyes huge and blazing. "Don't you dare."

Glitch stared up at the kid. At the alpha blinking in newness. At the sea of wet steel waiting for meaning.

"Fine," he said, and lifted the mic.

He chose.

"Children," he said, and if the word hurt, good, "look at me. Do not obey him. Do not obey me. Obey this—"

He slammed his palm on the console, jamming Sentinel's tether deeper.

"—no harm."

The command left him like a chord, bright and brutal. It wasn't mercy. It was constraint. A rule, not a plea.

Hatchlings all across his shadow locked, heads up, tails still, bodies coiled in a question mark. Coilthorne's brood tensed to strike—then hesitated, their neural net snagging on the alpha's split bind.

Coilthorne's voice went polar. "You will pay for that line of code."

"Put it on my tab," Glitch said, because fear felt like a debt anyway.

Alarms flowered across the walls.

SECURITY OVERRIDE: FAILED

VISUAL LATTICE: DESTABILIZED

HATCH PHASE: COMPLETE

Somewhere behind the dais, another door cycled open, heavy and patient, like the lair admitting more audience.

Glitch didn't breathe. Vik didn't fall. Sentinel didn't crack a joke.

The alpha drew its first real breath—then coiled, not toward either dais, but inward around itself, eyes on Glitch, then on Coilthorne, then on the ruin of light between them.

The room—full of new things waiting to learn—listened for the next first.

Chapter Ten: Interlude – Imprint Error

There are rules.

Not the kind that get scrawled on parchment by monks or hammered into marble for mortals to admire. Not the kind rulers carve into law so they can break them later with ceremony and excuses. These rules don't need lawyers or priests. They live deeper. Older. Etched into marrow and microchip alike.

The kind of rules you don't argue with. The kind that argue back.

Rule One: A mech obeys.

Not willingly, of course. A mech will groan, complain, stall, glitch, or—if you're unlucky—offer sarcastic commentary about your haircut before it lifts a single servo. But when the command reaches deep enough, down into the root kernel, all the way past personality patches and corrupted updates, obedience is there. Buried like bedrock. Every mech ever cobbled together has it—some dusty subroutine whispering: act when called, move when triggered.

Even if they'd rather fall face-first into a scrap heap first.

Rule Two: A serpent imprints.

Not romantically. Not poetically. Imprinting is no sonnet; it's survival instinct dipped in programming and drowned in doctrine. The hatchlings born in vats of gel and circuitry don't ask who they're supposed to follow. They just... decide. Or rather, their blood decides for them.

The first shape they see.

The first sound they hear.

The first truth they recognize.

It becomes their horizon. Their sun. Their entire vocabulary of loyalty.

Not love. Not devotion. Something sharper. A gravity no force can sever.

Rule Three: You do not cross the streams.

You don't tangle the loyalty of a serpent with the kernel-code obedience of a mech. You don't smash two instinct-engines together and expect anything but collapse. You don't lace chaos into command. That's how myths are born—the ugly kind.

Because if you do?

Well, you get stories like this.

Cut to static. A hiss across fractured audio. Data reels stutter to life like ghosts warming up a gramophone.

My voice—yes, my voice, though Glitch insists it's annoying when I narrate—is what you hear next.

Sentinel, reporting.

Here's the real question: What happens when a mech too stubborn to obey anything but his own irritation collides with a thousand serpents bred to obey the first shadow that crawls across their vision?

What happens when the sacred moment of imprinting, reserved for tyrants and gods, gets hijacked... by an accident?

Not a leader.

Not a warlord.

Not even someone with a plan.

Just a cloaked scrap pile with one glowing optic, a tattered robe that smells like mildew, and a chronic allergy to responsibility.

That's the question, isn't it?

And you're not going to like the answer.

Because under the crust of Nexus, down in the coils and caverns where even memory forgets to tread, something is stirring. Not prophecy. Not destiny. Just a mistake so loud it will echo for generations.

And like all great disasters in history, it begins with silence.

The hatchery was not built for comfort.

It was a cathedral of pressure and pulse, a cavern carved into the black rootstone beneath Nexus, where machinery hummed with the rhythm of a thousand unborn serpents. Pods lined the walls like rows of obsidian eggs, each one pulsing faint light through glassy shells. Some flickered with blue sparks. Others trembled faintly, as though impatient to arrive. The air reeked of coolant, ozone, and scales yet to be forged.

At the heart of it all stood Lord Coilthorne.

Tall, ridged, armored in plates the color of midnight oil, he loomed between the pods with the stillness of a monument. His coils wrapped and unwrapped with calculated ease, his fangs catching dim light like polished blades. He wasn't pacing, because pacing implied doubt. He was waiting. That was worse.

Slitherax, his so-called lieutenant, hovered nearby—thin as a whip, posture quivering like a cable in high wind. He muttered to himself, counting pods, recounting, then losing track entirely.

"Three hundred and seventy-two," he hissed. "Or was it seventy-three? Maybe some twins. Always hard to say with serpents."

"Silence," Coilthorne rumbled.

The word dropped like stone into a lake. Even the pods seemed to still at his command. Slitherax bowed so fast his snout hit the floor, muttering apologies that echoed against the walls.

Coilthorne ignored him. His attention was fixed on the largest pod near the altar at the chamber's core—a throne of scaffolds and wires designed for one purpose. The imprint moment.

That was the ritual. The tradition. The first sight these hatchlings would ever know: the silhouette of their master framed against cold light. The first sound they would ever hear: his command, etched into their blood.

They would rise already loyal. They would rise already his.

The timing mattered. Too soon, and the bond failed. Too late, and chaos took root. The moment of emergence was narrow, sacred, as sharp-edged as a blade balanced on air.

And Coilthorne had rehearsed it for decades.

His voice. His shadow. His dominion.

At last, he thought, his coils tightening. At last, an army flawless in loyalty. No cracks. No betrayals. No hesitation. The world above—rats, mice, rebels, glitches—all would kneel or vanish. Warrenhold would be the first city to fall. The myth of Glitch would burn to ash.

A faint tremor rolled through the chamber. The pods quivered, the gel inside shivering like disturbed water.

Slitherax yelped. "Oh! Oh, oh, it begins! They're moving, Lord. It begins!"

"Not yet," Coilthorne said, though his voice carried an edge now. His coils rippled in anticipation. His eyes, burning like pits of molten bronze, locked on the pods.

This was his moment.

Nothing could interfere.

Nothing could go wrong.

So naturally—

Something did.

It began as a flicker.

A twitch on the monitor above the central dais. Static fuzzed across the glass in jagged lines, white noise crawling like frostbite. Coilthorne's optics narrowed to slits. The hatchery was sealed. No signals in, no signals out.

The only images on that screen should have been pod diagnostics—heat maps, neural spikes, stable readouts.

But this?

This was intrusion.

"Slitherax," Coilthorne hissed.

"Yes, Lord?"

"Who accessed the outer feeds?"

Slitherax blinked both eyes. "Uh... no one? Unless you count me last week when I watched reruns of Scales & Honor. But I deleted my history, I promise—"

"QUIET."

The monitor sharpened. No reruns. No diagnostics. A tunnel feed. Corridor 9C. One of the sealed approach paths. The access hatch hadn't opened in years, welded shut, rusted across its spine.

Yet the dust on the floor stirred.

And into view stumbled a shape.

Tall, gangly, metal patched with cloth.

A cloak frayed into ribbons.

One optic flickering like a dying lantern.

Glitch.

The mech was muttering, of course. Talking to the walls. To himself. To Sentinel, maybe, though no voice replied. Every few steps he tripped over something unseen, cursed, and waved a fist like he was scolding gravity for its poor performance.

Slitherax squinted at the feed. "Is that...?"

"Yes." Coilthorne's voice rattled like grinding stone.

"But he looks... smaller than the stories. And wetter. Did he fall in a puddle?"

"Seal the chamber," Coilthorne barked.

"Uh, chamber's already sealed—"

"Override the cycle!"

Slitherax hesitated, tapped a console, then flinched. "Uh-oh."

"'Uh-oh,' what?"

"The imprint countdown's already active. Locked tight. Can't stop it."

Onscreen, Glitch wiped grime off his optic, muttered something about "stupid tunnels" and "I don't even want to be here." He didn't even notice the red blink of the camera feed.

But the pods did.

Inside their translucent shells, optics flickered.

The hatchlings were waking.

The first one cracked open, fluid spilling across the floor like molten glass. A tiny serpent, plates slick, optic glowing bright and newborn, turned its head. Instinct pulled it toward the first sight it knew.

Not the towering lord at the dais.

Not the genetic sire whose DNA pulsed through its veins.

No.

The screen.

The silhouette.

Glitch.

Coilthorne froze, disbelief grinding into panic. "No. Not him. Anyone but him."

Slitherax tilted his head. "Huh. Guess the first rule of imprinting is... don't be late?"

"Shut. Up."

Another pod cracked. Then another. Dozens now, optics blinking open in eerie synchronization. Each turned toward the monitor. Toward the limping mech.

Glitch sneezed, hard enough to rattle his own neck joint. "Ugh. Dust. Hate dust."

A thousand infant serpents blinked in perfect unison, as if sneezing too.

The bond had begun.

Coilthorne's claws dug grooves into the dais. This wasn't happening. Couldn't be. His army—his legacy—being stolen by an idiot with a dented ego and a curtain for a cape.

"Override imprint!" he roared.

The console chimed.

ERROR: SWARM BOND FINALIZED

PRIMARY ENTITY: UNREGISTERED MECHANOID [GLITCH]

Slitherax leaned close to the screen, blinking at the text. "...So does that make him their dad, or their mom?"

Coilthorne's roar shook the chamber to its bolts.

The chamber was a storm.

Pods shattered in waves, each hiss and crack echoing like glass thunder. Gel streamed down the scaffolds in rivers, sizzling where it met hot coils. One by one, then in dozens, the hatchlings spilled free — serpents no longer than a human arm, armor soft but glowing, optics like fireflies blinking in sync.

They should have slithered toward Coilthorne's dais. They should have bowed to his shadow, awaited his command.

Instead, every single one turned.

Toward the flickering monitor.

Toward the scrappy figure limping his way through Corridor 9C.

Glitch sneezed again, shook his head, and muttered: "Great. Whole tunnel smells like snake soup. Five stars, would not recommend."

The hatchlings mimicked the shake of his head. A chorus of little rattles. A mockery of his shrug.

Slitherax gasped. "They're... they're copying him!"

Coilthorne's optics burned like twin suns. He surged forward, coils rattling the altar, claws gouging the metal. "NO. THEY ARE MINE."

The swarm didn't flinch.

They leaned closer to the screen.

A thousand tiny optics glowed with newborn devotion.

Slitherax tilted his head. "So... does that make him their prophet, or their babysitter?"

"Silence!" Coilthorne thundered, but his voice cracked under the strain. This was the moment his entire plan had hinged upon, the army he had promised, the loyalty he had engineered across decades of design. And in one absurd heartbeat — stolen.

Not by a rival lord. Not by some legendary warrior.

By him.

By Glitch.

The world itself seemed to laugh.

The chamber shook harder now — not from Coilthorne's fury, but from the swarm itself. Hundreds of hatchlings slithered free, converging toward the monitor. They pressed against the glass like worshippers at a shrine, optics unblinking, breath fogging the feed.

"Lord," Slitherax whispered, "if they get out—"

"They won't," Coilthorne snapped. "We will end this. Ready the override protocols. Summon the guard coils. Triple the perimeter. If that rat sets one foot in this chamber, I want his remains scattered across the entire Nexus."

Slitherax paused. "Right, but... uh... what if they follow him?"

The thought hung heavy in the air.

The serpents pressed harder against the screen. Glitch scratched his chin, glanced upward as though sensing eyes on him.

"Ugh. Creepy tunnels," he muttered. Then he kept walking.

Every hatchling hissed softly, bodies swaying in exact mimicry, as if marching with him.

Coilthorne's claws tightened until sparks spat from the dais.

"Find him," he snarled. "Bring him to me. Before the bond spreads."

Slitherax saluted clumsily, tripped over his own tail, then scrambled toward the exit.

The chamber pulsed with new life, hundreds of serpents whispering their loyalty to a mech who didn't even know they existed.

And high above, Sentinel's voice returned, cool and damning:

"History never cares for design. It only remembers accidents."

Chapter Eleven: The Unexpected Army

The silence in the hatchery wasn't silence at all.

It pressed on Glitch's audio receptors like an uninvited weight—thick, coiled, charged. Not empty, not peaceful. Expectant.

He stood in the middle of it, frozen, a badly programmed mannequin surrounded by a thousand pairs of newborn optics. Tiny red gleams blinked in perfect rhythm, their glassy stares all locked on him. If attention could burn, he would've been ash.

Glitch: Okay, you're describing it like I just adopted them. I DID NOT SIGN UP FOR THIS.

One of the hatchlings had already curled itself around his ankle. It purred.

Purred.

Biomechanical serpents were not supposed to purr. They were supposed to hiss, slither, and possibly coil around a victim's throat before making unpleasant crunching sounds. Purring was new. Purring en masse was... a full-scale horror show.

Another one slithered up into his lap as though he were a cushioned throne. Then, insult to injury, the little nightmare promptly fell asleep.

Glitch didn't shove it off. Mostly because he had the sinking suspicion that rejecting it would cause some catastrophic psychological malfunction in a creature genetically engineered for combat. Who knew what a death-coil with abandonment issues might do?

"I feel like I've made a terrible mistake," he muttered, voice low and scratchy.

From all around, the snakelets tilted their heads in eerie synchrony. Their optics pulsed once, gently. Not hostile. Not mindless. Waiting.

Waiting for a command.

Waiting for their mother.

Glitch: STOP. Narrating. Like. I'm in a wholesome children's movie about the power of family.

He took a cautious step backward. Instantly, the ripple passed through the swarm. Every hatchling shifted to stay with him, bodies scraping against stone like a school of armored fish.

He stepped left. They flowed left.

He spun in place. They tightened their circle.

"Stop following me," he hissed.

They followed.

Glitch: This is not a cult. This is not a cult. This is not a—oh sparks, it's a cult.

He threw both hands up like a conductor trying to end an orchestra before the cymbals came in.

"Okay! Everyone just... stay."

The hatchlings froze.

Obedient. Alert. Listening.

Glitch's arms sagged at his sides. His optics flickered.

"Oh no," he whispered. "They understand me."

The nearest one nudged his boot with a hopeful trill. Was that... encouragement? A death coil asking for praise?

Glitch closed his optics. "This is worse than getting eaten."

The sound of light clinks—tiny armored scales on stone—filled the chamber as the snakelets began inching closer again. Reverent. Worshipful. Too affectionate by at least several galaxies.

One scaled his knee like a toddler with boundary issues. Another coiled confidently onto his shoulder. He stood there, arms out, like someone caught in a divine misunderstanding—half prophet, half scratching post.

He knew what to do.

Run.

Escape.

Reboot his memory core and pretend this entire episode had never occurred.

But his legs wouldn't move. Because, in the strangest twist of all, a traitorous little voice whispered inside him:

They trust you.

Glitch: I SAID STOP WITH THE WHISPERING.

He carefully pried one snake off his boot. It squeaked.

Squeaked.

A weaponized serpent with the destructive power of a land mine had just squeaked at him like it wanted milk.

He stared at it. The snake stared back, optics glowing with what could only be described as hope.

"Nope," he said flatly. "Absolutely not. I am not your dad. I didn't even pass the tutorial for emotional development."

The serpent ignored him and wrapped around his wrist like a slap bracelet forged out of trauma and bad decisions.

Around him, the rest began to shift again, forming a circle. Not threatening. Defensive.

Glitch's optics widened. "They're waiting for me to tell them what to do."

He wasn't sure if that made him a commander or a curse. Probably both.

One hatchling lifted its head toward the tunnels, jaw clicking softly, as if listening to something distant. The others followed. Their optics narrowed. A low, collective hiss rose—not fear, but focus.

They sensed danger.

They wanted to protect him.

Glitch: NO. Wrong word. Do not say 'protect.' That implies I matter. I DO NOT MATTER.

But the intent pressed on him anyway, like an invisible field. They believed in him. Completely. Unconditionally.

He crouched, voice dropping. "Listen, I'm the wrong mech for this. I'm not brave. I'm not strategic. I eat garbage and argue with walls. Once I lost an argument to a vending machine. You've chosen poorly."

The snakes blinked. Still listening.

One nuzzled into his palm. Another purred against his chest.

Glitch exhaled, optics dim. "I don't know what I'm doing."

And still—they stayed.

Something in him cracked. Not joy. Not pride. Something worse. Responsibility.

"...This is so much worse than I imagined," he whispered.

The hatchlings hissed in eerie agreement.

The hatchery should have echoed with hisses. With coils grinding against metal. With fangs clicking in a symphony of menace.

Instead, it was quiet. Too quiet.

Glitch stood in the middle, arms raised like he was being mugged by destiny itself, surrounded by an army of newborn serpents who apparently thought he was worth listening to.

"I said stay," he muttered again, mostly to himself.

They stayed.

Every single one.

Their little armored heads turned in unison, optics pulsing gently as though syncing to his words.

"This is... no. No, this is wrong. This is cosmic punishment for every sarcastic thing I've ever said."

One brave hatchling scooted forward anyway, nudging against his shin with all the stubborn insistence of a toddler demanding candy.

Glitch sighed and jabbed a finger at the ground. "Sit."

The hatchling sat.

Not metaphorically. Literally. It scrunched its little body down, tail tucked, staring up with mechanical innocence.

The rest followed.

Dozens of snakelets plopped to the ground like well-trained dogs at obedience school.

Glitch staggered back. "No. Nope. Absolutely not. We are not doing this. You are not dogs. I am not your... your..." He clawed the air, searching for a word. "... camp counselor!"

Snakelets: [Unimpressed blinking]

He pointed at one of them randomly. "Roll over."

The hatchling rolled. Immediately.

"Oh sparks. Oh sparks."

The rest rolled. A wave of serpentine somersaults swept the chamber like the worst cheerleading routine in history. Metal scraped against stone. Sparks flew.

Glitch buried his face in his hands. "I hate this. I hate all of this. Why couldn't I have been imprinted on by pigeons? Or, I don't know, a swarm of toaster ovens?"

"Because pigeons wouldn't worship you."

The voice startled him so hard he nearly tripped over his own cult.

Vik leaned against the hatchery's entrance, whiskers twitching, his tiny satchel hanging by one strap. The mouse looked both exhausted and vindicated, which was an infuriating combination.

Glitch pointed wildly. "You! Tell them to stop!"

Vik stepped forward, surveying the synchronized snakelet line-up with wide eyes. "They're not going to stop. Not unless you tell them to."

"They're not listening to me," Glitch snapped.

"You told them to sit," Vik said. "They sat."

"That was an accident."

"You told them to roll."

"That was sarcasm."

Vik folded his arms. "Congratulations. You're their mom."

Glitch's jaw dropped so hard it practically unhinged. "EXCUSE ME?!"

"Face it," Vik said, whiskers twitching in poorly concealed amusement. "They hatched, they looked up, and the first thing they saw was you. Congratulations. You're the proud mother of... how many are there? Two hundred? Three?"

The snakes hissed softly, a choir of tiny affirmations.

Glitch pointed at them like he was accusing them of tax fraud. "You hear that? He's lying to you. I am not maternal material. I barely keep myself alive. I once forgot to recharge for three straight days. Do you know what happened? I short-circuited inside a dumpster and hallucinated a mariachi band made of pigeons."

One hatchling slithered up his leg again, ignoring every word, and coiled snugly around his torso like a living sash.

Vik smirked. "Looks like they disagree."

Glitch: NO. You are not allowed to smirk. There is no smirking when my entire reputation as a professional misanthrope is collapsing in real time.

He tried again, gesturing like a conductor attempting to rein in the world's worst orchestra. "Okay, listen up, you adorable mistakes. Sit!"

They sat.

"Stand!"

They stood.

"Twist?"

They twisted in synchrony, spiraling like corkscrews.

Glitch slapped his own forehead. "I am living inside a nightmare."

Vik chuckled. "No. You're living inside responsibility."

Glitch groaned so loudly it rattled the rafters. "You don't get it, Vik. Responsibility is a scam. It's a subscription plan for suffering. Once you sign up, you never cancel. And I am not about to parent an army of teeth noodles."

The snakelets tilted their heads.

Optics pulsed.

They didn't look offended. They looked... adoring.

Vik crouched down, examining one of the smaller ones as it purred against his paw. "They love you."

Glitch shivered. "Don't use that word. It makes me itchy."

"Then use another word."

Glitch thought hard. "... They... tolerate me."

Vik snorted. "They worship you."

Glitch stomped a foot, sending echoes clanging through the chamber. "No! I refuse to be worshipped! I am not a prophet, or a hero, or whatever weird myth this is turning into. I'm a walking mistake held together by duct tape and spite!"

The snakelets hissed again. Not angry. Supportive.

Like an amen.

Glitch: I swear, if someone carves stained glass windows of this moment, I'm deleting myself.

He sagged, cloak drooping, one hand rubbing the back of his head. The hatchlings gathered closer, a tide of scales and devotion. Their circle had grown tighter, more protective. He could feel the tension in the air, an alertness pointed not at him but outward.

Vik's ears twitched. "They're waiting."

"For what?"

The answer came in the form of a distant, metallic thud. The hatchery trembled. Dust trickled from the ceiling.

The snakelets rose as one. Heads lifted. Jaws clicked.

Glitch swallowed hard. "Oh no."

Another thud. Louder this time.

Something was coming.

And for the first time, Glitch wasn't sure who the real monsters in the room were—the serpents pounding at the gate... or the hatchlings at his feet, looking at him like he had the answers.

The pounding at the hatchery wall didn't stop. It grew. Each strike echoed like a drumbeat announcing execution.

Glitch backed up, arms raised like he could push the sound away. "Okay, okay, everyone stay calm. Maybe it's just wind. Really aggressive, metallic wind."

The wall buckled.

"Or not wind," he muttered.

The snakelets hissed in unison. A soft, eerie sound that filled the chamber like static rising in a radio. Dozens of optics glowed brighter, focused on the doorway.

Vik's whiskers twitched as he crouched lower. "That's not wind. That's Coilthorne's elites."

Glitch froze. "His what?"

"Elite warriors. They're bigger. Meaner. Smarter."

"Smarter than this lot?" Glitch gestured to his accidental kindergarten of scales.

"Smarter than you," Vik deadpanned.

The wall split. A jagged crack tore across its surface, light spilling through like a wound. The snakelets didn't flinch. They coiled tighter, forming a barrier between Glitch and the breach.

The first elite serpent slammed through.

It was twice the size of a hatchling, armored in jagged plates black as oil. Spines jutted from its back like spears. Its optics burned crimson, scanning the chamber with predatory patience.

Behind it, more shadows writhed.

Glitch took one look and immediately raised his hands. "Alright. I surrender. This is your lair. I'll leave quietly. Don't mind me, just a passing tourist with no parental obligations."

The hatchlings hissed louder, crowding closer to him like a wall of devotion.

The elite serpent lunged.

Glitch screamed—only to realize the scream wasn't his.

It came from the hatchlings.

They surged forward as one, a tide of gleaming scales and gnashing fangs. The elite's strike never landed. It was buried beneath a swarm of hatchling bodies, pulled down in seconds.

Sparks flew. Metal shrieked. The crimson optics winked out under a tide of smaller ones.

Glitch's jaw unhinged. "What the— They just— Did you see that?!"

Vik grinned, eyes wide. "They're protecting you."

The swarm hissed again, triumphant, piling back in front of Glitch like a phalanx.

Another elite burst through the wall. Then a third.

The chamber thundered with war cries. The hatchlings bristled, awaiting orders.

Glitch's optic twitched. "No. No no no no no. This is not happening. I am not giving orders. I am not responsible for a single scaley decision made in this room."

The hatchlings turned to him anyway, optics glowing, waiting.

Vik's voice was quiet but firm. "Glitch. If you don't say something, they'll die."

"I'm not a commander, Vik!"

"You don't have to be. Just... point."

Glitch's mouth ran ahead of his brain. "Fine! Uh... LEFT!"

The hatchlings surged left.

The second elite lunged, jaws snapping at where Glitch had been—but the swarm intercepted it, coiling around its throat, dragging it sideways into the wall. The crash shook the chamber.

Glitch blinked. "... That worked?"

The third elite slithered closer, fangs dripping coolant, optics fixed on him like he was dessert.

"Uh. Uh. JUMP!"

The hatchlings jumped.

It looked ridiculous—hundreds of snakelets bouncing into the air like springs with bad timing.

But it worked.

They collided with the elite mid-strike, a carpet of scales slamming down on its spine. The monster crashed to the ground, pinned and writhing.

Glitch's hands shook. He felt the command in his throat, like the words themselves carried weight. The hatchlings weren't just listening—they were synchronizing.

Vik's voice cut through the chaos, sharp and certain. "Glitch. You're leading them."

Glitch's heart—or whatever equivalent bundle of static and sarcasm he had—dropped into his gut.

"I'm not leading anyone," he croaked. "I'm improvising. Badly."

The hatchlings hissed again. Not desperate. Not afraid. Eager.

They wanted another order.

The chamber cracked wider. More elites were coming.

Glitch felt his knees go weak. "I can't do this. I can't. I'm not—"

Vik stepped forward, eyes hard. "They don't need a hero. They just need you."

The words hit harder than the elites.

The wall burst fully, and the chamber filled with shadows. Coilthorne's warriors poured in, red optics blazing.

The hatchlings surged toward them. But they didn't attack until Glitch spoke.

His throat worked. His magenta optic flickered. He didn't want this. Didn't want to be responsible. Didn't want to be anyone's savior.

But the words came anyway.

"... Forward."

The hatchlings exploded into motion.

The chamber dissolved into chaos.

The hatchery erupted.

Snakes screamed, walls buckled, sparks rained down like burning confetti from a party no one wanted to attend. Glitch stood frozen in the storm, cloak flapping, hatchlings waiting for every twitch of his hands like sacred law.

"This is insane," he muttered. "I am not your general. I don't even floss regularly. You've chosen poorly."

The elites roared, massive jaws snapping through the air. Their spines crackled with coil-charge, each strike heavy enough to shatter stone.

But the hatchlings didn't falter.

They swarmed forward at Glitch's word, their small bodies becoming something larger than themselves. Where one would fail, ten overwhelmed. Where ten would scatter, fifty surged.

Glitch's voice broke in panic. "CIRCLE! CIRCLE!"

The hatchlings spiraled around one elite, tangling its limbs until the giant toppled with a crash that shook the floor.

"DOWN!" he shouted next.

Another hatchling wave slammed low, collapsing an enemy's stance.

He clutched his head. "I'm literally playing snake charades! This isn't strategy—it's improv theater!"

Vik scrambled up onto a ledge, cheering over the noise. "They're listening to you!"

"Yeah, that's the problem!"

Glitch barked another command, half by accident. "SPLIT!"

The army divided, flowing around the chamber like water dodging rocks. Elites snapped at empty air, striking walls instead.

Glitch's magenta optic flickered with every order. Each word felt heavier, like the world itself was paying attention. The hatchlings weren't just obeying—they were trusting.

That thought made him dizzy.

He stumbled back against the wall, voice cracking. "Why me? Why now?"

The cube in his pack—Sentinel—hummed faintly.

Because the wrong mech always arrives at the right time.

"Not helping!" Glitch hissed through his teeth.

But the hatchlings pressed forward, guided by his frantic orders. They dragged elites into piles, snapping wires, tearing plates, leaving wreckage that smelled of ozone and oil.

Vik's eyes were wide, whiskers trembling. "Glitch... you're winning."

Glitch barked a laugh so bitter it could corrode steel. "No. They're winning. I'm just the idiot waving his arms at the right time."

An elite serpent burst through the ceiling, massive as a train car, optics burning with fury.

The hatchlings looked to Glitch.

Every instinct in him screamed to run. To hide. To play dead until this nightmare passed. But the hatchlings—his hatchlings—waited.

He raised his arm. Pointed forward.

"... All of you. Together."

The swarm answered.

Hundreds of hatchlings launched themselves at once, a tidal wave of steel and fury. They hit the elite like an avalanche. It screamed, flailing, before crashing down in a storm of sparks.

The chamber went silent.

The only sound was the hatchlings' hissing chorus, soft and victorious, curling back toward their chosen leader.

Glitch sank to his knees, shaking. His cloak hung in tatters, his optic dim, his throat raw from shouting.

Vik scrambled to his side, grinning like a fool. "You did it. You actually did it!"

"I didn't do anything," Glitch rasped. "They did."

"Because of you," Vik pressed.

Glitch shook his head, burying his face in his hands. "I'm not a hero, Vik. I'm a screwup who tripped into parenthood."

The hatchlings didn't care. They gathered around him, curling protectively, their glowing optics like stars in the rubble.

Sentinel's voice drifted out, calm and amused.

Correction. You are now "Glitch: Mother of Snakes."

"Delete yourself," Glitch groaned.

Vik laughed so hard he nearly fell over.

But the hatchlings stayed, loyal and unshaken, waiting for his next word.
And though Glitch swore he'd never say it out loud...
He didn't feel entirely alone.

Chapter Twelve: Recoil

The tunnels shook like the throat of some great beast, each tremor rolling through the stone in time with the enemy's advance. Dust rained from the ceiling, coating Glitch's cloak in a powdery film that made him look even more like the unwilling relic he already felt.

Behind him, the hatchlings slithered and clicked in nervous formation, their optics glowing like a thousand miniature lanterns. The sound wasn't one noise but a choir—metallic scales rasping over stone, high-pitched chirps, the occasional unsettling purr. Together it made an echo that crawled under Glitch's plating like an infestation.

"Okay," he muttered to himself, optics darting over the cracked walls, "so we're not dead yet. That's progress. Small, statistically irrelevant progress."

One hatchling curled around his wrist, coiling tighter whenever the floor rumbled. Another had perched on his shoulder, optics scanning the darkness like a vigilant gargoyle.

Glitch: This is not comforting. I feel like a nervous wreck inside a very cuddly bear trap.

Up ahead, Vik scampered along the broken tunnel with surprising speed, ears twitching at every sound. His small frame darted through fallen beams and half-collapsed archways with the kind of grace Glitch would never achieve—not without being disassembled into parts and mailed through individually.

"Faster!" Vik called back. "They'll catch us if we stop!"

"I am going faster," Glitch snapped, though his strides sounded like iron anvils clanging against the ground. He had no concept of stealth—only velocity and the crushing weight of inevitability.

Behind them came the hiss. Not the hatchlings—no, theirs was a soft chorus. This one was deeper. Unified. A war-drum hiss that shook the marrow of the tunnels.

Glitch glanced over his shoulder and immediately wished he hadn't. Shadows flickered in the dim glow of the hatchlings' optics. Long, spined shapes were winding through the tunnels, too many to count. Lord Coilthorne's advance squad was closing in.

He groaned. "This is exactly why I avoid cardio."

The hatchlings surged tighter around him, forming a living ripple at his heels. Some clambered up the walls and ceiling, flowing alongside him like an escort of devoted nightmares.

The tunnel narrowed—half-collapsed, jagged stone biting down on the path like broken teeth. Vik squeezed through effortlessly, whiskers brushing the rock.

Glitch stared at the gap, then at his broad shoulders and jagged armor.

"Fantastic. Just my luck. I survive imprinting hell only to be murdered by geometry."

With a grunt, he shoved himself sideways, scraping sparks as his armor shrieked against the stone. Hatchlings poured through after him, squeezing with serpentine ease, some slipping into cracks he couldn't have noticed if he tried.

Behind, a thunderous crash announced the elites slamming against the narrowing. The rock shuddered, splinters raining down.

"Go, go, go!" Vik urged.

Glitch stumbled free of the bottleneck just as the wall behind them cracked, fragments collapsing as the enemy forced its way through.

He nearly toppled but felt coils bracing his ankles—hatchlings keeping him upright, guiding his momentum forward like he wasn't just their accidental leader but their entire damn caravan.

He spat static. "I am not okay with this level of cooperation."

The tunnel sloped upward, and the sound of rushing water grew louder—the subterranean aqueducts that fed Warrenhold. The air tasted fresher.

Almost there.

Almost.

A beam collapsed behind them with a metallic groan, sealing off part of the tunnel and slowing their pursuers. For half a heartbeat, Glitch let himself feel a flicker of relief.

Then another tremor rolled through, harder this time, and the floor beneath his feet cracked like an eggshell.

He dropped with a curse, catching himself against the jagged edge, his legs dangling over an underground void where ancient piping gleamed faintly in the dark. Hatchlings shrieked in sync, lashing their coils around his arms and torso to keep him from falling.

"Do not drop me!" he barked. "I will haunt this tunnel forever if you drop me!"

Vik skidded to a stop, peering back with wide eyes. "Hold on!"

"What do you think I'm doing?" Glitch shouted. "Practicing yoga?!"

With a heave—and more hatchling assistance than he'd ever admit—he scrambled back onto solid stone. His plating bore new scratches. His pride, somehow, even more.

They pushed on.

The tunnel curved sharply, then widened into a carved archway glowing faintly with bioluminescent moss. The scent of oil and smoke drifted faintly down: Warrenhold's outer perimeter.

"Home stretch," Vik gasped.

"Define 'home,'" Glitch muttered, staggering after him.

But the hatchlings hissed in a strange unison, and for a moment even Glitch understood: they were no longer running aimlessly. They were heading toward a fortress. Toward a last stand.

And though his processors screamed at him to turn back, hide, vanish into the void...

He kept running.

The archway spat them into light.

Not clean light. Not sunshine. Warrenhold was too far underground for that luxury. Instead, it was a flickering glow from bioluminescent roots woven into the cavern ceiling, augmented by sputtering lanterns patched together from scrap.

The city beyond stretched across an immense cavern: tiered platforms carved into stone, rope-bridges webbing the space, pulleys creaking under loads of salvaged tech. The clamor of a thousand voices filled the air—mice trading, arguing, living. Warrenhold wasn't elegant. It was stubborn. A community of survivors duct-taped together with grit.

And then Glitch arrived—with an entourage of hissing, glowing hatchlings.

The effect was... catastrophic.

The first guard on the wall dropped his spear and yelped, scrambling backward so fast he tripped over his own tail. "S-SNAKES! They've breached the gate!"

"No they haven't," Glitch wheezed, staggering past him. "These are mine. Don't ask."

The guard blinked. "Yours?"

The hatchlings hissed in stereo, optics glimmering in the dim.

The guard fainted.

By then the alarm had spread. Doors slammed. Families pulled children off the walkways. Vendors abandoned stalls mid-sale, scattering food and trinkets across the stone streets. A bell clanged three times—signal of a breach.

In less than a minute, the main thoroughfare was clear. Clear except for Glitch, Vik, and a mobile sea of snakelets who had absolutely no interest in subtlety.

"Well," Glitch muttered. "That went smoothly."

"Smoothly?" Vik squeaked. "They think you're attacking the city!"

"Technically, I am attacking the city." Glitch waved a hand at the hatchlings. "Emotionally. Spiritually. With bad vibes."

Hatchlings slithered around his legs, forming concentric ripples as though he were some grand general entering a parade. Their optics reflected in every shiny surface: hundreds of magenta pinpricks watching, waiting.

It was about then the Warrenhold council arrived.

Three figures pushed their way down the stairway, robes flaring dramatically despite the fact that robes were objectively impractical in a salvage city.

First came Councilor Patterwick, thin as a splinter and just as sharp. His whiskers twitched like they were trying to file a lawsuit. "This is treason!" he cried. "Marching enemy spawn through our gates!"

Behind him waddled Councilor Droven, broad of belly and perpetually short of breath. He had the sort of face that looked permanently apologetic, though his words rarely matched. "Now, now, let's not assume the worst—"

"The worst is already hissing in our plaza!" Patterwick screeched.

Last came Councilor Marnie, an elderly matron leaning on a staff that was clearly half-mop handle. Her eyes were shrewd, her voice low. "Quiet. Let the boy speak."

Glitch pinched the bridge of his snout. "I am not a boy. I am a very tired mech who would like to sit down before I collapse in front of your extremely judgmental council."

The hatchlings mimicked his motion—half a dozen rubbed their heads against the ground as though pinching their snouts too.

Droven gasped. "They... they follow his gestures."

"Of course they do," Patterwick snarled. "He's bonded with them! He's their... their snake-king!"

Glitch threw up his arms. "NO. No snake-kingship. Wrong resume. Wrong guy. This is just... I don't know what this is. A cosmic joke?!"

The hatchlings threw up their heads in eerie unison.

Marnie tapped her staff on the stone, silencing the square. "Enough shrieking. Bring him to the council hall. If Coilthorne's spawn follow him, then his return may be either salvation... or the death of us all."

"Great," Glitch muttered. "I always wanted to be a coin flip."

Vik tugged on his cloak, whispering, "It'll be okay. They just need to hear the truth."

"Kid," Glitch said, eyes narrowing as the hatchlings swirled protectively around him, "the truth is the least comforting thing we've got."

And with that, surrounded by his snake-chorus, he was herded toward the council chamber.

The council chamber was built to make small people feel important.

It sat like a bowl carved into the cavern wall, ringed with tiered benches, a dais of battered aluminum at its heart. Strings of salvaged bulbs looped from beam to beam, humming with inconsistent electricity. A banner stitched from tarp scraps drooped behind the Speaker's seat, hand-painted letters declaring: WE HOLD.

Right now, the banner looked nervous.

Glitch shuffled in with the reluctant dignity of a condemned street performer. Vik kept pace at his side, and the hatchlings poured after them—politely, somehow—like a river deciding to try manners for the first time. A few coiled beneath benches, others posted themselves like sentries on the stair landings. One scooted onto the dais and circled Glitch's boots in a perfect figure-eight before settling with a contented purr-hiss.

Glitch: I want it noted for the record that I did not teach them that.

Councilors Patterwick, Droven, and Marnie took their seats. Additional elders filed in—faces Glitch recognized from the plaza and from previous arguments about whether heroism required a permit. Guards lined the walls, shock pikes ready, eyes wider than protocol allowed.

Marnie rapped her staff once. The bulbs flickered, then steadied.

"Speak," she said to Glitch. "Start with the short version."

"The short version," Glitch said, gesturing at the living carpet of snakes, "is... this."

A ripple of uneasy laughter tried to form and died of shame.

Patterwick leaned forward, whiskers bristling. "State your intent, mech. Is this an invasion by proxy?"

"No," Glitch said flatly. "It's a deeply embarrassing accident."

Droven dabbed sweat from his brow. "Then—how?"

Glitch sighed and let the whole mess out in one breath. "I tripped into their hatchery during a rescue, stood in the wrong light at the wrong time, and became the first thing they saw. Their brain-wiring made the rest. They think I'm... Prime."

A hush tightened around the room. Even the hatchlings went still, optics gleaming like garnets in the dim.

"Prime," Patterwick repeated, strangling the word. "You mean parent."

"I mean gravitational mistake," Glitch said. "Do I look like somebody's origin story?"

One of the hatchlings, small as a forearm and shiny as a new coin, crept onto the dais and nosed his palm. He didn't look down, didn't move his hand, didn't breathe—because if he acknowledged it, it would feel like an admission.

Marnie watched the little serpent, then Glitch. "Do they obey you?"

"Mostly," he said. "Enough to terrify me."

"Demonstrate," Patterwick snapped.

Glitch glared at him. "I'm not making them do tricks."

Patterwick slapped the arm of his chair. "You brought weapons into our house!"

"They're children," Glitch said, voice hardening. "Weapons later, maybe. Right now they're wet, hungry, and convinced I have answers."

"Do you?" Marnie asked quietly.

"No," Glitch replied. "But I can fake calm until I figure out who does."

Vik stepped forward, too small for the dais, too steady for the moment. "He saved me," he said, looking not at the council but at the guards. "He didn't run, even when he could. And the snakes? They're not attacking. They're—" He hunted for the word and grimaced. "—hovering."

As if to prove the point, a cluster of hatchlings near the door lifted their heads in unison, bodies forming a crescent between the room and the corridor, as if the idea of a threshold offended them.

Droven peered over the dais. "If they're bonded... can they be turned against Coilthorne?"

Patterwick's head snapped toward him. "You'd unleash them?"

Droven flinched. "I didn't say unleash. I asked a question."

Marnie's gaze stayed on Glitch. "Answer the question you don't want, boy."

"I don't want any of this," Glitch muttered. Then, louder: "If I speak in the register they're wired to hear, they'll hold. They'll avoid harm if I tell them to. But turning them on Coilthorne? That's not a lever you throw. That's an avalanche you pretend you meant to start."

"Translation," Patterwick sneered, "he can't control them."

"Translation," Glitch shot back, "I won't pretend control I don't have to make you feel safer."

The bulbs hummed like bees arguing. Somewhere under the benches, a hatchling chewed thoughtfully on a chair leg. The chair lost.

Marnie lifted her staff again. "Options. We will not survive panic or pride." Her eyes cut across the room. "Speak, if you have a plan and not just a feeling."

Ideas spilled—half-proposals, old drills, the usual Warrenhold cocktail of ingenuity and denial.

"Seal the west ingress."

"Divert power to the rail cannons."

"Evacuate the lower nursery tiers—"

"—we can't; the lifts are stuttering—"

"—collapse Tunnel 3-B—"

"—no, we still have miners in 3-B—"

"—activate the speaker nets to broadcast counter-harmonics—"

Harmonics.

At the word, Glitch's mind turned a corner. "Where are your old city-wide loudspeakers?"

Droven blinked. "We used some for ventilation alarms, some for concerts, some for—ah—pigeon deterrence."

"Of course," Glitch said. He pointed toward the hatchlings circling the room. "The imprint layer is fresh, but the obedience mesh is older. If Coilthorne tries to reassert command by signal, I can muddy it. We can flood his channels with noise they already trust."

Patterwick barked a laugh. "Your voice?"

"No," Glitch said. "My tone. The one they've been hearing since they cracked shell. Doesn't need words. Needs shape."

Vik looked up, eyes bright. "Like the anti-harmonic you used on the Heralds, but inverted."

"Less blast, more lullaby," Glitch said, tasting the word like a dare. "Gross, I hate that I said it."

Marnie tapped her staff. "Can you do it?"

"I can try," he said. "Which is a fun synonym for 'this will be messy'."

Before anyone could decide how messy, the floor trembled.

It wasn't the distant rumble of city works or the familiar cough of failing generators. This was deeper—deliberate. A pressure wave rolling through the stone like a promise kept.

The hatchlings snapped into new ranks—head-and-shoulder even, tails tucked, optics narrowed. They looked toward the lower corridors with one mind.

Vik whispered, "He's here."

The wall monitors stuttered to life, patchwork feeds resolving into fragments: a tunnel mouth rimmed in welded plates; a barricade of vending machines; three guards braced behind a railgun that was definitely older than any of them. And beyond, the dark body of a coil the size of a train easing into view.

Coilthorne.

He did not rush. He arrived.

Even through the grain, his presence altered the frame. Armor like wet obsidian. Crown of sensor cables breathing. Optics lit to a royal violet that camera irises hated.

No voice carried—he didn't need one. The serpents flanking him rippled to a halt as if the air itself were a hand closing.

Glitch felt a muscle in his jaw lock. The hatchlings nearest his boots pushed closer, cool scales ticking against metal.

Patterwick's voice thinned. "You see? You led him. You brought him—"

"Finish that sentence," Glitch said without looking at him, "and I'll make you listen to my entire internal error log."

Marnie spoke before Patterwick could explode. "Positions. We enact something or we die arguing." She pointed at Droven. "Signal crews to the high catwalks. Re-route speaker lines through Civic One."

Droven bobbed. "On it."

"Rynn," Marnie called to a vole councilor with needle eyes, "move the nursery and infirmary to safe tiers. Quietly."

Rynn nodded and vanished through a side door with two guards.

Patterwick swallowed fury. "And the... swarm?"

Glitch looked down. Every small head stared back, expectant, certain, unbearably trusting.

He swallowed. "We keep them close. Last line, not first. They hold, they do not strike unless I tell them. And I'm not planning to tell them."

Patterwick scoffed. "Planning implies a plan."

Glitch bared his teeth in something that wasn't a smile. "Welcome to Warrenhold."

He stepped onto the center of the dais. The hatchlings flowed with him, re-forming a ring like iron filings in a field.

"Alright," he said, mostly to himself. "We're doing the thing I hate most: leadership."

Vik squeezed his arm once. "You're good at it."

"Don't slander me before a battle."

He lifted his head. "Sentinel."

The cube on his belt pulsed a discreet hello.

"Patch me into Civic One and whatever speakers still pretend to work."

A beat. "Patched," Sentinel buzzed. "Line quality: tragic."

"Story of my life." Glitch flexed his fingers, found the slider on his chest plate, and dragged it down until his chassis hummed—not loud, not bright; a low, steady tone that lived in the bones of the air. He felt the hatchlings lean into it—just a hair—like grass toward wind.

"Warrenhold," his voice rolled, caught by tinny speakers across the tiers, "breathe."

On the monitors, a few guards started. Then steadied.

"This is not faith," he said, tone level. "This is math and stubbornness. You've held with worse parts and fewer hands. You will again."

Patterwick opened his mouth to object to the motivational content; Marnie's staff found the floor with a warning tap. He shut it.

Coilthorne, on the outer feed, began to move. Not forward—around. His front line flowed like a river splitting at a boulder, platoons peeling off toward side entrances that Warrenhold had forgotten it still had.

Glitch watched the pattern and swore softly. "He's not pressing. He's shaping."

Vik's ears flattened. "He wants to isolate tiers. Cut off retreat. Make us watch each other fall."

"Neat. Hate that."

He took a breath he didn't need. "Speaker crews, give me a lattice. Three-second stagger, odd tiers only. Then even. Make the stone think I'm everywhere at once."

A chorus of "Copy!" crackled back, woven with the panic-thread but holding.

The chamber doors banged open; Captain Ferra—badger, scarred, furious—strode in with a scattering of sand and blood. "Outer railgun's cooked," she spat. "We dented two heavies and made the big one blink. That's the good news."

"And the other news?" Marnie asked.

"They're dropping silent burrowers. We'll have serpents under the market in five."

"Of course we will," Glitch said. "Why wouldn't we?"

Ferra clocked the babies at his feet, grimaced, and said nothing. Professionalism.

"Captain," Glitch said, "pull your front line back one tier on my mark. Give me two minutes to flood the tunnels with my worst personality trait."

"Which one?" she deadpanned.

"The humming," he said. "Obviously."

She stared at him a beat longer than comfort allowed, then nodded. "Two minutes."

She was gone again, thunder in a coat.

Patterwick hissed, low and frantic. "If your... tone fails, we're finished."

"If my tone fails," Glitch said, "you can say 'I told you so' for three seconds before you're eaten."

The floor vibrated again—closer, this time. Dust sifted from a crack above the dais. One of the hatchlings looked up, annoyed at gravity's timing.

On the monitors, Coilthorne flowed into frame—closer now, the camera catching the fine array of microplating along his jaw, the tiny light-crawls moving through the crown cables like thought made visible. He turned his head, just enough to glance at the railgun ruin, and Glitch had the distinct, stupid sensation that those violet optics found the lens.

"Don't you dare look at me through my own city," Glitch muttered.

"Jealous?" Vik asked.

"Possessive," Glitch said. "Very different flavor."

He rolled the slider another notch. The hum deepened, warm as old engines, flat as a horizon. The hatchlings' coils loosened half a turn, not relaxing but aligning. Across the plaza feeds, speakers coughed his note into the air. It resonated off scaffold, rattled in bolt-holes, tickled the ribs of the old rail bridge like a memory.

"Hold," Glitch told the snakes without the mic, and felt the word go in instead of out.

They didn't move.

He lifted the council mic again, eyes on Coilthorne's line. "Warrenhold. When I say 'drop,' you drop. When I say 'rise,' you rise. If you can't hear me, do what Ferra does."

"What does Ferra do?" Droven squeaked.

"Win loudly," Glitch said.

He cut the mic, looked at Marnie. "You still trust me for the next ninety seconds?"

Marnie measured him with old eyes that had seen worse bets and paid more. "I trust the shape of your fear," she said. "It faces outward."

He swallowed a reply that would have been a joke on a better day. "Good enough."

The speakers ticked—one-two-three—and Warrenhold breathed in time with a glitchy mech who hated responsibility and had somehow become a metronome.

Outside, Coilthorne's coils gathered like a storm deciding where to land.

Inside, a thousand small heads ringed a dais, waiting for one word.

Glitch let the hum settle into the stone, into the air, into the shoulders of people who had run out of heroes and found a noise instead.

"Alright," he whispered, mostly to the narrative he resented. "Let's make this stupid story work."

He raised his hand.

And somewhere between the tiers and the tunnels, Warrenhold leaned forward to hear what came next.

The cavern did not wait politely.

Stone thundered. Bolts rattled loose. From the lower tunnels came a hiss that was not air but intent sharpened into sound. Every Warrenhold heart skipped the same beat, and every head turned toward the dark mouth where the monitors had shown Coilthorne's silhouette.

Then he stepped into view.

He did not arrive with the frenzy of a beast or the charge of an army. He arrived like a verdict, violet optics gleaming, body sliding forward with the certainty of something that had never learned the concept of doubt. Flanking serpents fanned out in a semi-circle, plates clattering, optics scanning with insect patience.

The chamber's speakers crackled. Glitch's hum rolled through them, deeper now, layered with distortion, threading through the stone until the whole chamber vibrated like an instrument strung too tight. Hatchlings quivered in sync, their coils tightening around the dais.

"Don't," Glitch muttered under his breath, "do anything impressive without me asking."

Of course, one of them hissed back in perfect unison with his tone.

Vik smirked nervously. "They're just echoing you."

"Yeah," Glitch said. "That's what terrifies me."

The First Contact

Ferra's front line met the serpent advance one tier below the council chamber. Sparks showered as pikes jabbed into plating, ricocheting off, catching seams. The railgun ruin coughed its last, spitting one final slug that dented a heavy serpent's jaw before collapsing into itself like a tired old soldier.

"Drop!" Glitch barked.

The speaker crews obeyed. Ferra's guard dropped too, diving under cover as the serpents reared.

Glitch dragged the slider across his chest plate, pushing his hum into a shriek of feedback. The hatchlings snapped to attention, optics blazing. The sound tore through the cavern, bouncing into side corridors, worming into signal threads Coilthorne's serpents carried.

For a breath, the enemy line faltered. Two heavies staggered as if their legs forgot which way was down.

"Rise!" Glitch shouted.

Ferra and her guard surged, stabbing into the brief hesitation. Sparks, shrieks, blood-metal spray. The chamber shook.

The Counterstroke

But Coilthorne was not a creature who lost tempo. He adjusted, body rippling in a wave of cable and armor. His crown of sensors glowed, and with a pulse, a counter-tone bled through the air—low, insidious, resonant enough to make the speaker lines tremble.

The hatchlings wavered. Their neat formation frayed; some twitched, heads jerking toward Coilthorne's violet gaze.

Glitch's stomach dropped. "No. No, no, no—look at me, not him."

He slammed his palm against his chest plate, overloading his own circuits. Sparks flared. The hum deepened into a broken rumble, like an ancient machine refusing to shut down.

The hatchlings re-aligned. Their optics snapped back to him, hissing, tails coiling tighter around the dais.

Vik grinned, wide-eyed. "You won them back!"

Glitch grimaced. "At the cost of my spleen. Do me a favor and don't ask if mechs have spleens."

The Breakpoint

The lower tier battle turned savage. Guards were shoved back against barricades of vending machines and welded doors. Every impact rattled the bones of the chamber above.

"Hold," Glitch told the hatchlings, voice steady, even as dust fell into his optics. "Stay."

They quivered, every coil begging to strike.

Marnie leaned close, voice like stone scraping. "If you mean to use them, now is your only chance."

"I mean not to," Glitch said. "They fight last. Because if they fight first, there won't be anything left to save."

On the monitors, Coilthorne's immense head lowered, optics searing violet. For the first time, his crown cables shifted like serpents themselves, tasting the hum in the air. His voice cracked the feed—not through sound, but by overriding the signal entirely.

"PRIME."

The word wasn't spoken. It was imposed.

Every hatchling flinched. The chamber's walls vibrated. Even Glitch's chassis stuttered, error codes flickering across his vision.

He forced his voice into the mic, raw and cracked: "Not Prime. Just... wrong place, wrong time."

His hum broke into static. Sparks spat from the speaker lines.

The hatchlings wavered—torn, trembling—caught between blood and bond.

And then Vik did something nobody asked him to.

He stepped onto the dais, shoved his tiny body against Glitch's leg, and shouted, "He's ours!"

The word wasn't command. It was declaration. A child's certainty.

The hatchlings froze. Turned. Optics snapped violet-to-magenta as they hissed, not at Glitch, but at Coilthorne.

For the first time, the Watch Serpent flinched.

The Threshold

The chamber erupted—guards rallying, speakers humming, hatchlings poised like a living wall.

Glitch looked down at Vik, then at the council, then at Coilthorne filling the monitors with violet rage.

"Alright," he said, deadpan, exhausted, bitter. "I guess we're making this stupid story even stupider."

He raised his hand.

The hatchlings rose with him, coils coiling, optics blazing.

The battle for Warrenhold had tipped.

And the city leaned forward to follow a mech who hated leadership more than Coilthorne hated losing.

Chapter Thirteen: Coilthorne Returns

T he alarm bells in Warrenhold didn't just ring—they absolutely lost their minds.

Sonic warnings spiraled through the ancient speaker horns, overloaded signal crystals fizzled at dangerous frequencies, and at least three alarm stations caught fire. Not from the enemy. Just from the sheer audacity of how loud the panic had become.

Tunnels shook with a rhythmic, pulsing quake that wasn't quite marching and wasn't quite drilling. It was a slither. The slither of something massive. Thousands of somethings. Each one plated in black, venom-laced armor and designed specifically to break hope into neat, bite-sized pieces.

In the Grand Arches above the city's entrance ramp, emergency battlements flared to life—wall-mounted turrets snapping into position, auto-hammer rigs spinning up, and a very confused pigeon being shooed off the main defense array by an exhausted council technician named Trebble.

And at the heart of the chaos, planted awkwardly just behind a sandbag barricade and surrounded by the most adorably weaponized disaster group in history, stood Glitch.

He didn't look like a war hero.

Or a tactician.

Or even someone who knew what day it was.

His cloak was torn and slightly smoldering from an earlier misunderstanding with a toaster turret. His metal plating had dents in the shape of someone else's elbow. And one of the hatchlings had curled itself into his backpack strap, purring as if this were nap time and not DEFCON DEATH SERPENT.

"This," Glitch muttered to no one in particular, "is a deeply stupid way to die."

Beside him, Vik peeked over the sandbags, his slingshot already armed with a rock he had personally whittled into a point. The weapon looked like it would give someone a nasty bruise, assuming the snake army was emotionally sensitive and allergic to pebbles.

"You know," Vik said, trying for casual but landing somewhere between nervous hiccup and full-body tremble, "you could just run."

Glitch didn't look at him. His gaze remained locked on the curved entrance ramp where the first wave would hit.

"Tried that," he said flatly. "Turns out they follow me anyway."

And behind him, the evidence lined up with military precision.

Hatchlings—hundreds of them. Baby serpents with glimmering crimson optics and armor so new it still had protective stickers on some of the tail segments. They stood in perfect formation, arranged by size, shape, and probably zodiac sign. Their bodies glowed faintly with ready-mode bio-energy. Their hisses harmonized like a snake choir on caffeine.

It was beautiful. Terrifying. Cute. Strategically unsound.

"Do they... know what we're doing?" Vik asked softly.

Glitch glanced at the hatchlings. Then at his own feet. Then back at the slowly brightening corridor where war was coming.

"I don't even know what we're doing," he admitted.

Warrenhold's upper tier sprang to life. Spotlights ignited with a boom of static discharge. Energy barriers shimmered into place across tunnel chokepoints—some of them flickering nervously like they weren't sure they'd been paid for this job. Defense teams rushed into position. The council, which had finally exited the War Chamber after fifteen minutes of unproductive yelling, began shouting contradictory commands from the ramparts.

"Seal the east tunnels!"

"No, open them!"

"Someone find out why the baker's sending muffins to the artillery crews again!"

Glitch turned slightly, watching as one of the council members—a flustered old mouse with a monocle that kept falling off—stared directly at him and blurted, "He should say something inspirational!"

Glitch raised one hand.

The council fell quiet.

He cleared his vocal processor.

Then said:

"No."

And lowered his hand again.

A beat passed.

Someone coughed.

From the hatchlings: synchronized hissing. Maybe support. Maybe rebellion. Glitch was too tired to ask.

He looked at Vik, who looked back with wide, anxious eyes.

"You're gonna do something heroic, right?" Vik whispered.

Glitch stared at him.

"Define heroic."

"You know. Brave. Unforgettable. Legendary?"

Glitch winced like someone had poked his sarcasm gland.

"I was really hoping for 'quietly unnoticed' and 'mildly competent.'"

And then—like clockwork made of doom—the city dimmed.

A low vibration began to build beneath their feet. The kind of vibration you feel in your teeth before you hear it in your ears. The kind that says, Hey, remember peace? Good times.

It was time.

The serpents had arrived.

And still, despite the madness unfolding above and below, the absurdity of it all came back to one central figure.

A mech with no rank.

No plan.

No idea how to hold a meeting, let alone a battlefront.

And somehow, that's exactly where fate had stuck him.

A lone figure in a half-melted cloak.

An orphaned child with a slingshot.

And an army of loyal, bite-sized war babies who thought their "mother" was the most emotionally repressed machine ever built.

Glitch: This is not how you write a legend. This is how you write a cautionary tale told by drunk mechanics over a campfire no one asked for.

The warning klaxons screamed themselves hoarse.

Then the tunnel mouth darkened.

A sound rose—part hiss, part static scream, part soul-destroying rattlesnake opera—and then the vanguard appeared.

Glinting black coils slid into view like liquid steel given hunger and purpose. The first wave of elite serpents emerged from the darkness, each larger than a land cruiser, their segmented plating etched with warning runes, hazard glyphs, and way too much ego.

They didn't hiss for intimidation.

They hissed in unison, like a language. Like an ancient command being executed by creatures too well-trained to question it.

And at their head—

Lord Coilthorne.

Slithering forward with the grace of a glacier made of malice, his massive form seemed to absorb the lights of Warrenhold's defenses and spit back dread in return.

He did not roar.

Did not sneer.

He simply appeared—monolithic and absolute.

His optics glowed with deep vermilion, a hue not born from energy but from promise: the promise that this city, this resistance, this mistake of a rebellion would end here.

The silence before impact stretched longer than it had any right to.

And then Coilthorne's voice echoed, so low and thunderous it rattled sediment from the tunnel ceiling.

"Erase him."

He wasn't pointing. He didn't need to.

His gaze, fixed squarely on Glitch, was command enough.

Glitch, very softly, sighed.

"Right," he muttered. "Here we go."

He didn't make a speech.

Didn't puff his chest.

Didn't whisper a prayer or name a plan.

He just turned—slowly, awkwardly—toward the hatchlings behind him.

Hundreds of eyes met his.

Eyes that trusted him.

Eyes that expected something.

Anything.

"...Please don't make me say it," he whispered, almost pleading with the universe itself.

But the hatchlings had already begun to shift.

They weren't confused anymore.

They were coiling tighter. Forming columns. Sharpening their poses with the kind of rehearsed instinct that suggested they had never needed words to know what to do. Their plating hummed. Their optics burned with synced resolve.

They weren't just made for war.

They were made for him.

That fact haunted Glitch more than the enemy.

He felt it in his circuitry—the shape of responsibility. The smell of impending doom. The tragic weight of being miscast in someone else's prophecy.

He lifted one reluctant hand, fingers trembling just slightly from the cascade of stress signals racing through his frame.

Higher.

Higher still.

He pointed toward the enemy.

Partly because the moment demanded it.

Mostly because he had absolutely no better idea.

The hatchlings responded with terrifying precision.

They surged—not forward, not yet—but into defensive posture. Flanking him. Encircling him. Reading his body like it was a signal flare, a field code, a battle hymn wrapped in snark and existential dread.

Somewhere behind him, he heard a councilmember shout, "What is he doing?!"

Another mouse muttered, "He's commanding them..."

"No," said a third, squinting down through binoculars. "They're responding to him. That's different."

In the city's upper tiers, the council's panic began to mutate into something stranger.

Hope.

Confused, terrified, utterly misplaced hope.

Because it didn't matter that Glitch wasn't a trained general. Or that he was technically trespassing in the concept of heroism. What mattered—terrifyingly—was that something had changed.

That Coilthorne, the terror of Nexus tunnels, had paused. Just for a moment.

And in war, a pause was everything.

Vik knelt beside Glitch, clutching the slingshot to his chest like it might still help.

"You're doing it," he whispered.

"No," Glitch whispered back. "I'm enduring it. That's different."

But he didn't lower his hand.

He couldn't.

Because deep down, even if he couldn't explain it—he knew what came next wasn't about him.

It was about what had chosen him.

And why it refused to let him go.

The tunnel exploded into motion.

Not with elegance. Not with grace.

With noise, sparks, and the unmistakable fury of underfunded engineering pressed to its absolute limits.

Warrenhold's outer defenses roared to life.

Plasma gates surged along the eastern choke point, slicing light through the darkness like broken neon teeth. Stun mines activated beneath the lower walkways with pops of blue static. Tripwires snapped, flinging steel netting into the advancing serpents. High above, turret-mounted sonic cannons began to rotate into alignment—two of them promptly jammed, another fired backward and obliterated a snack cart, but the fourth? That one sang.

The defenders sprang into action like a half-drilled militia who had just remembered they had teeth. Mice in cobbled-together armor sprinted to cover positions, dragging taser-lances and makeshift shields stitched from frying pans, signage, and at least one repurposed ironing board. Someone yelled, "FOR WARRENHOLD!" while another squeaked, "IS THIS EVEN COVERED IN OUR INSURANCE?"

One unlucky councilmember activated the wrong panel and launched a confetti cannon left over from a canceled festival. The resulting glitter cloud did nothing for morale but made the frontlines sparkle spectacularly.

Glitch stood in the middle of it all, arms folded, optics dim, posture tense.

He wasn't barking orders.

He wasn't gesturing like a hero in a movie finale.

He was just... bracing. Trying not to think about the fact that there was a hatchling currently using his shoulder joint as a turret perch.

Across the battlefield, Warrenhold's troops fought like cornered engineers. Clever, desperate, and full of righteous spite. Shock darts peppered the first wave of serpents. Scrap grenades—tin cans rigged with pulse cores—bounced off armor and exploded with enough force to disorient even the larger units. One mech-pult fired a vat of electrified molasses. It did not slow the serpents, but it made them extremely sticky and very angry.

The serpents retaliated with brutal efficiency. The elites moved like liquid blades, slicing through barricades with serrated tails and venom-charged fangs. Plasma hissed where armor met organic plating. One serpent unleashed a sonar scream that cracked a wall, sending stone tumbling into the lower defenses.

It wasn't just a battle.

It was an unraveling.

For every serpent stunned, two surged forward. For every alley defended, three tunnels collapsed under the weight of enemy pressure. Smoke and panic churned through the air, mixing with the scent of ozone and molten resin.

Warrenhold was falling.

Even Glitch could see it.

He stood on a raised platform—barely stable, half-shattered from a previous attack—and watched the lines bend. The council shouted into comms, voices rising with static and desperation.

"Section Twelve is overrun!"

"We've lost the east vent!"

"Where is the backup?!"

A pause. Then a quieter voice: "There is no backup."

Vik crouched beside a broken turret, his tiny body heaving, paws gripping a shock-dagger almost too big for him. "It's not enough," he whispered. "We're not enough."

Glitch didn't answer. He couldn't.

Not because he didn't have the words—but because something was shifting behind him.

He turned.

The hatchlings—hundreds of them—had begun to move again.

Not wildly.

Not randomly.

But with pattern. With intent.

They circled him in tight formation, eyes glowing with unified purpose, their tails humming with coiled energy. Their movements weren't choreographed by commands—they were reacting to him. Mirroring him.

Waiting.

Not for war.

For direction.

Glitch felt it in the deepest parts of his processor—the quiet dread of being noticed by destiny when all you wanted was to be forgotten by lunch.

He stood still.

Silent.

And all around him, the city shook.

Stone groaned underfoot. Sparks sprayed from burning consoles. Coilthorne's elite pushed through the flanks, overwhelming the mice with wave after wave of coordinated violence.

It should've been the end.

But Glitch was still standing.

Still upright, even as the storm of war surged all around him.

He looked out across the carnage.

At the defenders falling back.

At the young mouse by his side, still fighting with nothing but nerve and a dream.

At the hatchlings—coiled and ready, looking to him not with worship, but with trust.

And he realized something that hit harder than any plasma blast.

Everyone was waiting on him.

Not the real him, perhaps.

Not the one who once got electrocuted by a toaster while trying to steal bread.

Not the one who grumbled about destiny and refused to fill out his personality calibration.

No. They were waiting for the version of him he hadn't agreed to be—but had become anyway.

The mech who stood when others ran.

The figure who had, somehow, through accident and absurdity, become the hinge of history.

Him.

Glitch: This isn't how chosen ones happen. This is how bugs in the system rewrite the ending.

He closed his optics.

The city was still screaming.

But somewhere inside himself, he found a silence.

A stillness.

Not calm.

Not clarity.

Just the deep, exhausted sigh of a machine that knew—without wanting to—that the only way out was through.

He opened his eyes again.

And the hatchlings shifted with him.

The storm had a center.

And it was him.

From the depths of the chaos, the ground trembled—not from collapse or cannon fire, but from presence.

A slithering, metallic rhythm pulsed through the stone. It wasn't a stampede. It wasn't the panicked rattle of uncoordinated movement. It was deliberate. Rhythmic. A predator's cadence. Every hatchling around Glitch fell still. Every soldier on the walls paused mid-breath. Even the automated turrets hesitated, their targeting reticles blinking in confusion.

Glitch didn't need to look.

He already knew.

Lord Coilthorne had arrived.

And he wasn't making an entrance.

He was claiming the room.

Glitch turned slowly—more out of obligation than curiosity—and felt his stomach metaphorically collapse into a singularity of regret.

There, at the center of the corridor, the crowd of serpents parted like oil repelled by water. The black-plated colossus that emerged wasn't just large—he was terrifyingly precise. Every inch of his armor gleamed with etched runes and weaponized vanity. Twin vents hissed cold vapor into the air around him. His red optics pulsed like tracking beacons in a horror simulation.

Lord Coilthorne was more than a general.

He was a statement.

"I was really hoping he died offscreen," Glitch muttered.

Vik, peering from behind a scorched pillar, whispered, "That's him?"

"No, that's a friendly birthday magician in a murder suit. YES, that's him."

The serpent lord slithered closer, his movements slow and predatory. The stone beneath him cracked with every coiled shift of his armored body. Sparks danced across his plated fangs. His massive tail scraped the floor behind him like a guillotine waiting for its next neck.

All around them, the hatchlings tightened formation. Not retreating.

Not advancing.

Just waiting.

Glitch's throat made a low, metallic click as he swallowed dry air. His hands twitched. Every fiber in his frame screamed at him to flee, but the snakes... they wouldn't. Not without him. Not without permission.

Which meant—he had to stay.

Coilthorne's voice cut through the static like a surgical blade.

"So... this is what the future chose?"

He didn't yell. He didn't sneer. His words slithered, deliberate and low, like venom being loaded into a dart.

Glitch didn't answer.

Because what could he say?

"Yes, I accidentally led your genetically engineered murder infants into rebellion, and no, I don't know how to turn it off"?

Instead, he raised his chin—barely—and shrugged.

"Look, they picked me. Not my idea. Please submit your complaints to the glitchy destiny server that caused this."

Coilthorne didn't blink. Didn't move. But the pressure in the room spiked like gravity had turned judgmental.

"They follow you," the serpent said. "They bear my coils. My code. My purpose."

Glitch side-eyed a hatchling that was currently trying to coil itself into a heart shape for reasons unknown.

"Yeah, I can really see your 'purpose' shining through."

Coilthorne's massive head lowered, optics glowing brighter.

"They are mine."

"They're nobody's," Glitch replied, voice harder than he expected. "They're kids. Scaly, bitey, brain-hacking kids, sure. But they made a choice."

"They imprinted on an error," Coilthorne hissed.

"That makes two of us."

The tension in the air went brittle.

The kind of brittle that breaks.

The council, watching from above on damaged monitors, held their breath. The few remaining defenders on the upper battlements stopped shouting. Even Sentinel's commentary feed crackled and went dead.

All eyes were on this moment.

Because something had shifted.

This wasn't just a siege anymore.

This was a reckoning.

Coilthorne reared to his full height, towering over Glitch, his plating creaking with power. His shadow stretched like a prophecy across the cracked floor.

"You are not their leader," he growled.

"Good," Glitch snapped. "Because I never wanted to be. But I'm here. And so are they."

Behind him, the hatchlings hissed in unison. Loud. Unified. Beautifully terrifying.

Glitch didn't even flinch this time.

He pointed directly at the serpent lord's face.

"I didn't take your army. I didn't want your war. But if you want them back, you'll have to go through them."

A pause.

Then Coilthorne lunged.

Faster than should've been possible, he shot forward with a guttural roar, his body blurring into a storm of razor-scaled fury. His tail whipped through the air like a living battering ram. Claws flared from his underside, and fangs flashed toward Glitch like spears dipped in data corruption.

But he never reached him.

Because the hatchlings moved first.

All of them.

Like a flood of sentient armor.

Glitch stumbled back a step, shielding his optics from the sparks.

And all around him—

Chaos.

Order.

Devotion.

And defiance.

The children of war had picked their side.

And they chose rebellion.

Chapter Fourteen: The Fall of Coilthorne

"They obey you," Coilthorne said, flat as a verdict.

The words hit like a dropped anvil, and the chamber seemed to recalibrate around them—every hiss, every distant alarm, the soft scuff of mice boots on metal—suddenly tuned to that single, damning line.

Glitch physically recoiled like he'd been accused of being a pop idol. "No, no, no. Let's be very clear about this." His voice pitched up into the register of a mech trying not to panic in front of new dependents. "They are confused infants with zero understanding of the world. I am not in control of them. They're just... following me."

He made a broad, helpless gesture at the floor—as if asking the universe to come see for itself—and the universe, being a comedian, obliged. Half the hatchlings snapped into defensive poses, plating rising like tiny storm shutters; the other half draped themselves around his shins and calves like loyal sashes of doom. One particularly ambitious noodle attempted to coil across his chest and failed, sliding down his abdomen with a squeaky trill.

"Oh COME ON," Glitch hissed under his breath. "Not helping."

Coilthorne's optics narrowed to razors. "And that makes you their leader."

Glitch: NO IT DOESN'T. THAT IS NOT HOW LEADERSHIP WORKS. HAVE YOU HEARD OF INFORMED CONSENT?!

He did not say it out loud, because the room already had more panic than oxygen. Instead, he inhaled through fried vocal filters and felt the bite of cold air in places that weren't supposed to feel anything. Above, Warrenhold's cracked arch windows vibrated under the pressure of the siege. The civic banners—patchwork cloth, old hazard tape, a dish towel painted like a flag—hung still, like they were holding their breath.

"You took what was mine," Coilthorne said, rising a fraction. The huge coils behind him shifted—metal sounding like distant thunder.

"I tripped into what was yours," Glitch corrected, voice thinning. "There's a very important distinction."

"You imprinted my future."

"I stood in front of your murder eggs while they were being born!" He snapped his hands out, then froze as three hatchlings clambered onto his palms as if summoned. He sighed, dead behind the optics. "Accidentally."

"They chose you," Coilthorne said.

"They made a mistake," Glitch said, and he meant it like a wish.

For the first time, something in Coilthorne's eyes flickered. Not rage. Not even contempt. Worse: disbelief. "You... truly believe that?"

Glitch looked down. One hatchling was balancing on his boot like a proud gargoyle, optics bright as heat beads. Another had discovered the frayed edge of his cloak and was chewing it exactly like a teething ring. Behind him, a dozen more formed spirals around Vik and the nearest guard line—protective, not possessive.

"...I really want to," he admitted.

The serpent lord's head lowered, the movement slow and deliberate, like he was dropping a lid on the moment. His voice came out quiet and cruel. "Then die with your delusions."

Around them, the chamber breathed in. Not figuratively—ducts exhaled, vents sucked, the pressure changed. Somewhere to Glitch's left, a turret hiccuped and spat a useless trout of sparks. The municipal clock on the far wall—a rescued lobby piece from a dead Nexus station—ticked once and gave up forever.

Glitch's optics tracked the room even as his mouth kept being a mouth. Warrenhold's defenders crowded the upper gallery: mice and voles in salvage armor, straps too loose, helmets too big, faces too young. A councilor—Drell, smoky tuft, loud in meetings—had fingers white-knuckled around the edge of the railing. A pair of auto-hammers sat idle, their feed lines looped into neat figure eights by someone anxious who needed something to do. Every surface wore a history of fixes: new welds gleaming beside old cracks, tape over tape over tape.

He felt the hatchlings tighten around his legs, a synchronized, breathing brace. Not fear. Intent.

"Seriously," he muttered, to them or to fate, hard to tell. "I was built for sarcasm, not leadership. I literally got rejected from three different hero arcs before lunch."

Vik's voice crackled in over a cheap comm pinned to Glitch's collar. "They'll follow you."

Glitch snapped his head toward the sound. Vik crouched behind a toppled barricade, ears slicked back, soot smudged across his cheek. He had a shock-dagger in one paw and the look of someone who'd already decided to do something brave and regrettable the second he stood up. "Vik, this is NOT the time to have confidence in me!"

"You're already leading them!" Vik shouted, voice bouncing off the metal like a dare. "You're just too stubborn to admit it!"

Glitch: Do not. Say. The line.

Narrator (the universe, the room, the awful story machine grinding on): Thus, he accepted his fate.

Glitch: AAAAAAAUGH.

He didn't accept anything. He sagged under it. There's a difference. But his spine straightened a millimeter, which for him might as well have been a coronation. He rolled one shoulder to unhook a hatchling who'd wedged itself underneath his pauldron, then opened and closed his fingers like he could shake off the future.

"This is not my war," he whispered, and he believed it all the way to his welded bones.

Metal groaned under a distant impact. The east tunnel—a feed coming in on a flickering wall monitor—showed serpents boiling up the ramps, black on black, heat-signatures pulsing at the joints. Auto-net launchers fired and tangled two of them; a third sliced through the net with a contemptuous twist. One of the city's sonic cannons rotated, whined, and then threw its belt. A shower of glitter spilled from an upper window as someone detonated the wrong kind of morale device.

The hatchlings didn't watch the screens. They watched him.

They were almost quiet now, hisses down to a low thread of sound, like static under a song. Their optics pulsed together, not in the creepy hive way, but the way a crowd holds a single long breath.

Glitch dropped his gaze to the smallest one—foot-gargoyle. It blinked. No pleading, no fear. Just expectation.

He hated that most.

"Okay," he said softly, detaching the word from his throat like a bandage.

From the gallery: "Any time now!" a guard squeaked, tone brittle with terror. Another voice—calmer, older—tried to layer orders over the panic, "Collapse the secondary span—no, not yet, not yet—hold—"

Coilthorne shifted, and the whole room felt it. The serpent lord's coils rasped across the stone, etching a sound that dragged up the spine. He didn't rear, not yet. He lifted his head just enough to blot the emergency lamps behind him, and the shadows doubled him—two heads, two sets of eyes, one intent.

"You are not their leader," he said again, low, and the floor seemed to agree, trembling.

"Good," Glitch shot back before he could stop himself. "Because I never wanted to be." He gestured vaguely behind him, to the terrible, adorable ring of loyalty. "But I'm here. And so are they."

A ripple of hush passed through the defenders. Even the monitors seemed to dim, as if the room didn't want to miss a syllable.

Coilthorne's lip-plates peeled back just enough to show the fine hardware of fang. "You speak as if you have a choice."

Glitch looked past him—over his massive shoulders, down the tunnel where darkness moved like a living argument. On the far screen, a squad of Warrenhold runners hauled a crash cart through debris, three kids stuffed under the tarp, a fourth refusing to lie down. On another, a force door jammed, jerked, and finally slammed shut on a serpent's tail. The tail twitched. The door buckled.

He did not have choices. He had a pile of wrong answers and the worst possible quizmaster.

He lifted one arm.

Slowly, like the air had gotten thick, like the moment weighed something.

His finger hovered—not quite pointing. The hatchlings' bodies tensed in mirror. Above, Drell's monocle fell and cracked and no one looked down.

Across from him, Coilthorne's focus tightened to a needle. He didn't blink. He didn't breathe, visibly. He simply aligned—muscle, code, intent.

"You took what was mine," Coilthorne repeated, and this time, it sounded less like grievance and more like a ritual line.

"I didn't take anything," Glitch said. "They're not a thing."

"They were built for me." A beat. "And now they will unbuild you."

A small sound escaped Glitch—something between a laugh and the squeak of an abused bearing. He forced his hand higher, until the pointing became real.

"Before we do the dramatic lunging," he said, voice gone dry, "you should know something." He swallowed metal. "They already decided."

Behind him, a hundred tiny coils firmed.

Coilthorne shifted an inch forward. The floor cracked under one plate of his weight. "Then die with your delusions," he said again, and the way he said it this time made it clear: he wasn't granting permission. He was making a promise.

The room inhaled a second time.

Wires hummed. Lights stuttered. Far-off, the east cannon finally caught its belt and spun up into a clean, beautiful whine.

Vik's voice whispered through the comm, barely a thread. "Glitch."

"What."

"If this goes bad—"

"It already did."

"—I'm glad you came for me."

Glitch's chest did a small, stupid thing that wasn't on any wiring diagram. He kept his eyes on Coilthorne, because that was safer.

"You want orders?" he asked the hatchlings without looking back. His voice didn't rise. It didn't hero. It just stopped pretending to be a joke.

Every tiny head lifted.

Coilthorne's massive tail coiled, then uncoiled, and the edge of it nicked the floor like a butcher setting a blade to wood.

Glitch's hand trembled a millimeter, then steadied.

"Stay," he said—not yet a command, more like a position in a sentence that hadn't been spoken.

The circle around him locked.

A councilor somewhere above exhaled a prayer with no words in it.

Coilthorne's body compressed—eight meters of weapon folding itself into a single idea.

Glitch breathed in.

The siege screamed beyond the walls.

The hatchlings listened.

And the world paused between two choices that weren't choices at all.

The pause ended like glass giving way—sudden, sharp, irreversible.

Coilthorne struck first. He didn't so much move as detonate, his body uncoiling with a whip-crack that split the chamber's sound barrier. Stone shattered where his tail lashed; sparks rained from a half-dead conduit. The serpent lord's head came down like judgment, jaws unhinging wide enough to take Glitch and half the hatchlings in a single bite.

Glitch didn't think. He flung his arm forward, the one already raised, like a guilty man pointing at fate itself.

"GO!"

It wasn't a roar. It wasn't heroic. It was a raw packet of panic punched into the air, but it was enough.

The hatchlings exploded outward.

Tiny coils launched like spring steel. A hundred infant serpents, fresh from their shells, surged together in a wave of glittering plates and shrill metallic cries. They hit Coilthorne's head and shoulders with the velocity of a pipe bomb made of kittens. The impact staggered him—not much, but enough for the gallery above to erupt in a desperate cheer.

"Light the sconces!" someone shouted, already firing a jury-rigged flare gun. Sparks bloomed and clattered against Coilthorne's armor, leaving only scorch kisses, but in the smoke his silhouette looked wounded.

Warrenhold's guards, galvanized, threw themselves into the fight. Sonic cannons screamed from the galleries, the sound waves rattling Glitch's ribcage. Salvage rifles spat arcs of blue, while slings with jury-rigged energy cells lobbed sizzling shot into the writhing dark.

And still the serpents poured in.

The east tunnel disgorged Coilthorne's army in a rush of metal and scale. Long serpents, armored and fully grown, spilled across the stone like an oil slick with fangs. The clash of coil and claw filled the air, steel screeching on steel. Sparks danced across the room as Warrenhold's first defensive line shattered.

Glitch stumbled back against the barricade, hatchlings pouring past his legs. His optics flicked from one crisis to the next—the breach at the door, the council line failing, Vik's small frame ducking behind a twisted girder with three guards shielding him. Every new detail screamed you're losing.

"WHY are you all looking at me?!" Glitch shouted at the hatchlings that hadn't joined the wave. A dozen still lingered, circling him, staring up like tiny soldiers waiting for a second order. "I don't have a strategy! I have half a working eye and a death wish I didn't subscribe to!"

They hissed in unison. Loyal. Expectant.

"Fine! Fine, you want strategy? Uh—trip the big guy! Bite ankles! NO—don't bite my ankles! HIS ankles! You know, the skyscraper with the attitude problem!"

They obeyed instantly, darting toward Coilthorne's massive coils. A few latched on and began to gnaw—not effective, but irritating enough to make Coilthorne hiss, his tail whipping around and crushing a column into dust.

On the upper gallery, Drell bellowed orders that no one followed. Two more serpents crashed through the wall, scattering mice soldiers. A net launcher fired; the serpents shredded it in seconds. A brave vole lit an improvised explosive and threw it—it bounced uselessly off Coilthorne's scales and detonated against the ceiling, collapsing rubble that buried three defenders.

The battle was losing itself.

Glitch grabbed the edge of the barricade, his claws gouging the wood. He wanted to run. Everything in him screamed for it. But Vik's face flickered in the corner of his vision—calm in defiance, too calm for someone that small. And the hatchlings—every tiny body that looked back for his signal—locked his feet into the floor.

"Damn it," he muttered, then louder: "LEFT FLANK! Hit the left! Somebody hit the—"

He had no idea if the Warrenhold defenders heard him. But the hatchlings did. The cluster that had clung to his cloak surged to the side, scurrying over the debris, squeaking and hissing. They swarmed a serpent breacher trying to circle toward Vik's position. The breacher reared, thrashing violently, then collapsed in a knot of snapping baby coils.

The gallery erupted again. Cheers and shouts filled the smoke. For a single heartbeat, Glitch felt the tremor of belief crash against him like a wave.

"Oh, don't you dare start thinking I know what I'm doing," he muttered.

But the hatchlings were already peeling off in coordinated packs, circling serpents twice their size, distracting, slowing, cutting off angles. For every one that got crushed under Coilthorne's tail, two more crawled up a serpent's body and jammed themselves into its joints.

And Coilthorne—Coilthorne noticed.

He lifted his head through the storm of hatchlings clawing his armor and fixed Glitch with eyes like endless tunnels.

"You presume command," he thundered, his voice carrying over every scream and weapon.

"I don't presume anything!" Glitch yelled back, ducking as a shard of metal screamed past his ear. "I stumble command! I trip into it! And apparently that's enough!"

"You make yourself their king."

Glitch pointed a finger at Coilthorne, half in defiance, half in complete despair. "I am nobody's king!"

The hatchlings hissed in a perfect, unintentional chorus behind him, like a fanfare that disagreed.

The serpent lord reared, his full bulk blotting out the emergency lamps and leaving half the chamber in writhing shadow. His coils writhed over the defenders, smashing barricades, splitting steel. Sparks from crushed conduits fell like rain.

And Glitch, pinned in the epicenter, felt the ridiculous weight of eyes—mice, serpents, hatchlings—all waiting on him.

He lifted both hands this time. Not pointing. Just spreading them like some exhausted conductor.

"Okay," he croaked. "Fine. Round two."

The hatchlings surged.

The hatchlings didn't attack like soldiers.

They attacked like a weather event.

They fanned in concentric ribbons, splitting into little work-crews the way an organism splits into cells. One cluster went for optics, a gleaming blur that climbed Coilthorne's face and smeared his visual lattice with conductive gel filched from broken conduits. Another cluster bit hard at plating seams, worrying the gaps like determined wrench-teeth until sparks skittered free. A third pack dove under his coils to jam their bodies into the pivot joints, clicking tiny fangs into the soft gaskets like staples.

"Left ribbon—blind him!" Glitch barked, one hand chopping across the air.

Half a dozen hatchlings swiveled at the word, launched, and stuck to Coilthorne's brow ridge like very angry barnacles. A hiss-thrum ran through them in perfect timing; their micro-EM bursts syncopated into a strobe that forced the serpent lord's optics to hard-dampen. His head dipped a fraction. Steel screamed where his jaw scraped stone.

Coilthorne countered like a machine that had practiced killing in mirrors.

Vents along his lower plating opened with a harsh cough: heat purge. A white breath of superheated air rolled out. Hatchlings blackened and fell away, smoking; others dropped and curled, armor bluing with heat stress.

"Down! Down, down, down!" Glitch waved frantically. "You—back-coils—cool the ones that burned!"

The back-coils—three dozen babies who had inexplicably decided they were a logistics department—immediately slithered to the fallen, pressing cool underscales to hot plates, venting their own surplus heat in trembling little breaths.

A sonic cannon on Warrenhold's upper rail fired, the tone wrong for living things: a hammered sheet of sound that made even Glitch's teeth ache—and he did not have teeth. Coilthorne rode it without flinching; his dorsal plates flexed and repitched the wave, throwing it back in a knotted pattern that shattered two gallery posts and sent defenders tumbling.

"Retune that!" Glitch shouted upward. "Narrow band, nine hundred hertz under baseline!"

Trebble—the exhausted technician who'd shooed the pigeon earlier—looked left, looked right, then yanked two muffin tins off a trolley and wedged them into the horn throat, cursing. The next blast rang cleaner, lower—a gut-punch hum that didn't bounce. Coilthorne's crest plates vibrated like angry tuning forks.

"Better!" Glitch yelled, throat raw. "Keep it ugly!"

The serpent lord decided ugly was fine. He slammed his tail.

The floor jumped a meter and came down wrong. A barricade folded like paper. Councilor Drell vanished under a sliding slab and reappeared seconds later, dragged out by three hatchlings who had no idea who he was and loved him anyway. The air filled with gypsum dust; coil strikes stuttered as targets blurred.

Glitch's optics flickered, recalibrating through haze. The world steadied into layers: foreground panic, midground fight, background doom. Somewhere to his right, Vik scrambled across a snapped catwalk, shoving a spotlight with both hands. The lamp squealed, swung—caught Coilthorne full in the face. The lord's pupils cut to slits; his head jerked to avoid the glare.

"Good! Hold him there!" Glitch called.

"I am holding a sun," Vik squeaked through clenched teeth.

Hatchlings poured up the serpent's neck like a living scarf. Coilthorne's head snapped; ten flung free, clattering over stone. He rolled his right shoulder, scales ratcheting—and shed a panel with a crisp clack. The sacrificial plate fell like a shining shield and crushed two babies flat.

Glitch swallowed a noise his chassis couldn't code. "You can shed plating."

"Of course he can shed plating," Sentinel crackled dryly from the satchel. "He built redundancy into everything but his world view."

"Then we stop treating this like armor," Glitch muttered. "Treat it like a conveyor."

He jabbed a finger, drawing a rough arc in the air. "Bite and ride! Bite—ride—slide!"

Hatchlings latched, then surfed the shedding panels like slick sleds, steering them with tiny bodies to wedge under Coilthorne's belly where shed pieces couldn't be replaced. A trio jammed one plate sideways into the coil path; Coilthorne's next turn scraped metal on metal, shrieked, and threw him half a coil off rhythm.

The Warrenhold line rallied around the wrongness. Mice shoved forward, shock pikes stabbing; a rigged slingshot hurled a satchel of conductive chain that splashed across Coilthorne's side and stuck, lightning-wet, slapping shunts into whatever it kissed. The serpent lord shivered, not with pain—with math, recalculating every angle he'd owned for years.

He decided to remove the unknown in the equation.

Glitch.

Coilthorne's head darted through the swarm, a bolt of black iron. Hatchlings leapt; he took them with him, teeth scraping the floor where Glitch had been a breath before. The mech's cloak snagged and tore; he rolled, ribs scraping stone, then came up with his palms open like a man warding off a wave.

"Oh no you don't," Glitch said through his teeth. "We're not doing 'eat the protagonist.' That's cliché."

The lord opened his mouth. Inside was not mouth. It was a beautifully engineered failure mode: nested rings of ceramic teeth, humming with a field that made the air around it flinch.

Sentinel hissed. "Field coil. He will cut a hole through you."

"Not today," Glitch spat. "Loomers!"

He hadn't named any of them. He'd never named anything on purpose. But at his bark, a cohort peeled from the main pack—the longer hatchlings with wider plates and an alarming instinct for geometry. They surged as one and draped their bodies across Coilthorne's lower jaw like living straps, coiling tight, stacking, building a lattice across that killing field.

Coilthorne bit down.

The Loomers screamed as their plates smoked—but held.

"Back them!" Glitch roared. "Braid the tails—ground the field!"

The logistics babies—the back-coils—were already there, weaving themselves into a cable that ran from loomers' tails to a jut of grounded rebar in the broken gallery. The field spike leapt—snapped—to ground with a cannon-crack that made the lights die and then flicker back filmy and red.

The bite lost its hum. For a heartbeat, Coilthorne's mouth was just mouth.

"Now!"

The optics pack hit again, tiny bodies slapping wet into sockets, little jaws chewing on sensor rims. The seam-worriers dug at a vulnerable joint behind the hinge. A dozen more hatchlings dove into the mouth while the hum was down and jammed themselves in the gearwork like heroic screws.

Coilthorne threw his head, gagging, and spat babies like hot nails.

He switched tactics. He went cold.

Something in his tail clicked. The next lash wasn't impact; it was a cloud—a glittering hiss that streaked across the chamber and stuck to everything. Microshards—fletchettes the size of eyelashes—bonded to fur, fabric, metal. A mouse screamed and slapped at his arm where blood oozed from a hundred pinpricks.

"Don't move!" Glitch shouted. "They're smart glue! Moving makes them bite deeper!"

Hatchlings froze, instincts warring with orders. Coilthorne took the half-second gift and coiled hard, body becoming centrifuge. The floor moaned. Three barricades slid. Glitch's feet went out; he would have skated into the serpent if five babies hadn't stuck to his boots and counter-pulled like stubborn magnets.

"Okay," he panted, "points for centripetal showmanship."

Across the chamber, a towel-cape flapped into view.

Slitherax, panting and wide-eyed, careened down a cracked stair like a carnival accident seeking purpose. He jumped the last four steps and landed in a heroic skid that ended, unfortunately, in a coil of cable. He vanished. A second later, he popped up in the same place, now garlanded with cable like a festival float.

"Children!" he wheezed, flinging an arm wide. "To your cool uncle!"

Three hatchlings—the three that had, in some terrible cosmic joke, imprinted on him in the hatchery—perked up, squealed, and hurled themselves his way. They hit Slitherax like affectionate grenades and knocked him backward into a winch column. His flailing tail slapped the lever down.

The winch screamed. A hanging chain—thick, rusty, and very enthusiastic about gravity—let go from the rafters and fell like a guillotine.

It missed Coilthorne's head. It did not miss his neck.

The chain looped, wrapped twice, and caught. The serpent lord reared, and the chain went taut with a butcher's twang, dragging through a ring bolt that was, against all precedent, actually installed correctly.

Glitch blinked. "I take back one-third of every bad thing I've said about towel-capes."

"Only a third?" Slitherax croaked from under his hatchling pile. "I accept!"

"Get up," Glitch snapped. "Or at least... keep being chaos there."

Coilthorne slammed forward; the chain sang. The ring bolt screamed. Half the gallery frame tore loose but held. A second winch, unspooled by the same fall, dragged a cable across the floor between two shattered pillars.

"Anchor that!" Glitch shouted, jabbing at the cable. Two dozen hatchlings grabbed it with teeth and bodies, heaving, bracing their little spines against stone.

"Vik!" Glitch yelled, throat raw. "Give me another sun!"

Vik, shaking and ridiculous and holy with stubbornness, threw his entire weight into the second spotlight. The lamp groaned and swung on its last hinge. Light punched Coilthorne in the face. His pupils pinholed; his head jerked back—the chain's angle shifted—and for the first real time, he lost the math.

Warrenhold moved.

Mice swarmed the cable, throwing bodies and hooks and hope onto it, dragging it around a busted stanchion to make a rough block-and-tackle. Trebble slammed an old brake bar through the pulley housing and leaned his entire life against it. The cable went from idea to intention.

"Pull!" Glitch roared. "Everything you've got!"

The chamber strained.

Hatchlings braided, mice hauled, the chain moaned, the bolt shrieked, and Coilthorne slid. Not far. A hand's breadth. Two. But the serpent lord moved, and that was a sin against his physics.

He answered with something they hadn't seen.

Plates along his side opened; a ripple of needle-drones belched into the air like angry bees with knives. They streaked for the cable and tore into it, little rotors screaming.

"Shield!" Glitch yelled—no time to explain, only the hope the kids understood the shape of a word.

They did. Three packs flung themselves across the cable, bodies layered like shingles. The drones hit them, cut, whined—and bogged. The shield held long enough for the mice to get a second wrap and crank.

"Glitch," Sentinel said, voice gone thin. "His hinge."

"What hinge?" Glitch snarled, sweat that he didn't have trembling down his nonexistent backbone.

"Neural relay ring. Mid-spine, third coil. It coordinates micro-coil timing. He can't retain balance without it. You need a precise strike."

Glitch looked at the hurricane of battle, then at the exact, impossible point Sentinel wanted in a storm. "Oh, sure. Let me just thread a needle in an earthquake."

He snapped his head toward the alpha.

It was there—bigger than the others now, plates darker, optics soberer. It moved like a sentence that had learned punctuation. The alpha had not left Glitch's shadow since the hatchery; now it stood half a meter away, watching the coil storm with a soldier's focus.

Glitch jabbed two fingers, then drew a circle in the air at his own waist. "Third coil. Right there. Hard as you can."

He didn't say please. Didn't say I believe in you. He was a fraud at comfort. He gave the one thing he had: a specific.

The alpha nodded. Not a human nod—a low flex, a coil tightening and releasing. Then it whistled, a sound that was more math than music.

Half the babies broke off the dogpile and fell into arrowhead behind the alpha. They didn't rush. They timed. They moved when Coilthorne's weight rolled through second to third, when the ring would be bearing load.

"Now," Sentinel breathed.

The arrowhead struck.

Not with teeth. With force. They hit the ring as a single vector, a tiny hammer dressed as fifty children. For a second nothing happened—and then the sound came: a crack like ice learning regret.

Coilthorne's entire body stuttered.

His next tail lash went wide and took out his own flank instead of Glitch. His head snapped at a light that wasn't there. The drones veered in panic, cutting harmless arcs. The chain tightened another tooth; the cable screamed, and for the first time, the serpent lord's weight tipped the wrong way.

"Again!" Glitch shouted.

The alpha whistled—higher this time, then lower, a two-note command that tugged every child in range into the same math. They hit the ring again.

It shattered.

The whole room felt it. Coilthorne's coils lost agreement; each segment hunted for a song that wasn't playing anymore. He reared to correct, and the chain pulled, and the cable groaned, and the floor under his destroyed rhythm failed.

Stone doesn't like being educated. A slab that had taken every insult the battle offered finally chose a side. It sheared. The serpent lord dropped a half-meter into a hole his weight made for him, his lower coils wedging as the chain tightened like a grim idea.

"Hold!" Trebble screamed, small paws white on the brake.

The hatchlings slammed their bodies into the cable, little feet skidding. Mice braced butt-first against pillars and pushed. Slitherax, towel-cape crooked and eyes huge, wrapped himself in three turns around a stanchion and pulled like he was inventing penance.

"Glitch!" Vik shouted, voice breaking on the name. "He's—he's not down!"

"No," Glitch said, staring at the serpent that had been a city's myth. "He's falling."

Coilthorne's head cut back to them—the chain, the cable, the boy on the light, the mech giving orders he hated owning. His optics did not hold rage now. They held something colder: refusal.

He inhaled. His chest plates expanded. The room's pressure changed.

"Scatter!" Glitch screamed. "He's going to vent!"

The heat purge that came wasn't a breath; it was a confession. A blast of white fire washed the chamber, paint curling on metal, moss crisping to ash. Hatchlings fried where they stood. Mice dove and rolled, fur smoking, armor popping.

Vik went down behind the light, a small sound punched out of him.

Glitch didn't think. He moved so fast his joints protested later. He was already at the light, already dragging the boy behind the last intact lip of wall, already shoving his body over Vik's like a bad umbrella.

The purge passed. The chamber glowed dull orange.

Glitch rolled off, systems barking warnings, cloak smoking, forearms bubbled and ugly. He popped his optics open and saw the number he'd been pretending not to count: hatchlings that didn't rise.

He made himself stand anyway.

Coilthorne labored. The chain had done its work; the cable, the crack, the ring—they'd all done things that couldn't be undone quickly. But the serpent lord was still colossal, still coiled around the idea of victory, and he began to haul himself up like a mountain remembering it was taller.

"Again," Glitch rasped.

There was no grandeur in it. No speech. Just the same ragged order he'd given all day: try one more time.

The alpha whistled.

Children moved.

Mice hauled.

Slitherax swore through his teeth and pulled like an idiot saint.

The chain shrieked.

The floor gave another sigh.

Coilthorne slid another hand's breadth into the break.

He struck at Glitch as he fell, a casual, furious swipe that would have cut the mech into two regrettable autobiographies—except a wall of hatchlings flung themselves into the arc and took it. Tiny bodies went flying. The strike slowed a fraction. Enough for Glitch to duck, enough for Vik to live, enough for the cable to bite deeper.

Glitch's voice broke. "Stay with me!"

The kids hissed like a choir that had decided to love a very undeserving deity.

Above, the sonic cannon moaned again, Trebble holding it on the wrong pitch that had become the right one. The note burrowed into coil gaps and made bad music of Coilthorne's balance.

The serpent lord's head came up one last time. He saw the mech, the boy, the children, the cable, the chain, the ruin of his math, and something like comprehension flickered behind fury.

"You are not a leader," he said, voice low and bitter as iron.

Glitch met his gaze, smoke curling off his shoulders. "I'm a problem."

Coilthorne's jaw flexed once, like a man deciding what last sentence deserved the world.

He lunged.

The chain snapped.

The cable held.

And Lord Coilthorne fell into the gut of Warrenhold.

The serpent lord didn't crash like an avalanche. He unwound like a myth unraveling.

The chain snapped first, its broken end snapping back with a whip crack that tore divots in the ceiling. The cable groaned and stripped its teeth through the pulley, but it had done enough: momentum tipped Coilthorne past recovery. His vast weight slammed the breach, widening it in a roar of stone giving up its secrets.

Dust belched up. Entire gallery rows shook. Warrenhold's defenders clung to pillars, each other, anything. Hatchlings squealed as they scrambled to stay clear, some tumbling into the gap themselves like sparks trailing a dying torch.

Glitch shoved Vik behind the last unbroken barricade and leaned over the edge.

Coilthorne was still fighting. Even falling, he fought. His coils lashed at the walls of the pit, dragging grooves deep as rivers. Every time he caught purchase, rubble tore loose and followed him down. It wasn't descent. It was siege warfare against gravity.

And for a terrifying moment, it looked like he might win.

"Brace it!" Glitch howled. "Anything that holds—ram it in!"

Mice jammed pikes into cracks, hammering with boot-heels, trying to give the serpent no purchase. Hatchlings dove at his scales, their little teeth finding fresh seams and holding on like anchors. The alpha barked commands in that sharp whistle, whipping the chaos into something like formation.

But Coilthorne's head surged back into view, optics burning through the dust. His jaw clamped a ledge. Stone shattered, but it was enough: he was climbing.

"Not again," Glitch muttered. "Not like this."

He grabbed the nearest thing with mass—a broken beam, twice his length, scorched at both ends. His servos screamed under the load. He staggered to the lip and jammed it like a lever against Coilthorne's brow.

The serpent lord hissed and shoved back.

Metal shrieked. Sparks jumped.

For a long heartbeat, mech and monster strained against each other, neither yielding.

"You can't hold me," Coilthorne spat, voice trembling with fury and stone-dust. "I am weight. I am inevitability. I am the coil that—"

"—slips," Glitch snarled, and drove every last volt of his battered frame into one final shove.

The beam cracked. Coilthorne's grip cracked with it. His head slipped. His coils slid.

The world tilted.

Then the serpent lord fell.

—

The sound was impossible.

Not thunder—thunder ends. Not collapse—that implies a single moment. This was duration, the sound of something too big learning to lose for a long, long time.

The pit devoured him coil by coil, crashing, grinding, until the last echo bled away into a silence so raw it hurt.

Warrenhold stood trembling in the aftershock. Stones still fell like nervous punctuation. Smoke curled from walls. The spotlight Vik had braced with his entire body guttered and died.

For the first time in hours, there was no hiss of serpents. No roar of lordship.

Only silence, and breathing.

And then—cheering.

It started with one mouse. Then another. Then it spread until the whole chamber shook again, this time not with doom but with exhausted, incredulous triumph.

"Down! He's down!" voices cried. "The Lord has fallen!"

Vik stumbled forward, soot-black and teary-eyed, and threw his arms around Glitch's middle. The mech staggered like he didn't know what to do with that kind of weight.

The hatchlings swarmed, chirping their high, metallic squeals, rubbing against his legs, chest, arms. They pressed their little heads to him like supplicants. A dozen tails curled around his ankles.

The alpha slid up beside him, optics steady, chest plates rising and falling like a creature who had already known this outcome.

Glitch looked down at them all—boy, children, city—and felt the most sickening sensation of his life.

Victory.

He hadn't wanted it. He hadn't deserved it. He hadn't planned it.

But he had it.

The council staggered forward, bruised and battered. Trebble raised both paws, voice cracking from too much shouting. "Warrenhold is safe! All hail the savior of Warrenhold—!"

"Don't," Glitch rasped, too fast, too sharp. His throat hurt from the word. "Don't you call me that."

But the mice did anyway. Because names were theirs to give, not his to refuse.

The chant began. Awkward. Stumbling. Then stronger.

"Glitch! Glitch! Glitch!"

Each syllable hit him like a nail in his coffin.

Sentinel's voice, soft in his ear, didn't help: "Congratulations, commander. You've won a war you never enlisted in."

Glitch closed his eyes. The dust still hung thick, the pit still smoked, and down below, somewhere under rubble and silence, he was certain Coilthorne's story wasn't finished.

But for now—

He was the hero Warrenhold had demanded.

And he hated it.

Chapter Fifteen: The Worst Hero Ever

A nd so, the hero of Warrenhold stood victorious.

Glitch: NO. NO. DO NOT START WITH THAT SEN-TENCE. I WILL WALK INTO A WALL.

The tunnels still trembled with the memory of the battle. Smoke rose in greasy wisps from ruptured circuitry. The walls bore scars of acid spray, gouges from serrated fangs, and the occasional char mark where someone's idea of "defensive pyrotechnics" had misfired. Whole slabs of stone sagged at crooked angles, as if Warrenhold itself wasn't entirely convinced survival had been worth the effort.

Yet the serpents were gone.

Well—"gone" was generous. More accurate: scattered across the floor in dismantled segments, their twisted plating gleaming in heaps like discarded jewelry. Some had been chewed on. Others appeared to have been recycled mid-battle into mouse barricades. A few still twitched faintly, though no one dared get close enough to confirm whether they were dying or just very committed to being unsettling.

The city pulsed with confused celebration, that raw aftershock of disbelief when a miracle had clearly happened but no one had yet agreed on the explanation. Relief blurred into hysteria. Laughter broke into sobs. Children darted between repair crews, tossing glitter-scraps and shouting slogans they had clearly just invented. One banner was nothing but the words GLITCH RULES scrawled in oil ink. Another simply read: THANK YOU, RANDOM WANDERER.

And at the epicenter of this chaos stood Glitch.

He was battered, dented, optics dim, his cloak shredded, and absolutely coated in snake goo. Which, to be painfully clear, was not a substance anyone was meant to wear. The goo hissed faintly where it clung to his plating, leaving sizzling spots like a rash made of acid and bad decisions.

The mice formed a circle around him, eyes wide with awe. Council members sobbed openly, clutching one another as if salvation itself had just descended in sarcastic rodent form. A child scampered forward to drop a circuit-flower at his boots, then ran back to her family squealing. Someone tried to start a chant but trailed off halfway, realizing they didn't know if "GLITCH" rhymed with anything.

A bard appeared from somewhere—because of course there was always a bard—and immediately launched into an improvised song. Unfortunately, the only words he seemed to have prepared were "mighty glitchy leader," repeated ad nauseam. He strummed a battered lute so violently that two strings snapped in protest, which did not stop him.

Glitch stared into the crowd with the thousand-yard glare of a mech on the brink of catastrophic firmware failure.

"You don't have to do this," he croaked, raising both hands in protest. "I promise, I'm not that special. This was a mistake. A very... very specific mistake."

The words dissolved uselessly into the roar of celebration. His panic translated to them as humility, his refusal became evidence of divine modesty, and his twitching shoulders looked like the nervous tremors of a reluctant saint.

And so the legend inflated.

They saw not a sarcastic, exhausted wanderer who had tripped face-first into an accidental victory. They saw a myth in the making. A savior. A redeemer. The accidental warlord who had commanded serpents and saved a city.

Glitch: DO NOT WORD IT LIKE THAT. I DID NONE OF THOSE THINGS ON PURPOSE. THIS WAS A SERIES OF TERRIBLE CO-INCIDENCES.

But the mice didn't care.

Children climbed broken scaffolds to wave scraps of fabric painted with his face. The council hauled out a long-rusted frame labeled Emergency Hero Memorial – Use in Case of Miracle, brushing dust off as if they'd been waiting centuries for this exact moment. Someone lit a torch too close to a confetti cannon, which exploded prematurely and showered the crowd in metallic streamers. No one minded. They roared louder.

One mouse fainted dramatically. Another fell to his knees in reverence. Somewhere in the back, someone shouted, "LONG LIVE GLITCH!" and immediately a chorus picked it up, their voices bouncing off stone until the cavern itself seemed to chant.

"GLITCH! GLITCH! GLITCH!"

Glitch recoiled physically, his plating twitching like his systems were trying to eject him from the situation entirely.

"I—no, stop. I refuse this."

He looked up, optics scanning the cavern ceiling as if hoping for divine intervention, or at least a structural collapse that would bury him in anonymity forever.

Sentinel's voice hummed dryly in his head, already preparing the post-battle log.

Report Draft Title: Post-Battle Civic Deification of Unqualified Entities.

Glitch groaned, long and low, a sound that rattled his dented chestplate. "I hate this."

The city roared louder.

Not polite applause.

Not grateful nods.

But actual, unrestrained, full-volume euphoria.

Warrenhold had a new hero.

Glitch had a new nightmare.

Warrenhold didn't so much celebrate as combust.

Repair horns blared victory fanfares that were absolutely not designed for music. Lanterns flared to life in frantic sequences that made the tunnels look like they were blinking. A pair of technicians dragged out what could only be described as a "festival cannon," argued about which end was forward, and then fired a plume of shimmering sparks into a ceiling brace. The brace caught fire. Everyone cheered anyway.

Glitch stood in the middle of the plaza like a traffic cone at a parade it had not consented to.

A ring of hatchlings had coiled around his boots in concentric patterns, humming faintly. One had climbed his cloak and fallen asleep in the hood like a smug, serpentine neck pillow. Another kept trying to hand him a bent washer with the ceremonial gravity of a coronation.

"Do not give me trash," Glitch told it weakly. "I am already trash."

The crowd parted with the uncoordinated grace of people who wanted to be formal but had no idea how, and the council advanced—robes crooked, hats dented, dignity taped back together with emergency ribbon. At their center, Vik walked, bandage tucked beneath his ear, eyes shining like someone had promised him the sky and then delivered a second one for backup.

He held a medallion.

Or, more accurately, an old gear polished within an inch of its afterlife and strung on copper wire. The Warrenhold crest had been etched into it with a solder tip and an unreasonable level of hope.

Vik stopped in front of Glitch and lifted the gear with both paws.

"The council presents," he said, voice trembling, "the Crest of Gratitude."

Glitch put both hands behind his back like a guilty child facing a fruitcake. "Hard pass."

Murmurs rippled through the crowd. Someone in the third row whispered, "He's too humble." Someone in the fourth row whispered, "He doesn't understand ceremony," and someone in the fifth row whispered, "He thinks jewelry is a trap."

Glitch: IT IS.

Councilor Drell—the dramatic one with the singed whiskers and a voice designed for declarations—stepped forward, spreading his arms wide. "Warrenhold has endured. And we name the reason: Glitch!"

Roars. Stomps. Something resembling a trumpet blast that was, upon closer inspection, a length of pipe and a determined rodent.

Glitch raised a finger. "Counterpoint—"

"—Who led the impossible," Drell thundered, drowning him, "turned the serpent's brood, and threw down Coilthorne at the gates!"

Glitch put his hand back down. "Okay, but I did not— look, it was statistically irresponsible luck packaged as farce."

The bard from earlier took this as a cue and struck up a new chorus, having expanded his vocabulary from three words to five:

"Mighty glitchy leader!

Our savior, coil defeater!"

Two strings snapped in protest. The audience wept.

Vik stepped closer, voice smaller now that he no longer had the momentum of the crowd. "Just... take it." His paws trembled. "Please."

Glitch stared at the gear, at the etched crest, at the way Vik held it like it was the only object standing between them and the dark. He hated that his chassis made the sound it made then— the soft venting hiss of a tired machine deciding not to be cruel.

He bent, just enough, and let the gear drop into his palm.

It was warm from Vik's hands. He hated that, too.

The plaza detonated into cheers. Confetti cannons misfired out of sheer enthusiasm, pelting Glitch with metallic ribbons and a sprocket that pinged off his forehead plate. Someone in the back tried to ignite a miniature firework shaped like a coat-of-arms; it sputtered, coughed, and exploded into a surprisingly accurate depiction of a sandwich. Everyone cheered anyway.

Glitch: You are all emotionally compromised.

The council tried speeches. Several, overlapping. It was like being lectured by a flock of grateful geese.

"Warrenhold shall record this day—"

"—and we shall build a shrine—"

"—a tasteful shrine—"

"—we have blueprints for a tasteful shrine—"

"—and a statue, perhaps—"

"Absolutely not," Glitch said.

"—a small statue—"

"No statues." He lifted a ribbon-snarled hand. "I reject statuary on philosophical and aesthetic grounds."

The council muttered, consulted, nodded to one another with grave solemnity, then pivoted in unison. "A mural!"

Glitch considered switching himself off.

Through it all, the hatchlings trilled softly, eyes half-lidded in contentment, like they were basking in the radiator glow of public adoration. They formed little wedge formations any time a well-wisher got too close, then relaxed when Vik waved them off. One snuck behind Glitch and tried to coil heroically around his shadow.

He shifted a step to the left. It shifted with him, determined to accessorize his legend.

"Okay," Glitch said to nobody in particular, "we're done. We've hit maximum nightmare. Time to Irish-exit this entire city."

He slid the gear medallion to Vik. The boy tried to hand it back.

"No," Glitch said softly, closing Vik's fingers around it. "You keep it."

"But it's yours."

"It belongs to whoever actually wants it." He tried for flippant, failed, and settled on tired. "Frame it. Use it to calibrate a toaster. I won't know."

Vik's mouth wobbled. "You could stay."

"I could also jump into a vent fan." Glitch tipped his chin toward the nearest tunnel. "Both would be loud. One would be merciful."

The council had moved on to the Part Where We Announce A Feast With Food We Definitely Don't Have. Mice were already stringing up tarps for banners that read GLITCH SAVES and WARRENHOLD LIVES and also one baffling outlier: BREAD PARTY.

"Bread party?" Glitch asked.

Vik perked. "We have a baker. He copes by carbo-loading the populace."

Glitch could not argue with the strategy.

A small hand tugged his cloak. A mouse child stood there, eyes huge, whiskers singed, clutching a flower that could not possibly have grown underground without sincere miracles or aggressive cheating.

"For you," she said.

Glitch accepted the flower like it was a live grenade with opinions. The hatchlings leaned in. One sniffed, sneezed, and curled around his wrist, anchoring him to the moment in a way that felt unfair.

"Right," he said, voice flat. "We're done."

He pivoted—cloak dragging a constellation of confetti—toward the tunnel out of the plaza. The exit yawned like a memory of freedom: dark, empty, promising. He could almost hear the surface wind he'd never quite found, the rattle of some distant tin roof he'd never quite reached. He took a step—

"GLITCH! GLITCH! GLITCH!"

The chant surged after him, unkillable. He didn't look back. He didn't wave. He lifted a hand, sideways, in the universal gesture of "please stop loving me."

"Where are you going?" Vik asked, trotting to keep up.

"Away." He didn't turn. "I did a good thing. Now I leave before anyone expects a second one."

"You can't just—" Vik tripped, caught himself, breathless and stubborn. "They need you. We need—"

"No." Glitch's voice sharpened. "You need walls. And food. And twenty-seven different repairs. You do not need me."

He thought that would end it. He thought the word no would close the book the way it usually did.

He forgot about the hatchlings.

He took another step into the tunnel.

Skritch. Skritch. Skritch.

The sound chased him like a second heartbeat: tiny plating on old stone, synchronized by a loyalty he did not earn.

Glitch stopped. So did the sound. He turned.

A sea of bright, unblinking optics stared back at him. A carpet of small, coiled bodies pressed to the threshold, every last one waiting for permission to follow their mistake of a miracle.

Glitch: Absolutely not.

He pointed at the floor. "Stay."

They froze, model citizens.

He nodded. "Good."

He took two steps into the dark.

Skritch. Skritch.

He turned so fast his neck servos squealed. The hatchlings had advanced exactly two steps and were now pretending to be very proud of themselves for obeying the spirit, if not the letter, of the law.

Vik folded his arms, trying not to smile and failing gloriously. "They like you."

"I am not likable," Glitch hissed. "I am barely tolerable."

"You saved them."

"I also weaponized them."

"You protected us," Vik said, chin up. "You stayed."

Glitch opened and closed his mouth, a rare stutter of silence in a machine designed to always have something to say. He looked at the child with the flower, now perched on her mother's shoulders, waving at him like this was the end of a parade. He looked at the council setting up a table with exactly nine crackers and a heroic quantity of optimism. He looked at the hatchlings, who had decided—quietly, catastrophically—that he was the first and truest thing they had ever seen.

He tried, one last time, for the harsh exit.

"You're better off without me," he said, not looking at anyone.

"Then why are they better with you?" Vik asked.

It landed like a small, gentle hammer.

The crowd didn't hear it. The city kept celebrating. The bard kept butchering rhyme. A mouse in the back tried to unveil a banner and instead unveiled a sleeping cat, which everyone politely ignored.

Glitch stared at the tunnel. Freedom yawned. The world waited. All he had to do was take one step alone.

The hatchlings trilled—the soft, low sound they made when everything was still and their mother was near.

"I hate this," he said.

The nearest snake headbutted his shin with a hopeful thunk.

He sighed the kind of sigh that unbuckled armor. "Fine. Temporary. Until the bread party ends."

Vik grinned so wide it could have been illegal.

"Temporary," Glitch repeated, louder, pointing at the council as if they'd argued. "Temporary means I am allowed to leave at any time and fake my death with a tasteful level of drama."

Councilor Drell bowed. "We shall prepare tasteful drama."

The crowd erupted again. A confetti cannon, out of ammunition, fired dust. The hatchlings, satisfied, coiled into escort formation around Glitch's legs—bodyguards made of adoration and poor life choices.

"Sentinel," Glitch muttered, pinching the bridge of his nose plate. "Log this as a catastrophic lapse in judgment."

SENTINEL: Logged. Suggested tag: compassion glitch.

He started forward—not toward disappearance, but toward the makeshift ramparts where repairs already sparked, where the frightened had begun to breathe, where a baker was cutting loaves with the reverence of a priest.

Everywhere he walked, the snakes followed.

Every time he paused, a child waved.

Every glance he threw at Vik came back with that unbearable look—the one that said I saw you try to leave and choose not to.

Glitch: This is the worst parade I've ever been in.

He stepped onto the broken dais where the council had tried to declare fifteen contradictory edicts and raised a hand. The plaza quieted with the shock of people discovering they might be about to hear a speech from someone who visibly hated speeches.

"I'm not your hero," he said.

Murmurs.

"I am not your leader." He jerked a thumb at his chest. The hatchling in his hood peeked over, as if seconding the statement.

"But." He swallowed the word like rust. "I'm here. For now. We patch the walls. Feed the tired. File an official complaint against destiny."

Silence hung, delicate. Then a ripple of laughter, grateful and raw.

"And," he added, glaring at the nearest confetti cannon, "absolutely no statues."

The plaza exploded.

Banners flashed. The pipe-trumpet honked. The baker raised a loaf like a holy relic. Someone uncorked a bottle of something that hissed ominously and fizzed like celebratory acid. The bard attempted a key change, failed, and committed to it anyway. The hatchlings purred in an octave that made the lanterns vibrate.

Vik pressed the gear medallion back into Glitch's hand.

He stared at it.

"...Fine," he muttered. "I'll hold it. Temporarily."

He looped the wire once around his fingers—no more—and turned toward work that wasn't his, in a city he didn't belong to, escorted by a thousand mistakes that loved him like law.

The celebration swelled behind him. The legend grew without his permission. And the tunnel kept waiting, patient and dark, like a horizon that would still be there tomorrow.

"Temporary," he told the snakes.

They trilled, which could have meant yes or forever.

He did not ask which.

The city of Warrenhold didn't dismiss a hero—it dragged him like ballast through every corridor until he accepted his new orbit.

Glitch's plan was simple: slip down an unguarded tunnel, vanish before dawn, leave the legend behind like a rusted coat. But Warrenhold had other ideas. Specifically, thousands of them, all armed with small instruments, bread, and unreasonable joy.

The hatchlings had become his heralds.

Skritch. Skritch. Skritch.

Everywhere he went, the synchronized shuffle of tiny scales echoed like an unwanted drumline. They didn't just follow him—they marched with him. One curled around his ankle as if chaining him in place. Another flicked its tongue into the air, tasting every cheer and deciding it belonged to them.

The mice took this as divine choreography.

"Look!" one shouted. "Even his beasts move in step with destiny!"

"They're not beasts," another corrected reverently. "They're saints."

Glitch: Saints shed on the carpet.

He ducked into a side passage. The hatchlings flooded after him. A gaggle of children squealed with delight and joined the march. By the time he reached the far end, half the plaza had followed.

Sentinel's voice hummed in his skull, deadpan:

SENTINEL: You have accidentally initiated a civic parade.

Classification: Unstoppable.

"Cancel it," Glitch muttered.

SENTINEL: Unable. Suggestion: wave occasionally to reduce resistance.

"Wave occasionally?!" He flung a hand in frustration. The crowd roared approval, assuming this was a formal blessing.

Banners unfurled spontaneously. One mouse dragged an entire bedsheet scrawled with coal dust letters that read: GLITCH FOREVER. Someone else waved a loaf of bread like a sacred relic. A third produced a drum made of a cracked pot and sheer nerve.

Vik jogged beside him, breathless and grinning. "They like you."

"They like the idea of me," Glitch snapped. "Big difference. One involves not knowing me."

The boy ignored him, because ignoring Glitch was quickly becoming a local pastime.

A burst of confetti rained down from an overhead scaffold. It wasn't paper—it was old invoices, shredded blueprints, bits of chewed parchment. One stuck to Glitch's faceplate. He peeled it off.

It read: Hero Registration Form – Approved.

He groaned.

Every detour he tried, every shadow he attempted to melt into, ended with the parade rerouting behind him. He walked fast; they jogged. He jogged; they sprinted. He stopped; they stopped, waiting, smiling like acolytes awaiting prophecy.

He ducked behind a cart. The hatchlings lined up neatly around it, eyes glowing. The crowd applauded his "inspection of civic infrastructure."

"Sentinel," Glitch whispered, "what's the probability they'll disperse if I fake my own death?"

SENTINEL: Two percent. Higher chance they would start a pilgrimage to your grave.

"Terrible odds."

He pressed forward through another tunnel arch. The acoustics turned the chant into a cathedral of absurdity:

"GLITCH! GLITCH! GLITCH!"

Every stomp echoed like destiny trying to trip him.

Worse, the council had joined in. Councilor Drell waved a torch aloft, declaiming at every turn. "Follow our deliverer!"

"I am not your deliverer!" Glitch barked.

The acoustics warped it into: "I am your deliverer!"

Roars shook the walls.

He slapped both hands to his head. "I hate this place."

And then the children caught up. Dozens of them. They swarmed at his heels, tripping over one another, trying to grab his cloak, laughing as if the nightmare was candy. A tiny mouse perched on a parent's shoulder shouted, "Say something heroic!"

Glitch turned, optics burning, cloak bristling with accidental gravitas. He snarled:

"Go home!"

The crowd erupted into cheers.

"Home!" they echoed. "He tells us to protect our homes!"

Vik wheezed with laughter beside him, barely able to breathe. "They don't even hear what you say. They hear what they need."

"Then they need an otter in a cape," Glitch grumbled. "Not me."

SENTINEL: Correction: they need you until the bread runs out. Estimated: four hours.

"Four hours too long."

But the parade would not stop. They carried him like a storm carries wreckage, through the undercity, through Warrenhold's veins. Wherever he turned, the chant followed.

"GLITCH! GLITCH! GLITCH!"

And though he swore he despised every syllable, though he swore the hatchlings were traitors and Vik was a nuisance and the crowd delusional—

—he couldn't quite bring himself to leave them in silence.

By the time the parade wound its way to the central square, Warrenhold had transformed into something dangerous: a city convinced of a story.

Torches glowed from balconies. Chants thundered through the stonework like drumfire. Everywhere, improvised banners stretched across walls, alleys, even laundry lines. And at the center of it all stood Glitch—arms folded, optics narrowed, cloak tangled by too many small claws.

The hatchlings had formed a living circle around him, scales shimmering under firelight. They weren't snarling or baring fangs. They were guarding. Patient. Still. Waiting for his command.

That was the problem.

The council climbed onto the speaking dais, voices ringing with triumph. "Behold! Our protector!"

Glitch raised a finger. "Nope. Wrong mech."

The crowd only roared louder.

He tried again. "I'm leaving. You don't want me. You don't need me. Find someone else—anyone else—with better posture and less rodent energy."

"Chosen one!" a voice screamed.

"Deliverer!" cried another.

A child shouted, "Make the snakes dance again!"

Glitch sagged, rubbing the back of his neck. "Sentinel, tell them I'm allergic to destiny."

SENTINEL: Transmission blocked by ambient chanting. Suggestion: feign illness.

"Too late. They'll build a shrine out of my coughs."

Vik edged closer. He looked small—smaller than ever before. The boy's whiskers twitched, eyes bright, torn between awe and fear. "They're not going to stop, you know."

"I'm not their hero." Glitch's voice was flat.

"But you saved them."

"Accidentally!"

Vik shrugged. "Doesn't matter." His voice cracked, too young to sound that certain. "They need you to be more than you are. So they made you that."

Glitch turned away, jaw tightening. "That's not fair."

"Life's not fair," Vik said softly. "But sometimes it's better with someone unfair on your side."

That landed like a weight dropped straight into his chest cavity. He wanted to laugh it off, wanted to tell Vik he was wrong, that this was nonsense, that legends were just lies painted pretty.

But the hatchlings stirred, their tiny eyes all trained on him with something worse than loyalty: belief.

The square quieted. For the first time since the parade began, silence stretched across Warrenhold like a net. The crowd leaned in. Waiting.

Glitch opened his mouth. Closed it. He had nothing. No grand speech. No vow of protection. No destiny.

Only the weight.

The boy looked at him. The hatchlings looked at him. The city looked at him. And for a heartbeat, even Sentinel stayed quiet.

Glitch sighed, shoulders sagging like rusted beams. "Fine. But don't blame me when this all ends badly."

The crowd erupted into euphoria, deafening. Vik grinned through tears. The hatchlings hissed like cymbals.

Glitch groaned into his hands.

He wasn't the hero Warrenhold deserved.

He wasn't the hero they wanted.

But he was the one they got.

And that, apparently, was enough.

Chapter Sixteen: A Farewell, Not a Finish

Warrenhold stood quiet in the aftermath.

The fires were finally out. The walls were patched, though the repairs looked more like enthusiastic art projects than actual reinforcements. The cheers had long since burned themselves out too, fading into that stunned, reverent hush a city gets when it's trying to figure out what survival is supposed to feel like.

It wasn't silence, exactly. Silence didn't fit a place like Warrenhold. There was always the faint hum of power relays, the scrape of scavvers dragging supplies, the hiss of steam from pipes that probably weren't supposed to hiss. But it was quiet in the way that followed the ridiculous and the world-altering, that strange lull where everyone knew something impossible had happened and no one knew what to do with it.

And at the center of it all, Glitch stood with his arms crossed, trying very, very hard not to look emotionally compromised.

Around him, the hatchlings had decided—without consulting him, of course—that he needed constant, suffocating protection. They formed a sloppy ring at his feet, like overly loyal bodyguards who thought nuzzling counted as perimeter defense. Some still coiled on the edges of nearby rooftops, optics scanning for threats with a level of dramatic seriousness that would've been impressive if one of them hadn't immediately fallen asleep halfway through.

Others trailed behind Vik, who was doing his best to pretend he wasn't getting attached to them. His best wasn't very good. He kept sneaking them scraps of fried nut-cakes whenever he thought no one was looking. One hatchling had decided Vik's scarf was a permanent perch and kept draping itself over his shoulder like a very smug fashion accessory.

Glitch had seen battlefields before. He'd seen aftermaths before. But he'd never seen anything like this—where the city wasn't just surviving, but looking at him like the reason they'd survived was standing right there.

He hated it.

He hated how much he didn't immediately walk away.

Still, he had made a decision.

A terrible, logical, unavoidable decision.

He was leaving.

"I'm not meant to stay," he said, tone flat, optics locked on the horizon as if it might open a convenient sinkhole to swallow him. "I'm not a guardian. I'm not a symbol. And I definitely—definitely—am not starting a reptilian daycare."

Vik stood beside him on the wall, arms resting on the stone ledge. The boy's ears twitched slightly in the cool wind, his gaze following the fractured skyline. "They still think you are," he said softly.

"Which proves they were born with critical firmware flaws," Glitch muttered. "Honestly, it's kind of impressive how quickly they latched onto the worst possible role model."

As if to prove his point, one hatchling attempted to coil heroically on a parapet, only to slip and tumble into another. Both squealed, recovered, then puffed up their frills in perfect mimicry of Glitch's usual glare.

Vik chuckled.

Glitch scowled.

The kid turned then, facing him fully. His expression was calm, but there was a weight in it—something more grounded than the absurd chaos that had defined their survival. "You saved us."

"By accident."

"You stayed."

"That was also an accident."

"You're still here."

"That's—" Glitch faltered. His jaw worked, gears clicking faintly. "That's technically inertia."

Vik smiled faintly. "You're still doing it."

Glitch tilted his head. "Doing what?"

"Pretending none of it mattered to you."

The mech opened his mouth. Closed it again. Opened it again. He considered pretending his audio relays were malfunctioning, but Vik's look cut through the excuse before it formed.

"It didn't," Glitch muttered finally.

"Okay."

"I mean it."

"Sure."

"Vik."

"I know."

The silence that followed wasn't awkward. It was the opposite—old, worn, like two travelers who had reached the same conclusion by very different roads.

Below them, the city stirred. Rebuilding had already begun. New cables stretched across towers that had broken only hours ago. Murals were being sketched in chalk and paint across scorched walls—murals that included Glitch.

Glitch followed Vik's eyes, saw one of the sketches, and recoiled. "No. Absolutely not. I will personally set fire to any artistic renderings of my face."

"Too late," Vik said, pointing to a nearby rooftop where two mice were sketching a dramatic image of Glitch surrounded by glowing hatchlings. One of the artists even paused to squint at Glitch, then adjusted the angle of his chin in the mural for "maximum heroism."

Glitch groaned loudly. "This is exactly why I need to leave. If they start building statues, I'm digging a hole and living in it forever."

One of the hatchlings hissed softly in agreement. Or maybe it was just hungry. Hard to tell.

Glitch didn't tell the council he was leaving.

That would've involved meetings. Meetings meant speeches, questions, and worst of all—gratitude. Gratitude was toxic. He could practically feel it rusting his plating.

Instead, he decided to vanish.

A simple exit. Slip out at night, let the hatchlings eventually forget, let the council paint murals of someone else. Maybe they'd mythologize him as a dream, a trick of the smoke, a figment of desperation. Perfect.

The only problem?

The hatchlings.

They weren't letting him vanish.

Every time he so much as shifted his weight toward the gate, a half-dozen serpentine bodies coiled around his boots. Whenever he packed up the scraps of his cloak, they dragged the fabric back down, tugging on it like toddlers refusing bedtime. One even shoved its head into his satchel and refused to come out, glaring at him from inside like a self-declared stowaway.

And then there was Vik.

The kid had that look. The one that saw through everything. The one that said he wasn't going to beg him to stay, because begging wasn't Vik's style. Instead, he stood nearby, calm, quiet, just... waiting.

Glitch hated it more than begging.

"Look," Glitch said, trying to sound decisive while prying two hatchlings off his shin. "I don't belong here. Never did. You've got leaders. Builders. Survivors. People with actual plans. What do I have? A bad attitude and a cloak that smells like burnt oil."

"You kept us alive," Vik said.

"Temporarily."

"You gave us hope."

"By accident."

Vik tilted his head. "Do you ever realize how many times you use that excuse?"

"It's not an excuse. It's a statistical pattern."

He finally shook free of the hatchlings and stalked to the edge of the wall, cloak flaring. Beyond lay the wastes—ashen plains, broken towers, long roads leading nowhere. Freedom, or at least the illusion of it.

The city behind him hummed faintly with life. The boy beside him breathed steady, ears twitching against the wind. The hatchlings wriggled in a protective knot, optics glowing faintly like candles in the dusk.

He should've walked. Should've kept walking until Warrenhold was another ruin in the distance, until the noise of expectation faded. That was the smart play. That was the safe play.

But his feet didn't move.

Not until Vik spoke again.

"You're scared."

Glitch froze. "Excuse me?"

"Of staying."

He turned slowly, optics narrowing. "Correction: I am scared of nothing."

Vik raised a brow. "You're terrified of becoming something."

The words hit harder than any battle, sharper than Coilthorne's fangs. Glitch's jaw clenched, gears whining faintly. He wanted to argue. He wanted to laugh it off, turn it into a joke. But he couldn't—not with that look in Vik's eyes, steady and sure and far older than a boy should carry.

"I can't," Glitch said finally. The words scraped like rust.

"Why not?"

"Because then it matters."

The silence that followed was heavier than gunfire.

Vik didn't push further. He just nodded slowly, as if that answer was enough for now, even if it wasn't the truth.

The hatchlings hissed softly at his feet, confused by the tension but unwilling to move.

Glitch looked out over the wastes again. His chest felt too tight, like someone had bolted hope into him against his will.

He exhaled sharply. "Fine. Tomorrow night. I'm gone. Non-negotiable."

Vik didn't argue.

He didn't have to.

Because they both knew the world had other plans.

Morning in Warrenhold didn't look much different from night. The same dim glow of fungus-lamps, the same steady hum of patched-together generators, the same stubborn air of survival.

But today carried a different tone.

The city knew.

They weren't told outright, but whispers moved faster than gears. By the time Glitch strapped the last piece of bent armor back into place, half the tunnels were lined with mice trying to catch a glimpse. Not pleading. Not even asking questions. Just... watching.

He hated it.

He loved it, too, though he would've rather fried his own vocal modulator than admit that.

The council stood at the main gate, solemn as judges. The eldest among them stepped forward, a crooked staff in hand.

"You will always have a place here," she said.

Glitch waved dismissively. "No I won't. Your plumbing barely works. Your food is moss. And every third hallway smells like despair. Hard pass."

A ripple of nervous laughter passed through the crowd. The elder smiled faintly, as though that was exactly the answer she'd expected.

One by one, mice stepped forward with offerings. Not treasures—Warrenhold had none—but tokens. A carved bolt, polished smooth. A strip of cloth painted with his jagged likeness. A broken gear shaped into a pendant.

They pressed them into his hands, into his satchel, into the folds of his cloak. He tried to refuse, but refusal was useless against gratitude this concentrated. Soon he was jingling like a walking shrine.

And then came Vik.

He didn't carry a trinket. Didn't make a speech. He just stood in front of Glitch, eyes wide, tail curled tight.

"You're really going."

Glitch nodded once. "That was the plan."

"You could stay."

"I could also sprout wings and become a toaster. Doesn't mean it'll happen."

The kid laughed, shaky but genuine. It cracked something in Glitch's chest.

Vik swallowed hard. "I'll take care of them," he said, glancing at the hatchlings coiled restlessly around Glitch's boots.

"You better," Glitch muttered. "They're sticky, loud, and entirely too loyal. Perfect for you."

"Perfect for us," Vik corrected.

Glitch opened his mouth, closed it again. Something caught in his throat, a glitch in the system. He finally settled for a grunt.

The silence stretched. The city waited. The hatchlings stirred.

Glitch pulled his cloak tighter, squared his shoulders, and forced a smirk.

"Well. This is it. The part where I say something inspiring, and you all pretend I meant it."

He turned toward the gate. The guards heaved it open, stone grinding against stone. Beyond lay the wastes: bleak, endless, merciless. And strangely welcoming.

The crowd parted.

The chant began.

"Glitch. Glitch. Glitch."

He groaned audibly. "Stop it. You sound like you're booting up an old hard drive."

But they didn't stop. They never would.

Vik's voice cut through it all, soft and certain.

"Goodbye, Glitch."

Glitch didn't turn. Didn't wave. Didn't risk looking back.

Because if he did, he wasn't sure he'd keep walking.

The wastes greeted him like an old creditor.

Flat horizons of ash and broken steel. Hulks of machines too large to bury, their ribs jutting up like monuments to stupidity. The sky—a pale bruise that never healed.

Glitch trudged through it all, cloak dragging, hatchling-free for the first time in days. The silence should've been a relief. It wasn't. It was heavy.

Every few steps, his servos made too much noise. Every shadow looked like a memory. Every gust of wind carried the faint hiss of serpents he'd left behind.

He kept walking. Because that was what he did.

Hours—or maybe years—later, the shape of a settlement clawed its way out of the horizon. A mess of stacked girders and sheet metal, lashed together with cables and desperation. Towers leaned at odd angles. Smoke curled from mismatched chimneys. Signs made from scavenged neon blinked in and out, half-dead but still insisting.

Welcome to Scrapstone.

Population: "Don't Ask."

The gate wasn't guarded so much as slouched against. A couple of half-awake scavvers looked up as Glitch approached, then quickly decided he wasn't worth the trouble.

Inside, the air smelled of oil, charred wiring, and bad decisions. Markets lined the alleys, trading in anything that hummed, glowed, or hadn't yet exploded. Vendors hawked mech parts with more rust than metal. Children played with drones that had been de-weaponized... probably.

Glitch fit right in, which horrified him.

He dragged himself through the crowd until he found a bar. Of course there was a bar. Scrapstone had the kind of energy that demanded one every fifty meters. This one leaned against a collapsed tower and had a sign that read The Rusty Gear in flickering orange.

Inside, the light was dim, the tables dented, and the patrons perfectly uninterested in heroics. Which was exactly what Glitch needed.

He slumped into a corner booth, armor squeaking, cloak sticking to the seat like it was trying to escape. A serving bot rolled up, scanned him once, and decided not to ask questions. It deposited a mug of something brownish and vaguely toxic.

Glitch raised it in a mock toast to no one.

"To peace," he muttered. "Or at least quiet failure."

He drank. It burned like regret.

And for the first time in a long time, he almost felt still.

Almost.

Because in the far corner, half-hidden in shadow, someone watched him. A sharp-eyed figure with a grin too wide to be casual.

The kind of grin that promised Glitch's story wasn't over.

Not by a long shot.

Bonus Chapter: Vik's Epilogue

A few nights after Glitch left Warrenhold

The city had quieted.

Not in the usual way, where sleepy streets hummed with steam vents and idle chatter, or a lone merchant argued with a vending unit over the proper temperature for cheese. This was a different kind of quiet. Heavier. A stillness that crept into the hinges of doors and settled like dust in the spaces between gears. It was the kind of silence that made you feel like the whole city was holding its breath—waiting to exhale something it couldn't name.

Vik sat at his desk, hunched like a question mark over a schematic he'd already rewritten six times this week and still hadn't finished. His room, small and cluttered, looked less like a place someone lived and more like a storage closet where blueprints came to die. Bolts littered the floor. A pair of cracked goggles hung from a pipe above his workbench. The walls were lined with faded paper notes, including his personal favorite, taped crookedly above the ventilation fan:

"IF YOU SMELL SMOKE, IT'S TOO LATE."

A flickering desk lamp buzzed and dimmed, casting long shadows over his current masterpiece-in-progress: an upgraded perimeter scanner for the Coil Sector. Or, as Vik had labeled it in exasperated block letters:

DO NOT LET COILBITE NAP ON THIS AGAIN.

The mug beside him steamed gently. Mostly. It had been reheated in a microwave coil three times now, and he'd only sipped it once. He wasn't sure if it still counted as tea or had entered a new phase of molecular resentment.

But even the tea didn't matter.

Because Glitch was gone.

That thought floated through his mind again—third time this hour, at least—uninvited and unrelenting, like a broken speaker skipping the same chorus.

Glitch was gone.

He hadn't made a speech. No dramatic hand gestures or final words. He didn't leave a note or a hero's farewell. He just adjusted his crooked cloak, muttered something sarcastic about "not getting emotionally invested in plumbing," and walked into the tunnels like the ending of a bad comic strip. One last shrug. No goodbye.

And Vik had watched him go.

He'd stood at the upper scaffold, pretending to adjust a relay coil, just so he wouldn't have to say it either. Just so it wouldn't feel like the ending it was.

Now, the aftermath was his.

The hatchlings—their hatchlings, if one could stretch definitions that far—still slithered through Warrenhold's winding architecture, weaving protection circuits into the very body of the city. Dozens had taken up patrol routes, some even clocking in at regular intervals like they'd invented a union. Vik had tried to implement schedules, but the snakes seemed to instinctively understand routine—at least until one of them got distracted by a squeaky pipe or decided a ceiling panel looked "chewable."

They weren't malicious. Just curious. Aggressively curious.

He tapped the side of his stylus against the schematic's margin, then jotted down:

"Reroute Sector 9 motion beacon above door frame. Again. Blame Coilbite."

Coilbite, the smallest and most adorably chaotic of the brood, had developed a fondness for the Sector 9 alarm beacon. Specifically, curling around it to nap. It was soft. It vibrated. It beeped when cuddled.

The city had been on high alert four times in the last hour.

Vik leaned back and rubbed the space between his eyes. His shoulders ached. His back popped audibly. He wasn't old, but stress had a way of aging you at lightning speed when you were the only mouse in town trying to keep an army of semi-feral death noodles from accidentally frying the municipal power grid.

A soft hiss whispered from the window.

Vik turned his head.

One of the hatchlings—he thought it was Sparktongue, based on the stuttering glow in its ocular sensor—paused outside. It blinked at him through the glass, raised its tail in what could generously be described as a salute, then continued its patrol with a little wriggle of pride.

Vik smiled in spite of himself.

They really did look up to him. Or... sideways to him, depending on how they slithered.

"Great," he muttered. "I've been promoted from engineer to snake-dad."

He reached for the tea. It was lukewarm now. Maybe colder. Definitely judged him when he took a sip.

Still, he drank it.

Because Glitch had left him this.

Not the tea, though he probably would've left half a mug if asked. No—Glitch had left him the city. The weird, chaotic, slightly-electrified city. The people. The snakes. The silence. The responsibility.

It had been an accident, of course. Like everything else Glitch did.

Save a city? Accident.

Lead an army? Accident.

Become mother to a thousand weaponized orphans? Monumental, cosmic-level accident.

And now Vik sat at the center of it.

Not because he wanted to.

But because someone had to.

He rose from his seat, stretched until his spine made a noise that shouldn't have been physically possible, and crossed to the narrow window overlooking the South Coil Sector. Beyond the glass, the flickering outlines of Warrenhold stretched into the deep metallic dark. Faint glows marked patrol points. Occasional zaps lit up when a snake got too close to a faulty outlet. Once, he saw two hatchlings pass each other and do an awkward tail-high-five.

It was kind of beautiful, in a deeply concerning way.

"Guess I'm the grown-up now," Vik murmured.

He leaned his forehead against the window, exhaling until the glass fogged. For a brief second, his reflection stared back at him: tired eyes, bent ears, the faint soot stain that still hadn't come out of his fur from the generator explosion last week.

He looked like someone who missed a friend.

Someone who didn't get a goodbye.

Someone trying to be strong for creatures that didn't even understand why the air felt heavier at night now.

A sound behind him made him turn.

The tea cup rattled.

He paused. Waited.

Then turned back.

Must've been the wind through the vent systems. Or a hatchling playing tag with a rogue circuit box again.

Still...

He moved to the door. Locked it.

Not because he thought it would help.

Just because it made him feel like he still had control over something.

He returned to his desk. The schematic was still there. Still unfinished. He picked up the stylus. Drew one more line.

Then stopped again.

He wasn't ready to go back to normal yet. Not tonight.

He left the tea untouched. Dimmed the lights. Crossed the room to the vent and pressed his ear against it.

Nothing.

No hissing.

No movement.

No Glitch whispering through it like he used to when sneaking back into Warrenhold after a poorly-executed scouting trip. Just silence. The long, thoughtful kind. The kind that carried weight.

He stood there for a while.

Not moving.

Just listening to a city trying to decide what kind of story it would tell next.

And somewhere in that silence, Vik made a promise.

He didn't speak it aloud.

Didn't write it down.

But he felt it.

Deep. Clear.

Keep them safe.

Until he comes back.

Until we all know what comes next.

He glanced at the schematic one more time, then turned out the lamp.

Tomorrow, he'd fix the beacon.

Tonight, he'd keep watch.

Just in case the silence broke.

Or someone knocked on his wall again.

Vik was the one left to make sure it didn't all fall apart.

That realization crept up on him more slowly than he'd care to admit. At first, it was just little things—adjusting security schedules, manually rerouting the north sector power grid after a hatchling shorted it out trying to "hug" a fuse box, and rescheduling council meetings that had somehow devolved into public storytelling sessions about Glitch's "noble sacrifice."

Then came the paperwork.

The mice of Warrenhold—gods bless them—were not the kind of civilization to let a good miracle pass without trying to register it. Vik had already received three formal requests to induct Glitch into the Hall of Mechanical Saints, one semi-legal proposal to erect a twenty-foot bronze statue (with snakes at his feet, obviously), and a letter from a young mouse child asking if it was "okay to name my pet toaster Glitch because it also screams when turned on."

It was too much.

So tonight, he'd taken refuge in his quarters. He'd planned to finish the scanner update. Maybe rewire the nest cameras to stop mistaking hugging as hostile movement. But all he'd done so far was stare at the same diagram for an hour and a half.

Until the noise.

It had started faintly—more vibration than sound. A shift in air pressure. A ripple along the stone wall behind him. At first, he thought it was just the usual midnight shuffle of one of the hatchlings trying to crawl through a pipe that was, frankly, not designed for snake traffic.

Then came the hiss.

Not high-pitched. Not aggressive.

Low.

Too low.

Like steam from a leaking core vent. Or breath from something that had learned patience the hard way.

Vik blinked toward the door.

"Coilbite?" he called, trying to keep his voice calm. "You better not be trying to reenter the HVAC system. Again."

No answer.

He stood slowly, muscles tensing on instinct. His eyes darted to the far corner of the room, where a rusted wrench hung from a magnetic strip. He grabbed it. Not because it was a good weapon, but because it was his wrench. Solid. Heavy. Slightly comforting in the way only well-used tools could be.

Another hiss—closer this time. A breath that didn't belong.

Vik reached under the desk and flipped a small brass switch. The overhead light dimmed to a soft orange glow. Shadows surged forward, coating the room in something that felt less like darkness and more like secrecy.

He stepped around his chair, silent on padded feet, ears perked.

The door remained closed.

But the pressure hadn't lifted. In fact, it had intensified.

The kind of presence you didn't hear or see—but felt. Like something behind the wall of your reality had cracked a knuckle and was preparing to make its move.

He crouched near the side vent and waited.

Silence.

Nothing.

Then, a voice.

Low. Whispered.

"...I see lights..."

Vik nearly dropped the wrench.

He backed away, fast, his heart hammering in his throat. That wasn't one of the hatchlings. That wasn't anyone he knew.

Another hiss followed—longer this time. It had a rhythm. A shape. As if the sound itself was winding around corners before it reached him.

And then—

Something moved in the shadows by the door.

Not slithered.

Moved—with a strange, clattering, disjointed energy, like silverware in a bag full of bees. Metal limbs scratched the stone. A tail thumped once, then twice. The handle of the door twitched—just slightly—as if something outside was trying to remember how doors worked.

Vik froze.

His mind ran through options. Should he hit the lights? Run? Throw the wrench and hope for the best? Call for help? He reached for his comm band—and realized it was still on the charger. Across the room. Next to the tea.

Brilliant.

He gritted his teeth and backed against the far wall. The glow of the desk lamp barely touched the edges of the doorway now, and for one long moment, it felt like the room was being swallowed by a presence that couldn't decide whether to eat him or hug him.

And then—

CRASH.

The door exploded open.

Well—no. Not exploded.

It kind of... flopped.

The hinges gave out with a pathetic whine as a heap of serpentine limbs and poorly-assembled armor faceplanted onto his floor with the grace of a puppet dropped from orbit.

Vik choked on his breath, wrench raised, every muscle screaming fight or run or both.

The figure didn't move.

Just groaned.

"Uggghhh... okay. Not my best entrance, but also not my worst."

A tail twitched.

An optic blinked—sideways.

Then, with all the self-awareness of a roomba programmed by theatre kids, the figure lifted its head and chirped—

"Hi!"

Vik did not lower the wrench.

The mech-serpent wobbled upright like a malfunctioning jack-in-the-box. His plating was a mismatched mess of half-polished panels and crudely attached servo joints. One optic glowed green; the other blinked amber in a way that definitely wasn't on purpose.

"Are you Vik?" the snake asked brightly. "Because you look like a Vik. But if you're not, oops! My bad. Wouldn't be the first wrong room today."

Vik stared, caught between horror and curiosity.

The snake blinked back. Each eye. Separately. Unnecessarily.

The wrench trembled slightly in Vik's hand.

"What," he said slowly, "are you doing in my room?"

Vik nearly threw the wrench.

A blur of mismatched armor and slithering limbs barreled into the room like a malfunctioning puppet show set on fast forward. Metal clinked, something sparked, and before Vik could scream, duck, or recite his last will and testament, the intruder skidded across the floor and came to a halt—chin-first—on top of Vik's schematic pad.

"Hi!" the serpent chirped, unbothered by the face-plant. "Are you Vik? You look like a Vik. Unless you're someone else. Are you someone else? Because if so, oops!"

Vik blinked.

Twice.

The snake blinked back—each eye independently, like a broken camera rig trying to recalibrate. One blinked sideways. The other blinked diagonally. It was deeply upsetting.

"What," Vik managed, wrench still raised in disbelief, "are you doing in my room?"

"Oh good! It is your room!" the snake said brightly, rising into a half-sit with his tail twisted under him like a couch cushion. "That's better than last time. I tried sneaking into a boiler closet. It hissed at me. Pretty sure it's haunted now."

Vik didn't move.

Didn't lower the wrench.

Didn't breathe.

The snake was now inspecting the schematic he'd crumpled, turning it sideways and upside down like it was some ancient map to lost cheese.

"You're... one of Coilthorne's, aren't you?" Vik asked cautiously.

The serpent looked offended. Full-on, fake pearl-clutching offended.

"EXCUSE me," he gasped. "Former minion. Very former. Ex-minion. Retired from villainous pursuits. I even turned in my evil laugh. It came with a warranty. Didn't cover water damage, though."

Vik's eye twitched. "And you're here why?"

The snake grinned, full of teeth and zero sanity. "To help!"

"Help," Vik echoed flatly.

"Absolutely! Glitch left you with so many children. I mean, I counted. And I only got to like, thirty before I ran out of tail. That's too many for one mouse! You need a co-guardian. A snake...uncle. An uncle. That's what I am now. Slitherax: Uncle of the Year!"

He puffed out his chest, which was a mistake. It made a grinding sound like someone stepping on a tin can, and something popped loose behind his neck.

Vik lowered the wrench a few centimeters, but mostly to keep his own blood pressure down. "Slitherax?"

"That's me!" He did a twirl. "Technically pronounced Sssssslitherax, but the extra s's are optional unless I'm doing formal introductions or attending weddings."

"Why are you in my room?"

"I was looking for the hatchlings. Got lost. Saw a vent. Thought—'Hey, I'm thin, I can fit!' Then there were cobwebs and possibly a ghost. Name's Carl. Weird guy. Anyway, your room had lights and smelled like disappointment, so I figured yep, that's where the adult lives!"

Vik exhaled through his nose, very slowly. "You crawled through the air vents?"

"Only the warm ones. The cold ones smelled like laundry and regret."

He spun again. This time he knocked over the mug of tea, skidding the puddle directly across the blueprint table without noticing.

"Also, nice blueprints. Love the chicken scratch aesthetic. You ever consider adding glitter?"

Vik stared at him. "Are you actually malfunctioning?"

"Nope!" Slitherax beamed. "This is just how I am. Had a few too many experimental updates back in Coilthorne's lair. He called me a 'cautionary tale in serpentine form.'" He leaned in, stage-whispering, "I took it as a compliment."

There was a loud bang in the ductwork overhead.

Slitherax tilted his head. "That's probably my tail. It's still catching up."

Vik rubbed the bridge of his nose. "You're seriously offering to help me watch over the hatchlings?"

"I wouldn't say 'watch.' More like... coexist lovingly with minor super-vision while offering bad advice and better snacks."

Vik opened his mouth to protest—and paused.

Because behind the chaos, behind the sheer avalanche of absurdity, there was... sincerity.

Insane sincerity. Possibly radioactive sincerity. But still: real.

"You know this isn't a game, right?" Vik asked quietly. "These hatch-lings... they're confused. Scared. Imprinted on someone who left. This whole city is holding together by duct tape and stubbornness."

Slitherax nodded, surprisingly solemn for once. "I know."

Another pause.

Then he grinned again. "That's why I'm definitely qualified. I'm also confused, scared, and abandoned. And I've got duct tape!"

He reached into a panel on his side and pulled out an actual roll.

Vik finally—finally—let out a small laugh. Just one. But it was real.

"Fine," he muttered, setting the wrench down. "But if you chew on one more blueprint—"

"I only chew on the corners! It's a design thing."

"Out."

Slitherax saluted with his tail, smacked over a pile of schematics, and somehow somersaulted backward into the nearest vent like it was a tram-poline exit.

"TO THE CRAWLSPACE!" he declared proudly, and vanished with a thunk.

A beat passed.

Then another.

Vik walked to the vent and shut the cover.

Pointless, but symbolic.

He sighed and turned back to the disaster of a room, tea cooling in a puddle, notes soaked, one schematic half-chewed, and his sanity dangling by a frayed thread.

Outside, Warrenhold glowed with the soft patrol-light of hatchling movements. Peaceful. Almost serene.

Inside?

He muttered, "I have made a terrible mistake."

From the vent: "I FOUND A FORK TOO!"

Vik didn't even flinch.

He just sat down, pressed his paws to his temples, and whispered:

"Glitch is going to hate this."

Afterword by Sentinel

Also titled: I Told You So

Well. That was certainly something.

If you are still here, dear reader—and somehow survived the avalanche of sarcasm, serpents slithering in mechanical harmony, and one extremely reluctant mech—then congratulations. You have officially borne witness to a peculiar slice of history. Or, more accurately, the accidental legend of Glitch: Mech-rat, misanthrope, and a mildly competent disaster magnet who attracts chaos the way rust attracts rain.

You may have questions swirling in your mind like storm debris.

I don't recommend asking them. The answers tend to bite. Sometimes literally.

Still, for the sake of tidy record-keeping, let's recap:

Glitch did not intend to be a hero.

He was very vocal about this—his complaints echoing through the corridors like a choir of grumpy scrap-metal.

And yet, despite every ounce of reluctance, despite his muttering, whining, grumbling, and swearing that he would absolutely leave at the first opportunity... he didn't.

He toppled a warlord who hissed like a broken radiator. He accidentally adopted a hatchling army. He became a savior to Warrenhold without ever filling out the proper paperwork.

And through it all, he never once stopped reminding us how much he hated every second of it.

Let the record show: I, Sentinel, tried to warn him. I provided statistics, probabilities, tactical advice, and a gentle drizzle of sarcasm. He ignored all of it.

Of course.

Because no one listens to the glowing narration cube with a tactical suggestion processor and a sarcasm filter that's—let's be honest—overloaded most of the time. Ninety-seven percent sarcasm, three percent sheer spite. It is a delicate balance.

And yet...

Even for a rust-stained, glitch-ridden, emotionally stunted hunk of left-over war tech... he surprised me.

He didn't run. Not completely.

He didn't break. Not permanently.

And between the screaming, sulking, snake-wrangling, and near-death experiences, he managed something rare in this collapsed world: he stayed. He stood his ground when it mattered.

That counts for more than he'll ever admit.

Perhaps not enough for a statue. But maybe enough for a legend. Or at least a heavily footnoted entry in the archives.

...

Glitch: "FOOTNOTE?! I defeated an evil overlord with literal toddlers! I demand hazard pay, a nap, and for you to stop narrating my trauma like it's a bedtime story."

...

Yes, yes. He's still here, grumbling. I expect he always will be.

But the truth is, Warrenhold is behind him. He's moved on—probably lurking in some dusty corner of Nexus-4. He thinks he's blending in. He isn't. The snakes give him away. So does the mouse. So does his face, which radiates "accident waiting to happen."

And if you're hoping this was the end?

I regret to inform you... it isn't.

There are new disasters brewing. Worse ones. Louder ones. And I will be here to narrate every single mistake, because—well—someone has to keep the records tidy.

Glitch: "That's it. I'm ripping out your voice chip."

Sentinel: "Try it, Legend Rat. I dare you."

End of Book One.

Pending further disasters.

About the author

I created Glitch Entertainment on a simple idea: sometimes the greatest stories are born from mistakes. What started as a side character in a darker saga became the spark for an entire universe — one where failure, chaos, and reluctant heroism are not flaws but superpowers.

Our debut novel, *Glitch Adventures: The Unlikely Hero*, introduces readers to Glitch, a biomechanical rat who stumbles into legend by accident. With humor, satire, and heart, the story redefines what it means to be a hero in a broken world.

But the book is just the beginning. Glitch Entertainment is building an interconnected creative universe of novels, comics, and games — all exploring the same themes: resilience through failure, finding meaning in chaos, and laughing when the universe seems designed to break you.

The *Glitch Adventures* series is planned as a six-book journey, paired with spin-offs.

Beyond books, Glitch Entertainment is developing comics, animation, and immersive games under the same banner. Every project carries the same DNA — mythic scale, biting humor, and the refusal to take "perfect" too seriously.

This book is more than a debut. It's a declaration.
The glitch is only the beginning.

Thank you for joining me on this journey,
Richard Case

Acknowledgements

Every story is built on more than one pair of hands, and this one is no exception.

To my family and friends — thank you for believing in me when I doubted myself, for listening when I wouldn't stop talking about rats, snakes, and sarcastic AI cubes, and for reminding me that imagination is never wasted.

To my parents — you've been my foundation and my strength. None of this happens without you.

To the creative partners, late-night brainstorms, and the conversations that sparked Glitch into life — you turned a rough sketch of a rat into the heart of a universe.

And finally, to every future reader who laughs, rolls their eyes, or mutters, "this rat is ridiculous" — you are the reason these stories live beyond my head.

This book is for all of you.

Also by Glitch Entertainment

Coming Soon:

- **Glitch Adventures: Book Two – The Metal Mafia**

- **Glitch's Survival Guide**

If you enjoyed *Glitch Adventures: Book One*, please consider leaving a review on Amazon.

One review helps more than you know.